HOLLYWOOD HANG TEN

For Julián —
With wishes for a
life full of good
books & reading.

Eve.

HOLLYWOOD HANG TEN

EVE GOLDBERG

This first edition published in 2017 by:

Thistle Publishing
36 Great Smith Street
London
SW1P 3BU

www.thistlepublishing.co.uk

CHAPTER 1

I had been at the office plenty of times without Uncle Lou, but this time was different. This time Lou wasn't at the post office, or picking up a deli sandwich, or out on a case somewhere. This time he was lying under a thin cotton blanket at the V.A. hospital with an oxygen tube up his nose, hooked up to a machine that monitored his breathing. This time, the doctor said, the two packs a day had finally caught up with him.

I stood just inside the doorway and looked around. The sun's rays slanted in through the large front window, catching the dust in the air. In the corner was a metal file cabinet, old and dented. Next to the file cabinet, Lou's desk was piled with papers, one sheet still threaded into his typewriter. I pulled the paper out and looked it over. He had been writing up a report on the Keplinger case. Mrs. Keplinger lived in Palm Springs, on the edge of a golf course. She was rich, lonely, and convinced that somebody was hitting golf balls onto her roof at night while she tried to sleep. Our job was to catch them at it.

The phone rang. I picked it up.

"Southland Investigations."

"Hello, is this Lou Zorn?" It was a woman's voice, anxious, almost panicky.

"Lou's not in. This is Ryan. How can I help you?"

"I left two messages with your answering service already this morning."

"I just got in. What can I do for you?"

"It's my son. He didn't come home from school yesterday and I'm starting to get, I mean, I don't think he was even at school yesterday, at least that's what his friend Nicholas said. Joey's not home, he's not at school, I don't know where he is. He's only 11 years old, and I'm scared, really starting to get worried. I don't have a lot of money, but I'll pay whatever you charge. Please, can you find him?"

"When was the last time you saw your son, Mrs. ...?"

"Flynn. Cora Flynn. It was two nights ago, Wednesday night, pretty late. I checked in on Joey when I got home. He was sleeping. But the next morning..."

She sucked in her breath. When she continued, her voice was shaky.

"Look, I'm at work and I can't leave right now, but is there any way you can come out here? I mean right away, if that's possible. I'm going out of my mind with worry."

I said yes. Then I got out a pencil and jotted down her work address: Building 8. Research. Pinnacle Studios.

***

Ten minutes later, I was cruising east on Santa Monica Boulevard toward Hollywood, past clapboard bungalows standing hip to hip with shoe stores and car dealers and glass-fronted drug stores hawking Brylcreem and Dr. Pepper, *Modern Screen* and Cutty Sark. It was just after 10:00 AM, and already getting hot. I rolled down the window, then cut up to Sunset and took a right.

The Strip was nearly deserted. The nightclubs — all neon swank after dark — had a ghostly abandoned look in the daylight, their lifeless marquees announcing Mort Sahl at the Crescendo, Johnny Rivers at Gazarri's, Dick Dale and the Del-Tones at Ciro's. If Uncle Lou had been with me, he'd be shaking his head and grumbling about how things had changed — and not in a good way. Back in the day, Lou had worked security for various Hollywood celebrities while he built up his private investigations firm. He loved to tell stories about Sinatra punching out some guy over a game of pool, Sammy Davis not-so-secretly dating Kim Novak, Judy Garland falling down drunk at the Macombo. "Who the fuck is Dick Dale?" he would have barked today if he hadn't been plugged into an oxygen tank at the V.A.

Lou had wanted to be a cop, but his gimpy war-leg kept him off the force. So he started up his own investigation agency, an outfit which consisted of himself... and eventually me. I had worked for him the last five years, since graduating high school class of '58. I'd run errands, type up reports, break him on all-night surveillance. Lou seemed to enjoy passing his know-how on to me. He taught me how to read upside down, how to follow a car in its blind spot, how to snap a decent photo on the sly without looking through the viewfinder.

I saw my uncle as a force of nature. He was short and stocky, had a deep gravelly voice, strong convictions, and a knack for solving even the most baffling case. Divorce, missing persons, hidden assets, midnight golf balls — you name it. Lou always took charge of the cases. I stayed in the background, which suited me just fine. The sidekick role left me plenty of time to surf.

Now, suddenly, here I was... 23 years old and on my first solo case. I tried to remember the tips Lou had given me over the years about an initial interview: listen to what a person does <u>not</u> say as much as what they do say; pay attention to body language; honor your first impressions, but be ready to modify them when new information presents itself.

Leaving the nightclubs and restaurants of the Strip behind, I drove through the unglamorous side streets of Hollywood — past the hulking concrete monoliths, windowless and beige, which housed the film processing labs, equipment rental houses, and sound mixing studios that made the movie business go.

At the northeast edge of Hollywood, where the scrub brush starts up again and the terrain begins to rise, was Pinnacle Studios. I turned into a wide driveway. Almost immediately, the nose of my car came up against a horizontal security bar with the green Pinnacle logo emblazoned across it. On my left was a kiosk flanked by a couple of coconut palms. A uniformed guard with the green Pinnacle logo on his cap stuck his head out of the kiosk. My white '61 Falcon, only two years old but in need of a wash, earned me a suspicious squint.

"State your business... sir." The guard didn't bother to hide the sarcasm on the "sir."

"Ryan Zorn. I have an appointment with Cora Flynn in Research."

The guard checked his clipboard, then waved me through with a scowl, as if I'd cheated him out of the chance to ruin someone's day.

The horizontal bar raised up, and I drove onto the lot. In an instant, I had left behind the hodge-podge randomness of L.A., and entered the meticulously manicured world of Pinnacle Studios. Although Pinnacle wasn't a major studio, it remained profitable year after year, churning out a stream of low-budget westerns and horror flicks, with the occasional historical drama thrown in for prestige. I cruised at the posted 15 miles per hour, up a spotless street lined with white Mediterranean-style buildings with red tiled roofs and covered walkways running along the front. Each building was topped with the green Pinnacle logo, followed by a number.

A woman stood in the shadows of Building 8's walkway. She was wearing a navy blue dress, cinched at the waist with a shiny red belt. She had a curvy figure, dark wavy hair that fell to her shoulders, and pale skin set off by red lipstick that matched the belt. As I got out of the car, she stubbed out her cigarette on the railing, crushed it under the toe of a low-heeled pump. I guessed her to be about 35 years old. Her skin was smooth, no wrinkles, but there was something brittle, even hard-edged around her mouth.

"Ryan?" she said, giving me a quick once-over.

I nodded.

"You're ... younger than I thought. I mean, not that it matters ... I just hope ... it's just that I'm worried and ... "

"We'll find your son, Mrs. Flynn."

"You can call me Cora."

She forced a smile. I extended my hand and we shook. Her nails were painted red, no wedding ring, and her handshake was limp like a lot of women's were. I wondered sometimes why nobody taught girls how to really grip the other person's hand when they shook.

"Thanks for getting here so quickly," Mrs. Flynn said. "Let's go inside. With all the lay-offs this summer, I'm the only one in Research right now, so we can talk."

I followed her into the coolness of a large, dimly lit room. The walls were lined with bookshelves and sturdy wooden file cabinets. At the center of the room was a large wooden table where a gooseneck lamp spotlighted an open book. More books were stacked on the table, many with thin strips of paper poking out from their pages. The room had the feel of being both overstuffed and vigorously organized.

Mrs. Flynn dropped into a chair and grabbed for her purse which was hanging over the back. She extracted a pack of Juicyfruit, popped a stick of gum into her mouth.

"No smoking allowed," she said with a nervous laugh. "Worst thing about this job."

She held out the pack of gum. "Want some?"

"No thanks. So, you said the last time you saw your son was Wednesday?"

"That's right. I had gone out with a couple of friends after work, and ... you know how it is, we had a few drinks, no big deal.

I checked on Joey when I got home like I always do. He was fast asleep."

"And the next morning?"

"Well, I . . . " She bit her lip. "I overslept a bit. I went in to wake Joey, but he wasn't in his room. I just assumed that he had left for school already."

"Is that common? That he gets himself to school like that?"

"He's done it before. Look, I do the best I can, okay?"

"Okay. So what about last night? Did you come straight home after work?"

"Of course I did," she said defensively. "Joey wasn't home, but that's not unusual. He often plays with his friends in the neighborhood until I get home, so I didn't think anything of it. But when I called over to Nicholas's — he's Joey's best friend in the neighborhood — he told me Joey wasn't at school yesterday. That's when I started to worry." Her eyes welled up. "He wasn't at school, and he never came home last night."

"Do you think he ran away?"

"Why would he?" She squinted at me, like I had accused her of something.

I shrugged. "I dunno. Kids do that. It happens."

"Joey and I are very close. He wouldn't do something like that to me."

Mrs. Flynn chewed her lip and looked down at her lap.

"Well," she admitted, "once we had an argument and he got really mad. But that was different. It was about a year ago. He ran out, saying he was going to live with his father. I got in the car and followed him. He didn't get very far. I found him down at the corner where our road meets Sunset, sitting at the bus stop. I reasoned with him, and he finally got in the car. Poor kid."

"Why poor kid?"

"Thinking that he could live with his father."

"Why couldn't he?"

She laughed, but there was no joy in it.

"Let's just say that when my husband left, he really left."

"So you're divorced."

She nodded. "Richard and I split up three years ago. I've only seen him a handful of times since then. Last Christmas he showed up with a present for Joey. No warning, just showed up. That's so Richard. Believe it or not he was once a regular, dependable guy. Had a good job teaching at UCLA."

"He's not at UCLA anymore?"

"Hardly." She shook her head, lost in her own thoughts for a few moments. "Something changed. I never understood what exactly. Richard tried to explain I suppose, in his own cryptic, philosophical way. I think what it boils down to is he just needed to change his life. Joey was eight when he left us. He screwed us financially, not a penny in child support or alimony. I guess I could take him to court, but what's the point... he says he has no money. Oh, excuse me," she said sarcastically, "he doesn't believe in money. That's why I work and have to leave Joey alone a lot. Do you think I feel good about that?"

It wasn't really a question, so I let it hang. The air in the room was still. I glanced over at the wooden file cabinets. Each drawer had a hand-printed label on the front: *Egypt, Rome, Old West, Civil War.* A buzzer sounded in the distance. A few seconds later, it stopped.

"So if Joey did run away," I said, "and he didn't go to his father's, where would he'd go?"

"I don't know. I just I don't know."

"And if he did go to his father's?"

"I don't... " she shook her head. Whatever she was going to say, she changed her mind. "For one thing, all we have is Richard's post office address. He's so damn secretive. No phone, no street address. His PO box is in Santa Maria, a little hick town north of Santa Barbara. That's all I know. He said he wanted to live 'close to nature' — whatever that means. Sometimes I think he's had a nervous breakdown or something. Each phone call, seldom that they are, he promises Joey that he can come visit him, but it never happens. And still Joey thinks his father walks on water."

As Mrs. Flynn descended into a bitter recollection of her failed marriage, I wondered to myself how long I should I let her go on. Lou's interviewing motto was: "Let em rip, then rein em in." I had sat in on interviews with Lou many times, but had done very little interviewing on my own.

"Mrs. Flynn," I cut in after a while, "did anything out of the ordinary happen on Wednesday, or maybe the day or two before?"

"Out of the ordinary? What do you mean?"

"Something that might cause Joey to run away. Like the other time, you said you had an argument. I'm asking because most missing children do turn out to be runaways."

She shook her head. I caught a flash of something in her eyes. I knew in that instant that Cora Flynn was holding something back.

"No" she said. "We didn't have an argument. Nothing like that."

"Or something else."

I waited. She fidgeted with her crumpled gum wrapper.

"That's what scares me the most," she said. "Nothing's happened. You hear ... you know, about kidnapping ... I don't know what to think, but I'm worried sick. I can barely concentrate on anything else."

"Have you called the police?"

"No!"

She stood up abruptly, walked a few paces, then turned and faced me.

"I don't want to involve the police. That's why I called you ... your agency. I need someone who will put all their energy into finding Joey. The police have so many cases, what's one boy to them?"

"Plenty. Finding missing persons is part of their job. They're good at it."

"I assume you are too."

"We are," I said. (Thinking to myself: *let's hope so.*) "But how would it hurt to have the police out looking also?"

"I told you: no police."

"Mrs. Flynn, is there something you're not telling me? Because most times that's one of the first things a parent does when their kid goes missing, is call the police."

"You ask a lot of questions."

"That's pretty much my job."

She smiled. She paced for another few steps, then turned back to me. She opened her mouth, was about to say something, but instead she slammed it shut. Finally she flopped back down onto the chair and sighed.

"A few months ago a County social worker came out to the house. She told me someone had reported that Joey was not being properly cared for. Do you know how humiliating that was? The social worker was sweet as can be, but behind that syrupy 'I'm here to help you and your family' crap, I knew she'd take Joey away from me in a quick minute if given half a chance. She checked the fridge, grilled me about my schedule, my habits. And on top of that, she wouldn't tell me who made the call. I'm fairly sure it was Mrs. Ackerman, Nicholas's mother. The way that woman looks at me .... I can feel her ... judging. Who's she to judge me? She's got a husband, money coming in. I'm working myself raw to support my child, while she's out planting geraniums."

We locked eyes. Hers burned with resentment. Eventually, she sighed and her expression softened up.

"Honestly Ryan, I'm afraid if I call the police, even if they do find Joey, they'll take him away from me."

"I don't think they'd do that."

"But you don't really know, do you?"

She was right: I didn't know much of anything for sure. Still, it seemed lame to worry about a social worker taking her son away in some hypothetical future when right now, in the real here and now, the boy was as gone as could be.

But I figured it wasn't going to do any good to tell this to Mrs. Flynn.

"Okay," I said. "I'll get on it right away. We charge $75 a day, plus expenses. I'll need a recent picture of Joey, and a list of his friends, relatives, anybody who might know something."

"Thank you, Ryan. I mean it."

Mrs. Flynn reached into her purse. She pulled a photo out of her wallet and handed it to me. Joey looked nothing like his mother. He had shaggy blonde hair, a turned up nose, blue eyes, and a few freckles.

"Also, I'll need that PO address for your husband."

"<u>Former</u> husband."

"Right. Sorry. And a photo of Mr. Flynn — as recent as possible."

"I've got some at home, but I can't leave work until five."

"Okay. I can get it tomorrow, although ... "

"Although what?"

"If I could get a photo of Mr. Flynn today it might help. The sooner I start pursuing this, the more likely we'll find Joey."

"Well ... " She looked at her watch, shook her head. "I'd never make it to the Palisades and back during lunch break."

"If you have an extra key, I could go out there myself."

"You mean let you into my house? When I'm not there?"

"Yeah. Basically."

"No, no, no. I don't think so."

I shrugged. "Okay. I can get it tomorrow."

Mrs. Flynn chewed on her gum for a while. I waited. I watched her and couldn't help thinking: This is a woman who is hiding something. Sure, I was essentially a stranger, and maybe she was just being cautious about who she let into her house. But something told me different.

“The key’s under the mat in the carport,” she said finally. “There’s a photo album on the bookshelf in my bedroom. Take whatever you need. As for Richard’s post office address, I’m not sure where I left my phone book, but it’s in the house somewhere. I’m sure you’ll find it.”

CHAPTER 2

I drove west on Sunset out of Hollywood, through Beverly Hills and Brentwood, around the big sweeping curve at Will Rogers State Park known for more than its share of killer car accidents, and into Pacific Palisades.

I turned up a quiet, tree-lined street of low-slung suburban ranchers with new, gleaming Rivieras and New Yorkers and Country Squires parked in spotless carports. It was the kind of neighborhood where housewives didn't check the prices at the grocery store, kids splashed around in backyard swimming pools, and Japanese gardeners arrived each week in their pick-ups to mow the lawn and trim the bird-of-paradise.

Cora Flynn's house sat at the end of a cul-de-sac under a couple of towering eucalyptus. The house was all glass and concrete, with a low flat roof, and a long, rectangular reflecting pool leading to the front door. It was modern and ritzy, but signs of neglect were everywhere. A blue Schwinn bike with a flat tire lay on its side in the driveway; the strip of grass that ran along the reflecting pool was parched the color of wheat; and the reflecting pool's dark water was littered with leaves.

I parked on the street, then walked into the carport and flipped up the mat where Mrs. Flynn said I'd find a key.

The door from the carport led into a kitchen with all-electric oven and stove, and a white round-edged Frigidaire with a top freezer. But despite the swanky appliances, a feeling of decay had settled over the room. The linoleum floors were scuffed. Dust balls had accumulated in the corners. A cupboard door hung open, exposing shelves bare of anything except a box of Lucky Charms and a jar of peanut butter.

Mrs. Flynn's bedroom was at the end of a hallway. The bed was made, but it was a half-assed job: the pink chenille bedspread pulled hastily over the pillows. On the night table was a glass with an amber puddle at the bottom. I could smell the booze from the doorway. Rum and Coke. My stomach clenched. The smell of my childhood.

I spotted the photo album and pulled it off the bookshelf. Wanting to escape the rum and coke stink, I thought about taking the album into another room, but forced myself to stay put and thumb carefully through the photos. A happy family beamed out at me: mother–father–baby . . . mother–father–boy . . . boy on bike . . . Christmas tree and boy . . . All the cookie-cutter shots that reveal nothing much about the people in them except that they had enough dough for a camera and knew how to move the right facial muscles when someone said "cheese."

I slipped out a color photo of mom–dad–boy, and tucked it Into the back of my spiral notebook.

Joey's bedroom was up the hall, just off the living room. His bed was unmade, blanket and top sheet crumpled in a heap against the wall. Above the bed hung a poster of Koufax and Drysdale, each bent forward in their pitching stance, lefty and righty, glove to glove. On a small, kid-sized desk was a record player with some 45s scattered around it: The Drifters' "Up on the Roof," The Four Seasons' "Walk Like A Man," the Beach Boys' Chuck Berry rip-off "Surfin' USA." I doubted Joey knew or cared that "Surfin' USA" was just "Sweet Little Sixteen" with a suntan. Chuck Berry knew it, you could bet on that. He was probably burning up right this minute in his Missouri prison cell just thinking about it.

Under the desk was a wastebasket containing an empty pack of Juicy Fruit gum, several Oh Henry! candy bar wrappers wrappers, and a single white envelope. I plucked out the envelope and examined it. It was addressed in a tight, jagged script to Joey Flynn. The postmark was too blurry to read. The top left corner of the envelope — where the return address should have been — was torn off. I slid the envelope into the back of my spiral notebook alongside the Flynn family photo.

Next: Mrs. Flynn's address book. It should have been easy to spot — by the phone, on the dining table. I searched all the usual, obvious places. But it wasn't there.

So, I searched the un-obvious places.

I finally found the address book in the sunken living room, wedged between the seat cushions of a black leather couch. I jotted down Richard Flynn's PO Box address and was about to leave when something caught my eye. In front of the couch was a glass coffee table which sat in the middle of a throw rug. The rug was black with a pattern of bright yellow, geometric shapes looking vaguely like leaves. The leaf shapes were clean-edged and bright. Except one. On the far corner of the rug one of the yellow leaves was infected by a dark fungus.

I bent down and examined the spot. The stain was a reddish-brown color. And it was larger than I first thought, extending into the black part of the rug where the stain was noticeable only because it caused the carpet fibers to clump and stick together. I touched the stain. Dry. I worked the carpet fibers between my fingers, dislodging some of the crumbly substance. Was it chocolate? Blood? Cherry soda? Ketchup? Paint? I had no idea.

If Lou were here, he'd know.

I put my nose to the rug and sniffed at the stain. I touched it to my lips, tasted a slight metallic tang. Not chocolate. Not cherry soda. Not ketchup. I dug into the carpet's thick pile where the liquid had saturated the threads and, insulated from the summer heat, still felt tacky to the touch. I flipped up the edge of the rug. Some of the liquid had soaked all the way through to the floor. I scraped at it with my fingernail. Not paint.

I went out to my car and got one of the small plastic baggies I kept in the glove compartment. Back inside the house, I scraped some of the caked, brown, possibly-blood, substance off the rug, and put it into the baggie.

I locked up the house and went out into the mid-day heat.

As I walked towards my car, I noticed a black Cadillac Eldorado parked halfway up the block. The Caddy was facing towards Sunset, its sleek tailfins jutting towards me. The windows were tinted. The car definitely had not been there a few minutes earlier when I came out for the plastic bag. I stood very still and listened. The Caddy's engine was purring. I thought about this for a minute. On the one hand, a Cadillac, even a new top of the line '63 Eldo, is par for the course in this kind of neighborhood. But dark-tinted windows? Not so much.

Just then, the Caddy eased away from the curb, made a smooth, arching U-turn, and began cruising slowly up the street, headed in my direction. Curiosity mixed with caution, I watched the Caddy when suddenly the driver hit the gas hard and peeled out. The tires squealed and smoked. Three thousand pounds of metal and chrome was barreling straight at me.

CHAPTER 3

Sun glinted off the front grille. The smell of smoke, rubber to concrete, drifted up my nostrils. The Caddy was closing in fast.

If I were paddling out and this had been a nasty breaker about to crash right on top of me, I'd know what to do. By now it was automatic. Head directly into the wave, grab the rails of my board, flip over sideways, stay underwater until the wave passes.

But this wasn't a wave.

I leaped towards my car, trying to put the Falcon's steel body between me and the metal monster. The Caddy swerved. Brakes squealed as the driver made a sharp (sharp for an Cadillac, that is) quick turn, nearly side-swiping my car.

A moment later, the Caddy was headed back towards Sunset, its tailfins disappearing around the bend.

I gulped air, breathed it out. Danger past. My muscles started to relax. Then it hit me:

I didn't get the plates. Shit.

I stood in the hot sun mentally kicking myself. Wishing I had paid better attention when Lou drilled me on memorizing license plates.

"You know the make and model of every car on the road, Ryan, but you can't keep three letters and three numbers straight in your head," he had complained to me more than once.

Back then, when Lou had tried teaching me the tricks of being alert to plate numbers, I couldn't have cared less. Now I cared.

Water under the bridge, Ryan. Let it go.

I waited on the sidewalk for a few more minutes, just to be sure the Caddy wasn't coming back. Then I walked up the block to the address Cora Flynn had given me. Ackerman. Home to Nicholas, Joey's best friend. It was Nicholas who had told her Joey wasn't at school on Thursday.

The Ackerman house was a beige rancher with a stacked stone chimney rising at the far end. A flower box overflowing with color ran across the front. In the carport was a turquoise Chevy Bel Air.

I rang the bell. Immediately, the high pitched yapping of a small dog started up from inside. Moments later I heard footsteps. The door opened a few inches and a face covered in cold cream poked out. The greasy white mask was framed by a circle of pink clip-on curlers. The door opened a few more inches. The woman behind the mask wore a pink terry cloth robe. In her arms was a small grey poodle. Two black holes at the center of the white mask peered out at me suspiciously.

"Yes?"

"I'm looking for Mrs. Ackerman."

"That's me."

I held out my card. "I'm a private investigator. I'm looking for Joey Flynn. He seems to be missing."

"Missing?" she exclaimed with alarm. "I knew that he . . . but . . . "

Mrs. Ackerman reached for my card, inadvertently jostling the poodle who took it out on me, snarling and showing his tiny razor-sharp teeth.

"That's enough, Buster," she said so mildly that the dog snarled one more time for good measure. She bent down so that her cold-creamed face nearly touched the dog's.

"You're such a good boy," she cooed. "Such a brave watch dog, aren't you?"

Then she turned back to me. "I don't know what to make of this. I mean, Cora said something, but… missing? A private investigator?" Her pink curlers jiggled when she shook her head, puzzled. "Honestly, though, I'm really not surprised. That was trouble waiting to happen."

"What'd you mean?"

Instead of answering, Mrs. Ackerman stuck her head further out the door and made a quick visual sweep of the street. Her eyes stopped momentarily on my car. The white Falcon was Lou's idea of the perfect PI ride. It was bland enough for surveillance, but still on the lower end of acceptable to people like Mrs. Ackerman. I would way rather be driving a T-Bird, but the Falcon's price was right, Lou kicked in for the insurance, and the rack for my board mounted in nothing flat.

Mrs. Ackerman glanced down at my business card again, then up at me.

"Do you want to come in?" she said.

"Sure. Thanks."

She hoisted the poodle up over her shoulder. Buster eyed me from his perch as I followed Mrs. Ackerman through a living room with floral upholstered furniture covered in plastic, and into a sunny kitchen with white Formica counters and table. She set Buster down onto a mat by a sliding glass door that opened up onto a kidney-shaped pool. The dog kept eyeing me.

"Hey, Buster," I said.

I crouched down. Keeping my open palm lower than the dog's chin, I slowly brought my hand towards him.

"Buster doesn't like strangers," Mrs. Ackerman warned.

"I like dogs," I answered.

"Do you have one?"

"No. Landlord doesn't allow pets."

"Too bad," she said.

"Hey, Buster," I repeated.

The dog sniffed my hand. He looked me in the eye and wagged his tiny pom-pom tail. I lifted my hand slowly, patted him on the head, and stood up. Buster watched me as I crossed the room. He growled half-heartedly, just to be sure I knew who was boss. Then he curled up and went to sleep.

"So, what did you mean about Joey, that trouble was waiting to happen?" I asked Mrs. Ackerman.

"It's that family," she said. "They're not normal. Doc Flynn, now why he's called 'Doc' I'll never know. He was a teacher, for god's sake, biology or botany, something like that. Not a real doctor. Anyway, Doc Flynn always seemed strange to me. Not that I've ever said anything. That's not my place. A few years ago he leaves his family, takes off with this, not that I'm prejudiced, but still, this Oriental woman. Now who does that? Up and leaves his family for no reason that I could ever find out. Not that Cora and I were close. I tried to be neighborly, but we just never ... we never *clicked* is how you'd say it these days. And now ... "

She took a sip of coffee, shook her head. "It's no wonder the child goes missing. Nobody home for him after school, Cora staying out late, bringing home ... men. But maybe that isn't for me to say."

She looked at me. I could tell she was itching to say more.

"Please continue, Mrs. Ackerman. Anything you can share with me might be important in finding Joey."

"Well, I'm not a gossip, but this is all very upsetting. I mean, I hope nothing has happened. Have you talked to anyone else in the neighborhood?"

I shook my head. "Not yet. So what about these men — did you meet any of them?"

"Of course not! I only know about them because of the strange cars parked there all night. And sometimes, if I just happened by coincidence to be out front gardening, I might see one leave in the morning."

By “coincidence” I figured Mrs. Ackerman meant that she spent a significant amount of time at her front window, peeking through the curtains.

“When was the last time you saw Joey?” I asked.

“Hmmm … a few days ago. He comes over to play with my Nicholas all the time. They practically grew up together, both being only children. They’re almost like brothers.”

“Do you remember what day that was?”

She thought for a moment. “Tuesday. Yes, it was definitely Tuesday. Nicholas has cello lessons on Tuesday, and I let Joey watch TV during the lesson. He had dinner with us, like he often does. I mean it’s that or the boy is all alone at home until who knows when.”

“How did Joey seem on Tuesday?”

“What do you mean?”

“Was he happy, or sad, or any different than usual?”

“Just normal, I would say. Joey’s a quiet boy.”

“Do you have any idea where he might be right now?”

“Certainly not! Why would I?”

She seemed alarmed by my question. Rookie mistake. I had put her on the defensive, and now I’d better mop it up quick.

“No reason, Mrs. Ackerman. I’m just covering all the bases. Is your son home? I’d like to talk with him, if that okay with you.”

“Of course it is … anything we can do to help. Nicholas gets home from school about 3:30 PM. Oh, no, 2:30 PM today because it’s the last school day before summer vacation. But I can tell you, he doesn’t know anything about this either. He would have said something to me if he did.”

Which told me exactly how much Mrs. Ackerman knew about 11-year-old boys.

I thanked her for her cooperation and said I’d be back. The poodle perked up when I pushed back my chair.

"Hey, Buster," I said, offering my open palm.

Buster sniffed at my hand. He looked up at me, cocked his head, then covered his face with his paws and went back to sleep.

***

I got into my car and I checked my watch. Just after 1:00 PM. I could hang around, interview another neighbor or two, then talk to Joey's friend Nicholas when he returned from school. But all that, I decided, could wait.

I drove back up Sunset, pulled into a gas station with a pay phone, and called Cora Flynn.

"Did you find out anything?" she said, her voice brittle and clipped with worry.

"Not too much, but I'm headed your way," I lied. "Can I come by the studio and talk?"

"What is it? Why can't we talk on the phone?"

"I need to show you something."

"Something about Joey?"

"Mrs. Flynn, I'll be out there in half an hour."

For the second time that day I drove east to Hollywood. I made it past Pinnacle's hostile gate keeper, cruised slowly to Building 8 where Cora Flynn was waiting for me out front.

"Let's walk," she said. "I need a smoke."

After lighting up, she practically bolted down the street. I fell into step with her as we headed away from Building 8.

"I'm going nuts sitting in there," she explained. "The phone rings and I nearly jump out of my skin. I can barely concentrate on work, so I guess it's a good thing the studio's slow. Seems like nobody knows what kind of pictures to make anymore. Word is *Cleopatra* went so far over-budget that Fox is headed for bankruptcy no matter how it does at the box office. And not even Pinnacle's immune … "

She was chattering non-stop in rapid-fire bursts, as if the barrage of words could keep her anxiety at bay. Or maybe she was just scared of what I was going to tell her if she gave me half a chance.

"... nothing in the pipeline. They even had me cleaning out some muckity-muck's office after he was fired. Just to keep me busy. Boring as hell, but I'm not complaining. At least I've got a job."

A clean-cut kid driving a golf cart with the green Pinnacle logo on its side passed us. The kid smiled and waved. Mrs. Flynn waved back. She forced a tight-lipped smile that to me read more like a grimace. I needed to get the conversation on track.

"Mrs. Flynn—"

"Cora."

"Cora. Did something spill on your living room rug recently?"

She looked at me quizzically. "Spill? I don't know ... why are you asking?"

"There's a stain on one corner."

"So there's a stain. I've got a kid so of course things spill. Joey could've spilled some cereal or something."

"It's not cereal. It's dark colored."

Mrs. Flynn shrugged. "Could be anything I guess."

"Did you or Joey cut yourself recently?"

She stopped abruptly. Her eyes widened and fear poured out.

"Are you saying there's blood on the rug?"

"I think so. And not just a drop or two."

"That's crazy. Blood? Don't you think I'd notice something like that?"

"I don't know. Would you?"

Mrs. Flynn shot me a furious glare. I thought she was going to let me have it, but the glare gave way to something else: A look of recognition? Just for an instant. Then her face went blank.

She turned away from me, lit another cigarette off the lipstick-smeared stub in her hand. We walked in silence for a while. We had left the red-roofed office buildings behind and were now passing through an Old West set. Splintered plank sidewalk. Hitching post. Fake wooden store fronts. Generic signage painted to look old and weather-worn and historic. *Trading Post... Hotel... Sheriff... Dry Goods...* Signs you've see in a hundred cheap westerns. The *Saloon* sign hung crooked above an expertly broken window.

I thought about how to handle Mrs. Flynn. I was certain she was hiding something. But who didn't have secrets? I just hoped that whatever she was hiding wouldn't block me from finding her son. I fished the torn envelope out of my back pocket and handed it to her. She studied it.

"That's Richard's handwriting. Where'd you get this?"

"From Joey's room."

"The return address—"

"I'm betting Joey took it with him."

"Do you still think he ran away to his father's?"

"For lack of any better idea, yes."

She shook her head, thinking. "No. It just doesn't make sense. I mean how would he get there? And where would he actually go? To a damn post office? And beyond all that, WHY? Why would he do something like that to me?"

"I don't know."

Mrs. Flynn dragged hard on her cigarette. We had circled the Old West set, past the Pioneer Church and the horse corral. Now we were on the backside of town, walking behind the building facades where their missing back walls exposed a web of electrical wires, beams, pipes, ladders, and the scaffolding that held the Saloon and the Trading Post shells in place.

"About Wednesday night," Mrs. Flynn began. She hesitated and bit her lip. "Maybe it's nothing, and... it's all kind of fuzzy, but I went out with some of the girls from work for a few drinks and I... maybe I had a bit too much to drink."

"Okay."

"What I'm trying to say is...I met a man there. We...he came back to my house."

"Just the two of you?"

She nodded. "It's not easy for me to tell you this, but that's how it is. If you want to judge me there's nothing I can do about it. He was gone in the morning."

"This man, did you know him?"

"I'd never seen him before," she mumbled, looking down at the ground.

I had an urge to shake her. Not because I gave a damn who she slept with or why. *You brought a stranger back to your house, the next day your son goes missing, and you waited until now to tell me!* I wanted to shout. But I didn't. I stayed cool. I kept my voice in neutral. "Stay detached," Lou always said. "Try not to display emotion in an interview."

"What did this guy look like?" I asked.

"Umm...big, really big...blonde hair, blonder even than yours."

"Big-tall, or big-fat?"

"Not fat. Just big. Big like a football player."

"How old?"

"I don't know. It was dark. Thirty maybe, thirty-five, forty."

"What bar?"

"Kelbo's. We go there sometimes after work."

"The one on Pico or Fairfax?"

"Pico."

I pulled out my spiral notebook and a pen.

"Which friends were with you? I'd like to talk with them."

"It wouldn't do any good. My girlfriends had all left by then. You really think this has anything to do with Joey?"

"It might. You said the guy came back to your house. Did he drive his own car?"

"I assume so. I told you, I don't remember too much about that night."

"What more do you remember?" I asked casually. I was getting to know Mrs. Flynn and how the smallest thing, a slight tone of voice, could switch on her defenses.

"I checked on Joey. I definitely remember that. He was asleep. After that . . ." she ran her fingers through her dark wavy hair, tugging at the strands as if she were trying to pull out a memory. "After that . . ."

She dropped her cigarette butt and ground it into the pavement with her heel. I had the feeling she was stalling for time.

We walked in silence for a few minutes, turned a corner. All at once we had returned to the modern world of white-washed office buildings with shaded walkways and red-tiled roofs. When we got to Building 8, Mrs. Flynn finally broke the silence.

"Now that I think about it," she said, not looking at me as she spoke, "you're probably right about Joey going to his father's. I mean with the envelope and everything, I'm almost certain that's where he went. I think that's the best place to start looking."

Nice dodge away from the guy at Kelbo's, I thought.

CHAPTER 4

By the time I got back to the office, the sun was dropping and the air was cooling off. I checked with the answering service: no urgent calls, nothing I'd have to deal with tonight. Finally, I called the VA hospital. A nurse with a slow Southern drawl told me that my uncle was sleeping and I should call back in the morning.

"I will," I said. "How's Lou doing?"

"He has his good days and his bad," she said vaguely.

"How about today?"

"It's best you speak with a doctor about medical matters. But I'll be sure to let Mr. Zorn know you called."

I thanked her and we hung up. It had been a few days since I'd visited Lou. I felt bad about it, but since it was due to work, I knew Lou would understand.

I sat down at Lou's desk and unwrapped a fat roast beef sandwich from Zucky's. Just the smell made me hungry. I realized that I hadn't eaten since breakfast. I gazed out the window as I ate. Across the street was a nursery specializing in bonsai. A small man in a pith helmet and khaki jacket was locking the nursery gate. Next door to the nursery, a red neon BAIL BONDS sign flickered on. The West L.A. Police Station was just around the corner, so the bail bonds joint did a decent business, 24/7.

This was the time of day Lou and I would often talk about his cases — our cases, he would call them — or just shoot the shit about life. I wondered if we'd ever do that again. Lou had put off going to the doctor for months, until he no longer had enough breath to walk from his house to his car. The doctor characterized his emphysema as 'severe.' I didn't understand any of the doc-talk about bronchial obstruction or disruption of alveo-somethings, but it didn't take a genius to figure out where it was all leading.

"Hold down the fort, kid," Lou had said in a weak, raspy whisper the last time I'd visited him at the VA. "I'm counting on you."

That was new and different: Lou counting on me. I didn't know exactly how I felt about that, except that it was strange and I knew for sure that I didn't want to let him down. Couldn't let him down. Lou had never let me down, he'd always been there for my mother and me. Now it was my turn. Ready or not, that's how it was.

I finished the sandwich and sorted through the mail — a few bills and a flyer advertising a vacuum cleaner shaped like a flying saucer.

Then I drove over to Kelbo's.

It took me a few seconds to adjust to the dark. Kelbo's was a Polynesian-themed restaurant with pineapple-shaped lanterns, hand carved tikis, and a high ceiling draped with fishing nets. I threaded my way past booths disguised as thatched huts where families hunkered over plates of sweet spareribs, shish kabobs, and blue drinks topped with paper umbrellas.

I pushed aside a curtain of shells and entered the bar. Japanese lanterns and dried porcupine fish hung from the ceiling. The bar itself was a mammoth slab of dark polished wood. The bartender, tall with a cleft chin and a stubble of beard, was wiping down some glasses with a rag.

It was still early. The sole customer sat on a stool at the far end of the bar — a middle-aged man in shirtsleeves staring listlessly into his drink. He was clean-shaven with wiry grey hair. He had a taut, sinewy body; small but packed with muscle. He looked like a man who wanted to be alone with his liquor.

I ordered a Schlitz, sliding a five across the wood slab to the bartender.

"Keep the change," I said.

"Let's see some ID."

I showed him my driver's license. He made a big deal of comparing me to my picture. I was used to it. He finally brought me the beer.

"Been working here long?" I asked, trying to sound nonchalant.

He looked at me warily, knowing, as bartenders always do, that I wanted something.

"Long enough."

I put my card on the bar so that the writing faced him.

"I'm looking for a guy who was in here Wednesday night."

He picked up the card and looked it over. His face hardened. He slapped the card back down on the bar.

"We don't give out information about our customers."

"I understand, but —"

"No, buddy, I don't think you do."

"Take it easy, man. I get it. I'm a PI. My clients depend on me keeping things quiet too. I'm not asking you to snitch on some sleaze ball going out on his wife. I'm looking for a missing kid. This customer, he might know something about it."

"Sorry, no can do."

The bartender turned away from me. He picked up a glass from the drain board and began polishing it.

"Hey, Mike, give the kid a break." The voice came from the wiry man at the far end of the bar. He flicked me a crisp salute off his brow. "You're Lou Zorn's kid, aren't you?"

"He's my uncle."

The man picked up his drink and moved over to a barstool near mine.

"Alex Terekov. Detective Sergeant, Hollywood Division. I remember seeing you over at West LA. a few times. How's Lou doing?"

"Not so good."

"Sorry to hear it. That son-of-a-bitch is a survivor, though. He'll make it through this... if anybody can."

"I hope so."

"He and my old patrol partner were at Guadalcanal together. Saved my partner's ass at Henderson Field."

"You in the Pacific too?"

"Aleutians. Seventh Infantry." He raised his glass. "Here's to frozen tundra, frost bite, and coming home to sunny fucking paradise."

The detective drained his glass, then held it up for a refill. The bartender drifted over and picked up the empty.

"Mike, while you're at it, help this kid out," Terekov said. "He's one of the good guys."

"Sure thing, Detective," the bartender replied. There was a sullen edge to his voice. He'd cooperate, but not happily.

Mike The Bartender poured a shot of scotch for Terekov and set it down on a fresh napkin. The detective picked up his drink and ambled back down to the far end of the bar. The bartender turned to me.

"Okay, buddy, I guess it's your lucky day."

"The guy I'm looking for is thirty to forty, big guy, real light blonde hair, lighter than mine even. Left with a woman at closing Wednesday night."

"Any particular woman?" the bartender said with a smirk.

"Name's Cora Flynn. Do you remember the guy or not?"

"Yeah, I remember him. Hair's white as snow."

"White?"

"That's what I said."

"Seen him before?"

"Nope. Never saw him before and hope I never see him again."

"Why's that?"

"Cuz he was a creep."

"How so?"

"Picking up on ... on the lady when she was already out of it, is what I mean. You know the type."

"What type?"

"A creep. Like I told you. I watched him all night. Circling like a vulture. He kept his distance, but was checking her out. Then he goes in for the dead meat at the end. Disgusting. No respect at all."

I nodded slowly, wondering how far I could push this guy before he'd clam up.

"Did they leave together?" I asked.

"More or less."

"What do you mean?"

"He kind of carried her out."

"What about the woman? She a regular?"

"Comes and goes."

"Can you tell me anything else about her?"

He shrugged. "Nice lady. But I've had to call her a cab a few too many times."

Mike The Bartender picked up another glass from the drain board and started to dry it. "So Cora's kid is missing, huh. I didn't even know she had one."

I nodded. I took a few sips of my beer, waiting to see if he'd say anything else. I didn't like alcohol, not even beer, but sometimes you gotta do what you gotta do. The bartender busied himself with what bartenders do: rearranging glasses that didn't need to be rearranged, checking levels on bottles he already checked ten minuets ago.

"This white haired guy," I said, "if he comes in again, would you let me know?"

I tapped my card which was still on the bar and pushed it towards Mike the Bartender.

He didn't pick it up. He glanced over at Terekov who had lit a cigarette and was staring at the smoke as it wafted up into the hanging lanterns and bloated, spiny fish. Terekov could have been thinking deep thoughts, or thinking nothing at all. Either way, Mike The Bartender and I both knew he was listening to our every word. Almost imperceptivity, Terekov nodded. The bartender turned back to me.

"Sure," he said. "No problem. If I see the creep, I'll give you a call."

CHAPTER 5

It was dark by the time I got home. I parked in the alley behind my apartment, a two-story duplex with peeling plaster and no heat. The duplex had been built in the 1920s, the golden age of Venice Beach. Back then — when gondolas glided along the pristine canals, tourists soaked in the salt-water plunge, and Sarah Bernhardt performed at the pleasure pier — Venice had been proclaimed the "safest beach in the country." Now it was pretty much a slum.

I climbed the rickety wooden steps to the second floor landing, careful to avoid the splintered hand railing. Decades of salt air had taken its toll on the place, and the landlord sure as hell wasn't doing anything about it.

I unlocked the door and went inside. Even after living here almost two years, I still got a kind of thrill each time I walked in. This was MY apartment. MY place. As long as I was able to come up with the rent each month, I had a home. The single big, airy room (plus bathroom) was plenty for me. More than plenty.

I kicked off my shoes and pulled a cold tonic water from the fridge. The "kitchen," which occupied one corner of the room, consisted of a tiny fridge, a hot plate, and a red vinyl dinette table with four matching chairs that I had picked up cheap at the Salvation Army. On the other side of the room was a Murphy bed that pulled out of the wall, a dresser, and a sagging couch that I had inherited from a buddy when he moved up in the world. Next to the dinette set, on the west-facing wall, a sliding glass door opened to a balcony where I kept my surfboard. The slider was the landlord's single concession to fixing the place up. The view from the balcony was the backside of an old brick building that housed a liquor store with a few apartments above it. Beyond that was the beach. I couldn't see it, but it was there.

My apartment had two main attractions: the rent was cheap, and I could hear the surf breaking just a few hundred feet away. As an added bonus, my downstairs neighbors, Tom and Tina Crawford, had become friends. Tom worked the line at the Ford plant in Pico Rivera. Tina waited tables at Chasen's, a swanky Hollywood joint where tips were famously large. He was Negro and she was white. We all liked the same music, so they never complained when I blasted the hi-fi. Now and again I'd run into them up at Shelly's Manne-Hole in Hollywood or down at The Lighthouse in Hermosa Beach. Sometimes we'd all go together.

I opened the slider to the balcony. Cool ocean air flowed into the room. I switched on the radio, catching the tail end of a Mingus cut just as the phone rang.

"Ryan, where have you been? I've been calling you all evening."

"Working, Mom. The usual. You see Lou today?"

"I went to the hospital, but they wouldn't let me into his room. The nurse said he needs his rest. I'm worried, Ryan."

"I know."

"I just wish there was something I could do."

"I know."

"And he's going downhill so fast. You remember last year, the doctor said his only chance was to quit smoking, cold turkey, right then and there. But did he listen?"

"It's the past, Mom. Forget about it."

"I just don't want to lose him. First your father … "

We both fell silent.

I had no real memories of my father. He died when I was two. His unit had been captured during the war by the Japanese in the Philippines. My father and a couple thousand other prisoners were force-marched across the Bataan Peninsula with almost no food or water for weeks. Most of the them died along the way. The Army said my father may have died of starvation, dysentery, dehydration, or a shot to the head while trying to escape. Or any combination of the above. They never recovered his body.

I only knew my father from photographs, from my mother's memories, and Uncle Lou's. Lou had come back from the war hobbling, but alive. He made it his life's mission to be sure his brother's widow and kid were taken care of. He married, but never had children of his own.

Growing up, I remember Lou's wife seemed perpetually irritated by both me and my mother. Our once a week dinners together were her personal hell. If she could have made us both evaporate, she would have. After Lou's divorce, he had a live-in girlfriend — she was a good-looking blonde with a horsy laugh and a gambling problem — but the relationship didn't last. After that, it was just the three of us against the world.

"Ryan," my mother was saying on the phone, "Are you there?"

"I'm here, Mom."

"Come by soon, okay."

"Yeah," I said, "I will."

I hung up the phone, feeling shitty. I wanted to say something to my mother, something to make her feel better. But anything I said would be bogus. How do you comfort someone when there is no comfort, no good news, to be found in the truth? My father was gone, and Lou was on his way out.

I switched off the radio. Then I tossed a toothbrush and a change of clothes into a brown paper grocery bag, negotiated the flimsy stairs back down to the alley, and hopped into my car.

***

The Greyhound bus station in Santa Monica was nearly deserted. An elderly woman with a cane sat by herself in a chair near the ticket counter, knitting something red white and blue. I checked the bus schedule above the ticket counter. The northbound line ran twice daily and included a stop in Santa Maria. I asked the tired-looking man behind the counter if he had been on duty Wednesday night or Thursday morning. He shook his head, pointed to a Negro janitor who was sweeping the floor.

"He was," the clerk claimed.

I went over to the janitor and asked him if he'd seen a boy hanging around a few nights ago. I showed him the photo of Joey Flynn. The janitor took his time examining the photograph.

"Sorry, mister," he said, shaking his head. "Didn't see him."

He handed the photo back to me.

I got back into my car, swung onto the coast highway and headed north. I figured it would take about four hours to get to Santa Maria. I'd find a cheap motel, then get an early morning start on my search for the boy.

I'd been driving Pacific Coast Highway since high school. PCH is the road that leads to all surfing spots from San Diego to Santa Cruz. Despite its name, PCH is actually less a highway and more a narrow snaking blacktop that hugs the twisty California coastline. It's squeezed between high crumbling cliffs on one side, and a steep drop-off to the ocean on the other.

Tonight, with no street lights and only a sliver of moon, PCH was just miles of serpentine darkness. I could smell the ocean, but couldn't see it. And I could only hope that the occasional headlights coming from the other direction stayed on their own side of the road. Driving PCH at night took a certain steady alertness and attention. I liked the drive. I liked the sound of tires rolling across the smooth asphalt. I liked having time to think.

My mind drifted to Joey Flynn, a sandy-haired 11-year-old, who, according to his mother, would never run away because "he wouldn't do something like that to me." And who, again according to his mother, thought his father walked on water. I hoped Joey had run away to his fantasy father. That the worst to happen was he'd find out the father wasn't so perfect after all. I hoped Joey's disappearance had nothing to do with the stain on the carpet which might or might not be blood. As for Mrs. Flynn, what did I know about her so far? One minute she gushed information, a mother desperate to find her son. The next minute she clammed up. She claimed to remember almost nothing about the night Joey disappeared. I figured either she was hiding something, or she was a blackout drunk.

I knew something about blackout drunks.

Growing up, I lived with my mother in a tiny apartment on Venice Beach. It was supposed to be a temporary place until my father returned from the war. But he never did. So we stayed in that apartment, and Venice Beach became my home. During the war, my mother had worked as a welder up at Hughes Aircraft in Culver City. When the war ended, she kept working at Hughes, but had to give up her spot on the line for a lower-paying secretarial position. She paid an elderly couple up the block to watch me until she came home from work. Sometimes that wasn't until the next day.

When the elderly couple moved away, my mother decided I didn't need them anyway and was old enough to take care of myself. By the time I was Joey Flynn's age, I was cleaning up my mother's puke, putting her to bed, making excuses to her boss when she was too hung over to show up for work. I didn't think too much about it. I just did what had to be done.

Then in high school, I watched in amazement as my mother found AA, got sober, and started to put her life together. All of a sudden I was free from having to worry about her all the time

Somehow she'd hung onto her job at Hughes. She started making friends in AA. She saved enough money to buy a new car. She even joined a bowling league and started dating a guy from AA who also liked to bowl. And I was free from gearing my life around making sure she was okay.

Not that everything was easy sailing all the time. Mom had a couple of slips. Once she wound up in County lock-up after driving onto Clover Field and hitting a parked plane. It had been a few years since she last slipped, but she wasn't dating the bowling guy anymore, and I knew she was lonely. Her loneliness made me worry. I could picture her right now: sitting in her recliner with a pack of Newport menthols and an Orange Fanta, watching Johnny Carson, and worrying about Uncle Lou.

***

It was 2:00 AM when I reached Santa Maria. I checked into the first motel I could find, and sacked out for the night. The next morning, I went across the street to a diner, picked up some coffee and a donut, a sandwich for later, and the local newspaper. I asked the waitress where I could find the central post office. She told me there was only one post office in Santa Maria, and pointed me towards it.

The town was wide open and flat — part cowboy, part Mexican, and part modern Deluxe. I passed a motel advertising telephones in every room. Another motel offered Magic Fingers vibrating beds. The movie theater on Broadway was showing *Donovan's Reef.* Maybe they'd get *Cleopatra* by Christmas.

The post office was in a brick building the color of sand. An American flag drooped listlessly from a pole on the roof. I went inside and located Doc Flynn's PO box. Then I crossed the street, got into my car, rolled down the windows, and settled in.

If this had been a weekday, I would have gone down to the County Courthouse to check whether Flynn had any liens or lawsuits, any kind of public record which might reveal a street address. That sort of research was the side of the business I'd been doing for Lou for years. But this was Saturday. County offices closed. I'd have to be patient — and lucky.

Keeping one eye on the post office entrance, I opened the newspaper and scanned it. I learned that a new Presbyterian church was being built to accommodate the growing Santa Maria population; that the high school football coach was retiring; that President Kennedy was in Berlin visiting Checkpoint Charlie. There was a quote from Kennedy saying, "All free men, wherever they may live, are citizens of Berlin, and therefore, as a free man, I take pride in the words, 'Ich bin ein Berliner.'"

Ich bin ein Berliner. What did that mean? And: *We are all citizens of Berlin?* Lou would have something to say about that.

Some movement caught my eye. I looked up from the paper and watched a leather-faced man wearing a cowboy hat and boots saunter into the post office. He emerged in a few minutes with some letters in his hand. Not Flynn.

A while later, an overweight woman pushing a baby stroller went into the PO. At noon I ate the sandwich, got out of the car, and stretched. A few more customers went in and out of the PO. None were Flynn. By three o'clock I was cursing Cora Flynn for insisting that no police be involved in the search for her son. One visit to the local Sheriff and I might have located Flynn in minutes.

An hour later I was cursing myself for wasting a day that I could have spent searching for the big white-haired man from Kelbo's. What idiot parks in front of a post office on the slimmest chance that one particular man might show up on one particular day?

Then I saw him. I flipped to the back of my spiral notebook and examined the Flynn family photo. I looked back up a the man walking near my car. Doc Flynn was no longer a smiling, clean-cut, suit-and-tie college professor. Not by a long shot.

CHAPTER 6

He was rail thin and had a bushy beard streaked with grey. He wore a faded denim shirt, jeans, and mud-caked work boots. As he passed by my car, I had a brief but decent look at his face. There was a strange, wild look in his eyes. Something off-kilter. Something that instantly put an end to my idea that Joey might be a simple runaway hanging out with his dad.

I was still holding the photo when Doc Flynn emerged from the PO. He was carrying a small package wrapped in brown paper. He got into a dirty Ford pick-up and took off. I waited until he turned the corner, then cranked the key in the ignition.

I tailed Flynn's truck out of Santa Maria and up into the hills east of town, keeping a respectable distance and a couple of curves between us. The hills were covered with chaparral and the occasional stand of oak or madrone. The air was dry and smelled of sage. Eventually the paved road gave way to dirt. To keep out of sight, I had to lag further and further back until all I was tailing was the churned-up dust.

I followed the cloud of dust past a jagged outcropping of rock, rounded a blind curve.

Suddenly, I hit the brakes.

Fuck!!!!

I had nearly smashed into Flynn's pick-up which was parked diagonally across the road. Flynn was standing by his truck, holding a shotgun. The barrel was pointed at my windshield.

"Get out," he said. "Hands on your head."

Flynn was smiling. Grinning, actually. Like this was all an amusing prank. It crossed my mind that he might be insane.

"I said: get out," he repeated. "Hands on your head."

I got out and put my hands on my head.

"Sit down," he said.

I sat down.

I had never had a gun pointed at me before. I felt my muscles start to tense up. Don't panic, I told myself. This is just another wave. Count to three. Stay alert.

Flynn set the shotgun on the ground, then pat searched my body. He pulled the wallet out of my back pocket, looked through it, tossed it onto the dirt. Without taking his eyes off me, he picked up the shotgun again. He took a couple of steps back, and pointed it at my head.

"What's your story, man?" he said.

"I'm a private investigator. Your ex-wife hired me to find your son."

"No shit?" He grinned again.

"He's been missing since Wednesday and she thinks he might be up here."

"How do I know you're not a cop?"

"Because if I were a cop there'd be four of me, or maybe ten, and we'd show up fully loaded just before dawn and right about now you'd be sitting in a cell somewhere screaming bloody murder for me to unshackle you so you could call your lawyer or take a piss."

Flynn laughed. It was a deep, belly laugh that shook his whole body. He was really enjoying himself.

"In other words," he said, "a cop wouldn't be so dense as to get himself caught in the act by an old fart like me."

"That about sums it up."

He chuckled. Then he walked over to my car and pulled the keys from the ignition. He walked backwards, keeping the gun trained in my direction. Without turning away from me, he removed a jumble of rope from his truck's flatbed.

"Put your hands behind your back."

"Is this really necessary, Mr. Flynn? I'm not here to cause you any trouble. I just want to find Joey. Is he here?"

Flynn said nothing. He moved towards me and flicked the tip of the gun barrel against my arm.

"Alright, alright," I said. "Be cool."

I put my hands behind my back and he tied my wrists together with the rope. He worked faster and more efficiently than I expected. When I tried to wiggle my wrists, they wouldn't budge.

"Okay wise guy," Doc Flynn commanded, "get in the truck."

"What about my car?"

"Don't worry about that. We'll take care of it."

"Who's 'we'?"

"Don't worry about that either. Just get in the truck."

I got into the truck. We drove up the dirt road in silence. Soon, on the right, appeared a high chain-link fence topped with coils of razor wire. All I could see behind the fence was more scrub brush and a few trees. Flynn drove along the chain-link until we reached an iron gate flanked by two stone pedestals. The gate swung open as we approached. We drove through and the gate closed behind us.

Flynn maneuvered the truck up a pitted gravel road. We seemed to be in some kind of primitive compound or ranch. We passed a ragged wood shack... a clearing with a vegetable garden... a mud hut about the size and shape of a camping tent. Flynn braked in front of a small log cabin with a steep pitched roof. Two metal patio chairs sat on the front porch. The cabin had a door, but oddly, no windows.

He got out of the truck and opened the passenger door.

"Get out," he said mildly.

I slid off the seat awkwardly, hands behind my back, and followed him into the cabin.

I was in a very dark room. A sliver of light leaked in between some wall planks, and a bit more entered through a small hole in the center of the ceiling that could have been an improvised skylight or a construction mistake.

"Relax," Doc Flynn said. "Have a seat."

I looked around for a chair, but there were none. The only piece of furniture was a shabby bureau pushed up against one wall. In the middle of the room was an oriental rug with an intricate pattern only vaguely visible in the darkness. I sat down on the rug, but I didn't relax. Flynn leaned his shotgun against the wall. He sat down on the rug directly in front of me, a bit too close for comfort. He stared intently directly into my eyes.

"So Ryan, have you read any William James?" he asked, as if this were the most logical question in the world.

"Excuse me?"

"James. William James. Brother to Henry. Pioneering psychologist and philosopher. Intrepid explorer of mystical experience, the world beyond and within."

He watched me expectantly, waiting for a reply. I probably appeared as baffled as I felt.

Flynn chuckled. "Is that a no?"

I shrugged.

"How about Huxley?" he probed. "*Brave New World. Doors of Perception.*"

Who was this guy? What did he want from me? I knew what I wanted from him: I wanted not to die. He wasn't holding the gun anymore; that was progress. In a straight-up physical fight I believed I could get the best of him.

"Look, Mr. Flynn, I don't know what this is all about, but if we're having an English lit exam, could you untie my hands first? My brain works better that way."

He ignored my lame humor. “No Huxley, huh? What about marijuana? Tried it?” He was grinning again.

Maybe Doc Flynn was insane. Or maybe he was something else. There was something about him that reminded me of Big Daddy and the other cats who hung out Venice West Café and the Gas House, beat joints on the Boardwalk crammed with chess tables, bongos, and poetry written on the walls. The cops were always trying to shut down these places, citing reasons like “reading poetry without a license.” The beat scene wasn’t my thing, but the Boardwalk was my backyard, so I’d been dropping by ever since I was a teenager. It’s where I first got into jazz, listening to Buddy Collette and Shelley Manne and Shorty Rogers jam at Venice West.

Flynn wasn’t letting it drop. “Marijuana,” he repeated. “Pot. Weed. Have you smoked it or not?”

“Sure. Couple of times.”

“How was the experience?”

“Fine.”

“Come on wise guy, enough of the one word answers. What was it like?”

“I got buzzed.”

“And?”

“Music sounded awesome.”

“Ah yes, music. Sound. The sensory plane. So you liked it?”

“Sure.”

“Excellent. Promising start. Now it’s time to graduate. Not to disparage the sensory plane, but there’s so much more.”

Flynn stood up abruptly. He grabbed the shotgun and left the cabin. I heard the key turn in the lock. I thought about trying to kick the door in and making a run for it, but I didn’t figure I’d get very far. Doc Flynn might be crazy, but he wasn’t stupid. Besides, if Joey was here, I didn’t want to blow the opportunity to find him.

A few minutes later, Flynn returned without the gun. He locked the door to the cabin and put the keys in his back pocket. He was carrying a package that looked like the one I'd seen him collect at the post office. It was about the size of a transistor radio. Flynn sat down on the rug and unwrapped it. Inside was a cardboard box. Inside the box was a plastic bag. And inside the bag, sandwiched between two sheets of cardboard, was a stack of blotter paper dyed bright orange. Each sheet of paper was about four inches square. Flynn counted the sheets, handling them delicately. The sheets were scored with black lines into a grid of small squares. Carefully, he tore off two of the squares and held them up.

"Lysergic acid diethylamide. LSD. Synthesized from ergotamine, a chemical derived from ergot. That's a grain fungus that typically grows on rye. Pretty nifty, don't you think?"

He grinned like a proud father. I guess I was supposed to be impressed. I might have been, if I'd known what he was talking about.

"What we've come up with is a hallucinogen similar to those found in the peyote cactus and psilocybin mushroom, both of which have been utilized by many ancient civilizations. Here ... "

Flynn scooted across the rug so that he was behind me. He untied my hands. I shook out my wrists to get the blood circulating again. He handed me one of the tiny paper squares. I didn't take it.

"Twenty-five micrograms. I strongly suggest you try it." He popped the other square into his mouth and grinned. "See. It's easy."

"Maybe some other time," I said flatly.

"No time like the present."

I shrugged.

"Really Ryan, there's nothing to be frightened of. For eons, shamans have used the psychoactive alkaloids occurring naturally in plants to contact the spirit world of their ancestors. Tribal priests throughout the Americas use psychedelics to empower themselves with supernatural visions. Now we — you and I — through the marriage of modern science and ancient herbology, have the ability to transcend our ordinary consciousness, to experience layers of reality that have thus far been hidden from modern man."

"I'm just here to find Joey."

"So you say." His tone had changed. The glint of amusement in his eyes turned to cold steel. I liked the grinning Doc Flynn better.

"Why would I lie?" I said.

"Why does anybody lie? To protect yourself, to protect someone or something you care about, for financial gain, for social or political gain, to appear virtuous, to manipulate your environment, out of insecurity, pathology — do you want me to continue?"

"I'm being straight with you, Mr. Flynn. And if Joey is here, I'd think you'd want to let his mother know that he's safe. If he is safe."

"I appreciate the 'Mister,' but it's unnecessary, inaccurate, and ineffective. Look, I'm giving you a unique opportunity. If you're too puritanical or uptight to appreciate this opportunity, then so be it. I thought you were a pretty hip guy, but I may have misjudged. So here are some terms you might understand better: I don't know you. I don't trust you. If you want me to be open with you, you'll have to take a risk."

He extended his hand with the tiny square of orange paper towards my mouth like he was feeding a carrot to a horse.

I thought it over. I had smoked weed. It was no big deal. What the hell. I took the orange paper and put it in my mouth. It tasted like paper.

"Chew," said Flynn.

I chewed until the paper dissolved. I stared at Flynn. He stared back. Nothing happened. Then Flynn lay down on his back and shut his eyes. The keys to the cabin door were beneath him in his back pocket. Maybe he would pass out and I could take the keys and go looking for Joey. I'd just wait it out and see.

I looked around the darkened room, at the chunky log wall, the ancient bureau, the locked door. I looked back at Flynn. His eyes were shut and he was smiling. His arms hung loosely at his side. He looked as relaxed and untroubled as a teabag in a warm cup of water. That's when I noticed that he was vibrating, the edges around his clothes were glowing, radiating gold and yellow, like a halo, each color blurring into the next. I lay down and shut my eyes and watched the gold halo turn to butterflies on my eye lids. I opened my eyes and a swarm of butterflies ... is it called a swarm? a flock? a pack? ... flew in through the hole at the top of the cabin ceiling. Hundreds of butterflies landed on my body, fluttering, lightly touching the skin on my arms. Then the butterflies rose off my skin and flew up through the hole in the ceiling.

I opened my eyes. I hadn't noticed before the exquisite wood grain of the cabin walls and ceiling. The wood grain flowed like a river ... flowing like a river, not just the grain but the logs themselves were flowing ... and now the air was flowing and the wood grain river flowed into the air. I closed my eyes and the river of air flowed into my eyes, forming spirals on my eyelids.

I opened my eyes again. Flynn was sitting cross-legged on the rug. His eyes were closed. His hair was on fire but it must not have been a very hot fire because it didn't seem to bother him.

"Flynn?" Somebody was speaking. I looked around the room, but nobody else was there. Flynn opened his eyes and grinned. The fire in his hair was changing colors, from red to orange to blue, the colors swirling.

"I think your hair is on fire," I said.

"That could be. Infinity means anything is possible."

Flynn stood up. He walked to the door and unlocked it. When he opened the door, a whoosh of light flowed in. I thought for a moment that the light might knock him over, but instead it swirled harmlessly around him like water in a stream flowing around a rock. Flynn moved his hand in a way that I knew meant he wanted me to stand up.

I followed Doc Flynn out of the cabin and across the wooden porch. We walked slowly, very very slowly, each footstep a rocking motion, heel down, toe down, heel up, toe up, the boards creaking with each step. I had never noticed before how many sounds there are in a footstep. On a surfboard, you pay attention to what your feet are doing, but I had never paid attention to my feet walking across a wooden porch.

And now packed dirt.

And now gravel.

We crunched our way across a gravel road. I looked up. The sky was in full blazing sunset. I stared transfixed at the sky. I heard the crunching sound again. Flynn was walking up the gravel road. I hurried to catch up with him. We left the road and entered an oak grove. Waves of green were coming off the quivering leaves which vibrated in the air currents that we created as we walked, single file, like the prow of a boat sending ripples in our wake.

The oak forest opened up to a chaparral savannah. We climbed a hill. *I'm on a mission.* The words had floated into my head. They seemed completely right and true and obvious. Flynn stopped, turned, grinned, and nodded as if he heard me. Had I said my thoughts out loud? *We know everything we need to know, we've just forgotten.* The words came to me in Doc Flynn's voice. Did he say that out loud?

At the top of the hill we sat down and gazed into the trees and shrubs below. We just sat there, saying nothing. After a while, I noticed that the earth was breathing. The scrub brush and the oaks were all breathing in unison with the earth. My own breathing was in sync with the earth's breathing. Everything was breathing together, all part of the same breath. *Wow*, I thought. *Wow, wow, wow.*

I followed Flynn back to the cabin in the dark. I lay down on the rug and closed my eyes. *I am on a mission. I am on a mission to save somebody. Someone who needs saving. I've always been on this mission, but I had forgotten. That's why I'm here right now: To remember. This is a key. Don't forget this moment, engrave it on your brain.* I thought about the keys in Flynn's pocket and laughed. *Don't forget this, this is important..*

I opened my eyes and sat up. Flynn was gone. A bird was standing on the rug where he had been sitting. The bird looked at me. The bird was brown with a bright orange underbelly and streaks of white and black on his head. I wondered why the bird didn't fly away. Birds usually fly away when they are this close to a human. It took me a moment to realize that of course the bird didn't need to fly away because I wasn't going to hurt it. The bird looked at me and winked. I'd never seen a bird wink before. I reminded myself to tell Uncle Lou about the winking bird. He'd get a kick out of that. Then the bird flew up to the ceiling and out the hole in the roof.

I closed my eyes and fell asleep. When I opened my eyes again, Doc Flynn was sitting cross-legged on the rug, staring at me. Next to him was a boy with shaggy blonde hair and blue eyes. For a moment I thought it was me.

CHAPTER 7

Joey Flynn's body was rigid and his eyes were focused on me. He didn't seem frightened, just alert. On the other side of Doc Flynn knelt a woman. She was small and Asian. Her long black hair was tied back in a pony tail. In one hand she held a plastic cup.

"What day is it?" I asked nobody in particular.

Doc Flynn answered. "Sunday."

The small Asian woman said, "Are you thirsty?"

I licked my lips and nodded. My mouth was dry as sand. The woman put the cup in my hand. The cup felt cold and wet. After I drank the best, clearest, coolest, purest water I had ever drank, I turned to the boy.

"Are you Joey?" I asked.

"Yes."

"Can I take you home to your mother? She misses you."

Joey looked at his father.

"Ask your question, son. Go ahead. It's best to face the truth."

The boy swallowed. "Is the man dead?" he asked. Fear had crept into his eyes.

"Which man?" I said.

"The one I hit. He was slapping my mom and yelling, so I hit him."

"Did he have white hair?"

The boy nodded. "I didn't mean to kill him. I just wanted him to stop hurting my mom."

"What'd you hit him with?"

"Frying pan."

"You knocked him out?"

Joey shrugged. "I dunno. He fell and didn't get up. Is he dead?"

"No. He's not dead."

"Am I going to jail?"

"Not a chance. He's not dead. Besides, you were only trying to protect your mother, right?"

He nodded. "So ... they won't take me away from my mom?"

"No. They won't."

Nobody said anything for a while, so I lay down on the rug and shut my eyes. I watched the blood cells flow through the veins in my eyelids, wondering if the butterflies would return. I heard people talking. I fell asleep. I woke up and looked around. The Asian woman was gone, but Doc Flynn and the boy were still sitting on the rug, looking at me. Flynn had changed his shirt. I sat up.

"I'm ready to go home now," Joey said.

I looked over at Doc Flynn. He shrugged. "It's Joey's decision. He owns his own life."

He owns his own life. I pondered that. Do we own our own lives? But no profound thoughts came to me on the subject.

"Misako called Cora while you were sleeping," Flynn said. "Cora wants you to drive Joey home. She's said she'd leave work early and be at the house by the time you get there."

My mind was fuzzy. There were questions I wanted to ask, but I couldn't quite focus on what they were.

"Isn't it Sunday?" I said finally.

Flynn shook his head. "That was yesterday. It's Monday now."

Monday. I tried willing my brain to click into detective mode — or at least reasonably normal mode.

"I thought you didn't have a phone," I said.

Flynn shrugged. "You thought wrong."

CHAPTER 8

Joey sat in the passenger seat, staring out the window. We rode in silence, out of the mountains and down to the coast where morning fog lay thick on the water.

I was glad for the silence. Ghost images and sounds were floating through my mind: crunching gravel, quivering leaves, breathing earth, the words: "I am on a mission," the sense of purpose that was so clear and absolute just hours ago but was now getting thin and vague like the ocean mist evaporating in the morning sun.

As we neared Santa Barbara, Joey said he was hungry. We stopped at a grocery store and I bought a package of Fig Newtons and two apples. Curiously, I wasn't hungry, although it seemed like days since I'd last eaten.

The food seemed to perk Joey up. He fidgeted with the radio dial. When all he could find was a country western station, he switched off the radio and turned to me.

"My dad says you're a private eye."

"Yup."

"So you're like Stu Bailey on *77 Sunset Strip*?"

"Something like that. But without the swanky office, or the pretty secretary, or wrapping up each case in an hour."

"Your secretary's ugly?"

I laughed. "Actually, you're looking right at him."

"But you're the private eye."

"At the moment I'm both. Maybe when I hit the big time I'll have a pretty secretary like Stu Bailey and his pals."

"Do you own a gun?"

"Yup."

"Can I see it?"

"Nope."

Joey pushed on the button to the glove compartment, but it was locked.

"Is it in there?" he asked.

"You're a smart kid. That's why I keep it locked."

"But if you need your gun in a pinch, wouldn't it take too long to get it out?"

"See, that's why you can't believe everything on TV. Real life PI stuff isn't all about guns and bad guys and shooting."

"Well, if I was a private eye, I'd carry my gun on me at all times."

"And have a pretty secretary?"

Joey's cheeks reddened. We drove for a while in silence again.

We cruised through Carpenteria, passed the cut-off road to Rincon Point. Rincon was one of my favorite surfing spots. This time of year the surf was mushy, but come winter Rincon had a big, peeling right break that curled around the rocks. And another perk: it hadn't yet been discovered by the surfer-wannabes who drove in from the Valley, Nebraska, you name it, and cluttered up the water. I blamed it on The Beach Boys. Their tunes were tight with catchy hooks, and they were inspiring half the country to converge on California each summer.

"Do you have a girlfriend?" Joey asked.

His question jerked my mind off the beach and back into the car.

"I used to."

"What's her name?"

"Allison."

"Why not anymore?"

"She dumped me."

"Why?"

"You'd have to ask her."

Joey looked at me with a puzzled expression, then turned away. I knew my answer was dopey.

"I guess we just grew apart," I added.

Joey pushed the button on the glove compartment a few times.

"My dad has a girlfriend," he said.

"Misako?"

"Yeah."

"You like her?"

"She's okay."

I waited for him to continue, but he didn't.

"Joey," I said after a while, "you up for it if I ask you a few questions?"

"Like what?"

"About the night you ran away from home."

He wrinkled up his nose. "I guess."

"That white-haired man who was hitting your mom, you ever seen him before?"

"No."

"You sure?"

"I'm sure."

"Ever seen anybody else hurt your mom?"

"No."

"You said the man was yelling. Did you hear what he was yelling about?"

"He was swearing. He said… can I say the word?

"Go ahead."

"He said 'bitch'.

"Okay. What else?"

"I don't really remember. I just knew he was hurting my mom and I had to make him stop."

"Sure, I understand. I know you were just protecting her. Relax about that, okay?"

Joey shrugged. He started to press the glove compartment button again. I got the feeling that he was shutting down.

"When I was your age," I said, "I lived alone with my mother too."

The click click click of the glove compartment button stopped. I looked over at Joey. He began pressing on the button again, but lazily. I had his full attention.

"And if some man had slapped my mother," I continued, "or hurt her in any way, I would have done just what you did. I would have wanted to beat the shit out of him."

"I tried to hit him, but he pushed me."

"Probably swatted you away like a fly."

Joey nodded. "Yeah."

"So how'd you get yourself way up to Santa Maria in the middle of the night?"

There was a long silence.

"Do I have to tell you?"

"I'd like to know."

"Well . . . I'd better not."

"Why's that?"

Joey shrugged and looked away.

We drove in silence again. Past the bluffs at Point Dune . . . past the Malibu cliffs with their trails zig-zagged down to hidden beaches . . . past the Malibu Pier where a flock of seagulls had gathered on the asphalt outside the Fosters Freeze, pecking at bits of free burger buns and fries . . . past a billboard advertising Coppertone Suntan Lotion . . . past another billboard hawking the Kodak Instamatic camera.

"Photos!" Joey suddenly blurted out. "He was yelling about photos. 'Where are the photos?! Where fucking photos!?' He was yelling. It woke me up."

"The white-haired man said that?"

Joey nodded.

"What photos was he talking about?"

"I don't know. That's just what he said."

I nodded. "Good job, man. You've got a good memory."

Joey beamed. Then his voice went dark again. "How come you're sure he's not dead?"

"Because he was gone when your mother woke up in the morning. Dead men don't just walk away."

"That means he might come back."

"It's possible."

"He might come back and hit my mom again."

I had nothing to say to this. I didn't know who the man was or what he wanted, or what he was capable of. Joey turned towards me. He stared directly at me just like his father had done sitting cross-legged in the cabin.

"Can you do something to keep him from coming back?" he asked.

"I don't know."

"Why not?"

I shrugged. What could I tell him? That a job is a job, and this job would end when I dropped him off at home. That Lou's number one rule is Don't Make It Personal, but at the same time there was something tugging at me inside to help Joey out, to make sure the white-haired goon never came back. To fix it so Joey didn't have to be alone all day and deal with a mother who drinks. It didn't make a lot sense to me, and I knew it wouldn't make any sense to Joey. So I stayed quiet and kept driving.

We turned off the coast highway, wound up Sunset through the Palisades, turned onto Joey's street. As we pulled up to the curb at Joey's house, the front door flung open. Cora Flynn stood motionless in the doorway. Her eyes landed on Joey, then her head swiveled sideways towards the house. Something was wrong.

CHAPTER 9

She could have been just a mother hurrying, eager to reunite with her son. But something was off. She stumbled on the stone path that ran alongside the reflecting pond and nearly fell.

Joey jumped out of the car and rushed towards his mother. I watched from the car as they embraced. Mrs. Flynn held onto Joey. After a few seconds, he squirmed to get away. I got out of the car and walked towards them. Up close, I saw that Mrs. Flynn's face was a mess: mascara ran down her cheeks, and her eyes were red. I smelled booze on her breath.

"Somebody's broken in," she said.

"What?" I looked towards the house. The curtains were drawn across the windows.

"What happened, Mom?" Joey's eyes were wide with alarm.

"I... I just got home a while ago. I tried to clean up. I really did. I didn't want you coming home to this, baby... but it's... it's hopeless."

"Stay right there," I said, moving past them. Mrs. Flynn froze. But Joey started to follow me.

"Stay with your mother, Joey," I commanded. "Wait here until I come back out."

I went inside the house. The place was trashed. Shelves were emptied out, books and record albums tossed onto the floor, drawers pulled opened, papers strewn about. I made a quick search of the house, going room to room. No room had been spared. In the bathroom, heaped on the floor was a jumble of towels and pill bottles, soaps and lotions and lipsticks. In all three bedrooms, sheets and blankets had been ripped off the beds, mattresses overturned, clothes piled on the floor. Joey's 45s had been pulled out of their covers and tossed onto his overturned mattress. In the kitchen, the cabinets hung open and the floor was a clutter of broken dishes and utensils. The Lucky Charms cereal box was ripped to shreds.

I went back outside and found Joey and his mother standing together by the front door. Mrs. Flynn's hand was resting on Joey's shoulder. I wasn't sure if she was holding him back, or using him for support.

"Can we come in now?" she asked.

"Might as well. The dining area's about the only place that's not trashed. But try to touch as little as possible. The police might want to dust for prints."

Mrs. Flynn shot me a look. The NO POLICE look.

The three of us sat at the teak dining table where I had a direct view of the ransacked living room. Joey was wide-eyed, checking everything out. Mrs. Flynn chose the seat facing the wall. She reached for a cigarette. Her hands were shaking.

"I feel horrible," she said. "It's like we've been invaded."

"Can I see my room?" Joey asked, looking at me.

"In a while," I said, then turned to Mrs. Flynn. "You haven't called the police yet?"

"No. I… I'd rather not. I mean what's done is done, right? What can the police do about it now?"

"Probably nothing. But now and then they do nab a bad guy or two."

"Dad doesn't like cops," Joey said.

"There you go," Mrs. Flynn said, as if this closed the discussion.

I didn't know what to do or say next. My brain felt locked up and fuzzy at the same time. But like it or not, Joey and his mother were depending on me right now. I pictured the ocean on a calm day, low rollers under a grey sky. My brain started to unlock. I turned to Mrs. Flynn.

"Have you noticed anything missing?"

"I'm not sure. I haven't looked real closely. Everything is such as mess."

"Do you keep cash in the house?"

"Only what's in my purse. And a few dollars for Joey, in case of emergency." She turned to her son. "But you took that the other night, didn't you?"

Joey nodded with a hangdog expression.

"What about jewelry?" I said.

"I don't know. I was trying to clean up."

From what I could tell, she had been doing more drinking than cleaning up.

"I'd like you to go check and see if anything's been stolen," I said. "Cash or jewelry or medication. Anything."

"Now?"

"Yes. I'll stay here with Joey."

Mrs. Flynn stood up and walked down the hall. When she was out of sight, Joey turned to me.

"Is it my fault?"

"What do you mean?"

"If I hadn't run away . . . I mean summer vacation started today and maybe . . . if I'd been home . . ." Joey trailed off. He looked down at his hands.

"Hey, listen up. This is not your fault. None of it. You're just a kid. All this is grown-up stuff."

Joey shrugged. A few words from me wasn't going to change how he felt.

When Mrs. Flynn returned, she was carrying a pink satin-lined box. The lid was hanging open from a single hinge like a loose tooth. Inside was a tangled mass of jewelry.

"It was all on the floor," she said. "I'm not positive, but I don't think anything is missing. I don't have any real expensive pieces anyway."

Joey turned to me. "Can I go to my room now?"

"Okay, let's check it out."

I walked with Joey to his room. We stopped at the threshold and took in the mayhem. Joey stood very still. His face was blank.

"I'll clean it up," he said.

I helped him put the mattress back on its box springs, then left him to the rest. By the time I returned to the dining area, Mrs. Flynn had miraculously found an unbroken glass and was pouring herself some scotch. I sat down across from her.

I said, "You know this wasn't a robbery, right?"

She nodded, lit a cigarette, and took a long drag.

"Mrs. Flynn, I'm not sure what's going on here, and it seems like you don't want to tell me, but doesn't it bother you that whatever is happening, you and your son may be in danger?"

"We'll be fine."

"I think you should call the police."

"No police. I already told you." She shook her head, but the back and forth went on a bit too long, and her head starting to droop.

"Then what *are* you going to do?" I said.

"Look, you found Joey and I'm truly grateful for that. But I can handle my own life from here."

It sounded like a speech from a B-movie, but she had a point. How was this any of my business? I had accomplished the job she hired me for. I should pat myself on the back: *Good job, Ryan.* I should cruise over to the VA and describe the whole crazy thing to Lou. I should get some sleep, wax my board, and hit the waves in the morning.

I should have been stoked to be done with the case. I should have just shut up and gone home.

"Sometimes it's hard to handle things all by ourselves," I said instead.

"Are you insinuating that I can't take care of my own life?" Her eyes flashed with anger. She stood up and rummaged through her purse. "What do I owe you? I'll write you a check."

"Please, Mrs. Flynn. Sit down. I didn't mean anything."

"Now you're being plain dishonest."

She was right.

Neither of us said anything for a while. A car engine started up somewhere nearby. A dog barked.

"We're fine," Mrs. Flynn said. "Okay? I appreciate your concern, but Joey and I are fine."

"Alright. One question though. Where's the black rug?"

She jerked her body around to face the living room.

"Well, I.... I don't know." She walked to the top of the three steps which led down the sunken living room. "Where is it?"

"You didn't do something with it? Take it to the dry cleaners or something?"

"No," she said adamantly. "What are you talking about? Where is the rug!"

"I think all this has something to do with the photos."

"Photos?"

Lou always emphasized how important it is to watch people's faces. I watched Cora Flynn's. I saw confusion... then fear... then anger.

"I need you to leave now, Ryan. I have a lot to do here. You can send me the bill later if you'd rather."

I ignored her request. "Here's what I'm thinking," I said. "I'm thinking the guy at Kelbo's picked you up Wednesday night not because he wanted to get his paws on you, but because he wanted to get his paws on some photos. He didn't find the photos because Joey knocked him out before he could. Today he came back to get them. He saw blood on the rug, possibly his own from when

Joey hit him, so he got rid of it. Does that sound about right to you so far?"

Mrs. Flynn didn't answer. She glared at me. Then she sat down at the dining table and knocked back the rest of her scotch. When the only thing left in her glass was a lump of melting ice, she put her elbows on the table, dropped her head to her hands, and began to kneed her forehead. I watched and waited. If I hadn't been so focused on Cora Flynn massaging her forehead, I might have noticed the shadow of a 11-year-old boy who was hiding in the hallway behind the door.

Mrs. Flynn finally lifted her head from her hands.

"Why do you think this?" she asked.

"Joey heard the man yelling about photos. He said the man was big and had white hair. That matched the description I got from the bartender at Kelbo's."

"I don't remember much from that night. It's kind of blurry."

I nodded. "I understand. But here's the question: Did the Kelbo's guy find the photos <u>this</u> time? Because if he didn't, it stands to reason he'll be back."

I stood up and pulled my car keys from my pocket, ready to leave.

"Hey," Mrs. Flynn slurred, "I thought we were having a conversation."

With a rubbery arm, she motioned vaguely towards the chair. I sat down. She took another long drag on her cigarette. *So this is what it's like to handle a case on my own*, I thought. Landing smack in the middle of peoples' messed up and troubled lives. I liked it better when Lou did the heavy lifting. Running errands was a whole lot easier and less complicated. Was I even cut out for this work? But before I could descend further into doubt, Mrs. Flynn spoke up.

"Remember Chip Jordan?" she said, seemingly out of nowhere.

"Sure. Who doesn't?" I was intrigued by this unexpected new topic.

"Well, a few weeks ago I was sorting through Victor Dargin's files. If you read the trades then you know—"

"I don't."

"Mr. Dargin is ... rather was a VP at Pinnacle. Head of production. He'd been there for years. Then about a month ago he was fired. Escorted out is more like it. Word on the lot is he had a blow-out with the execs in New York. Anyway, I don't know about all that, but whatever happened, it was sudden. Things were slow in Research — dead is more like it — so I was asked to go though Dargin's files, decide what to toss, what to keep in the office for his replacement, what to store in the archives. That's when I came across the photos."

"Of Chip Jordan?"

She nodded. "But they weren't ordinary publicity stills. They were personal."

"What do you mean?"

"One showed him sitting by a swimming pool with another man. Another showed him and that same man — swimming. And in the last one, he and the man are in the water at the side of the pool."

"Who was the other man?"

"Beats me. The thing is, all the photos were autographed. So right away I'm thinking maybe they're worth something. I had been worrying how to come up with the money to send Joey to summer camp, nothing fancy, just day camp while I was at work, and here were these photos, in an unmarked folder in the back of a filing cabinet. Autographed. I know it must sound like I'm making excuses, but that's just how it was. What year did Chip Jordan die?"

Chip Jordan had been a childhood idol of mine. In grade school, my buddies and I all wanted to be as cool as Chip. He had come on the scene just before Brando or Dean, and we considered him to be as cool as they got.

I remember asking Lou why a rich and famous movie star like Chip Jordan would kill himself. Lou said something about money not being everything, and other words of wisdom that didn't make much sense to me at the time.

"Around '51 or '52," I said.

"So you see," Mrs. Flynn said defensively, "by the time I found them, the photos must have been sitting there for over a decade. So I took one. Big deal. I brought it over to a memorabilia shop in Hollywood to find out what it was worth. Tinseltown Treasures. The man running the shop gave me a hundred dollars cash on the spot, practically begged me for more if I had any. A few days later, I brought him the other two photos and he paid me another hundred each."

"That's a lot of dough."

"Frankly, I was relieved to be done with them. I didn't feel guilty, I mean nobody was ever going to miss those old photos... well, maybe a little guilty. But mostly I was nervous. Ever since then I've been scared that somehow the studio would find out, that I'd get caught and lose my job."

"Did you give the memorabilia shop man your name or phone number? Some way to get in contact with you?"

"No. He asked for my phone number, but I wouldn't give it to him. I'm not that stupid."

"And the guy at Kelbo's?"

Mrs. Flynn shook her head. She took a drag on her cigarette. I noticed that her hands weren't shaking anymore.

"Summer camp money," she muttered. "It didn't seem like such a big deal at the time, but now it's like a bad dream that I can't wake up from. If only I could turn back the clock a couple of weeks, I'd put those stupid photos into a Pinnacle archive box, label it, seal it up, and send it over to the vault."

"Did you tell anybody else about the photos," I asked. "Anybody at all."

"No. Absolutely not. I'm not a fool."

She finished off her cigarette and crushed it out in the empty glass.

"That funny little man who ran the shop," she said, "there was something strange about him."

"What kind of strange?"

"I don't know exactly, but he was so keen for those pictures. Could he have followed me? I told him I didn't have any more. Could that ... that other man ...? Oh, I don't know."

She lit another cigarette. I kept quiet and waited.

"Maybe you could talk to him," she said finally. "The man at the shop. Tell him I don't have any more photos. Tell him to stop. Make it all go away."

"I could talk to him, but I don't know if it would do any good. We don't even know that he did anything."

"It had to be him."

"What does he look like?"

"Little and bald. And both times I went there he was dressed in white." She made a small noise that could have been a giggle. "He reminded me of an ice cream cone."

CHAPTER 10

Tinseltown Treasures was located in an old brick building on a seedy Hollywood side street, jammed between a dry cleaners and an abandoned theatre. Next to the cleaners was a Chinese restaurant with a plate glass window so grimy that it was hard to see through it. I hadn't eaten since the Fig Newtons in the car with Joey that morning, but even the grumbling in my stomach wasn't enough to get me into the Chinese joint.

Tinseltown's front window was plastered with vintage movie posters. A bell jingled above the door when I opened it. I shut the door behind me and the bell jingled again.

With one step, I left behind the grubby streets of "real" Hollywood, and entered a different world. Movie posters covered the walls; some were behind glass in elaborate frames, others were simply taped to the wall. *Dr. Cyclops, Grand Hotel, Christmas In July, Mutiny on the Bounty, Mildred Pierce.* The center of the room was filled with rows of file cabinets, flat oversized horizontal drawers, and shelves bulging with movie-themed knick knacks. At the back of the store was a counter and cash register. A short pudgy man with a round pink face, white mustache, and a fringe of white fluff circling his bald head, stepped out from behind the counter. He wore a white linen suit, a red and white polka dot bowtie, and a red satin vest. Where Mrs. Flynn had seen 'ice cream cone,' I saw one part barbershop quartet, one part professor/wizard in *The Wizard of Oz.*

"May I help you, sir?" the little man asked.

"Just browsing."

"Wonderful. Wonderful. Take all the time you need." He put his hands together as if in prayer. "If you need any assistance, please don't hesitate to ask. Oscar Panozzo at your service."

"Thanks."

I ambled up one of the aisles. My first objective was to see how Chip Jordan photo prices compared with similar items. I opened one of the file drawers at random and began flipping through the photos. Immediately, I felt Oscar Panozzo's presence behind me. He was inching closer. Now he was looking over my shoulder, practically breathing in my ear. I ignored him. The photos were old. None were autographed. The only movie star I recognized was Rudolph Valentino.

"Ah, the Silent Era," whispered Panozzo.

I turned around. Panozzo took a couple of tiny steps back.

"I don't mean to disturb you, sir," he said, "but it's so rare that someone of your youth has an enthusiasm for the marvelous era of silent cinema. Here at Tinseltown, you'd be thrilled to know, we have the largest collection of Silent Era lobby cards in the United States."

The little bald man was beaming.

"Actually, I'm not really interested in the silent era," I said.

"Oh." He looked crestfallen.

"Do you have any James Dean? Or Marlon Brando?"

"Certainly! We have full sheets, lobby cards, production stills, head shots of nearly every significant Hollywood movie star since D.W. Griffith said 'roll em'."

"How about a Brando?"

"Ah! Of course! Come with me. I have an absolute treasure for you!"

I followed Panozzo down the aisle. He opened one of the low horizontal drawers. Brando — full lipped, scowling, a bandolier draped across his body — stared up at me.

"Voilà!" Panozzo exclaimed "*One Eyed Jacks*! Originally scheduled to be directed by Stanley Kubrick, but Brando took over. Starred in and directed! A tragic tale of betrayal and revenge. The movie, that is."

Panozzo chucked, eyeing me to see if I got the joke. I smiled.

"This poster is dreadfully rare," he continued. "You'll be the envy of all your pals with this one."

"I never saw the movie."

"Which is hardly surprising. American audiences virtually ignored this masterpiece. Now the French ..."

I couldn't help but like the little guy. Maybe it was his enthusiasm for movies that seemed so innocent, almost childlike.

"... are true connoisseurs of the cinema. Do you know what a full-sheet *Cinderfella* goes for in Paris?"

"Nope."

"A lot. Trust me."

"That's Jerry Lewis, right?"

"Correct you are! Now I'll admit Lewis is no Orson Welles. One might say his is a more subtle genius. Sometimes it takes a foreign sensibility to appreciate—"

"Actually," I interrupted, "I'm looking for something autographed."

I hated to cut the little guy off, he was enjoying himself so much, but I didn't have all day.

"Of course, of course," Panozzo responded enthusiastically. "Not a problem at all."

He scurried off to another aisle, me trailing behind. He tugged open a metal file drawer and pulled out a black and white glossy photo of Brando in his signature tight T-shirt. *To Connie. Regards, Marlon Brando,* was scribbled across it.

"Streetcar," Panozzo said as he handed me the photo.

"Yes. That's more like it. What does this go for?" I asked.

"Well ..." Panozzo's eyes were glowing. He was savoring the moment. "I couldn't possibly let this extraordinary gem go for less than ... ten dollars. Minimum. And that's only because I can tell you are a true connoisseur."

"Ten dollars. That's kind of steep."

"Sir, this is Brando!"

"Well, how about James Dean?"

"Even more valuable. After all, tragically, Mr. Dean will not be signing any more autographs. Ever. So the supply is finite. I have nothing, absolutely nothing in an autographed James Dean for less than fifteen dollars."

"I see. What about Chip Jordan?"

"Huh?" Panozzo took a sharp intake of breath. His whole body seemed to freeze up. I watched his eyes. I saw fear. Then a quick recovery.

"Certainly. Chip Jordan. We have several. All quite valuable of course, due to Mr. Jordan' heartbreaking demise."

He filled away the Brando photo, flipped through some folders in the same drawer, handed me a black and white glossy. It was a moody publicity still — Chip Jordan with a black fedora slanted down over his forehead, a cigarette dangling from his mouth. James Dean before James Dean.

"How much for this one?" I asked.

"Twenty dollars," Panozzo replied. "Now keep in mind, this is a rare autographed Jordan. One of a kind. I couldn't let it go for a penny less than twenty."

"Hmmm." I handed the photo back to him. "Actually, I was looking for something more candid. Maybe Chip Jordan out by a swimming pool?"

Panozzo starred at me. His eyes narrowed. He squinted at me.

"Who are you, mister?"

"A friend of mine sold you a couple of Chip Jordan photos recently. I'd like to see them."

"I'm sorry," he said icily. "This is all we have."

Panozzo handed me the folder. I flipped through the photos: all standard publicity shots. None autographed. None with a swimming pool. I handed the folder back.

"You paid my friend a hundred bucks apiece for those photos. Seems like a lot, given what these others go for."

"First, I have not the slightest idea what you are referring to. And secondly, we cater to niche collectors all over the world. You'd be surprised how values fluctuate. Now, is there anything further I can help you with?"

"What'd you do with the Chip Jordan photos?"

"Sir, our transactions are private."

"What is this — a Swiss bank?"

We sized each other up. Panozzo was no taller than 5'6" and wore a polka dot bow-tie. I was 6'1" with an upper body hardened by years of paddling through the Pacific surf. Panozzo clutched the pale paper folder to his chest and took a step back.

"My friend wants you to know," I said, "that she doesn't have any more of those photos. She will never have any more. She wants to be left alone."

"Excuse me?" He looked genuinely confused.

"You know what I'm talking about."

"I certainly do not."

"Just stay away from her. You and your thug."

"Thug? This is preposterous, sir. I have absolutely no knowledge of what you're referring to."

"Either way," I said, "you've been warned."

I tried to sound menacing, but menacing didn't come naturally to me. And the look of alarm on Oscar Panozzo's round pink face almost had me wanting to take it back. Was he telling the truth? If so, then I had just frightened an innocent little man who wanted nothing more than to be surrounded by his Joan Crawford and Rudolph Valentino movie posters.

CHAPTER 11

I left Tinseltown, got into my car, and headed south on La Brea. I was still thinking about Oscar Panozzo, still feeling lousy about scaring the guy, when I got the feeling that I was being followed.

I checked the rear view mirror. Traffic was heavy as cars flowed out of Hollywood and downtown on their evening commute. At the corner of LaBrea and Pico, I hung a right at Lucy's Drive-Thru. I kept checking the mirror as I headed west on Pico. It didn't take long to spot the black Cadillac El Dorado about six cars back. Fairfax... La Cienega... Robertson.... the Caddy was still back there. Just past Overland, I hung an abrupt right. I entered a leafy residential neighborhood, the streets lined with small Spanish-style homes.

I zig-zagged through the neighborhood, checking my rear view mirror every few seconds. No black Caddy. Eventually I returned to Pico. If someone had been following me, they weren't now.

I pulled into the alley behind my apartment and parked between a trash dumpster and the speed limit sign that pretty much everyone ignored. Fifteen miles per hour? Forget it. The official name for the alley was Speedway. It was a narrow one-way street that ran parallel to the beach and begged to be speeded on. This was my territory. Home.

Just as I was getting out of my car, the nose of the black El Dorado appeared up ahead as it turned onto Speedway from a side street. The Caddy came zooming down the alley, going the wrong way on the one-way corridor. It screeched to a halt alongside my car. The barrel of a Colt .45 poked out the driver's side window, pointed in the direction of my head.

"Don't move," a man's voice commanded from inside the car.

The Caddy's front door thrust open, pinning me between the two cars. A large hulking man with white hair got out.

My muscles tightened and my heart sped up. I looked this way and that, searching for a way out. The hulk grabbed my shoulders and shoved me inside his car. For a big man, he was quick and agile. My body folded. Crunched face down between the seatback and the steering wheel, I was smothered in the smell of leather and cigarettes.

The hulk pushed me over to the passenger side as if I were a sack of laundry. I tried to struggle against the massive arm that held me down, but it did no good. Fighting against this guy would be about as effective as fighting the ocean's spin cycle in a wipe-out. When the surf is churning you up like you're a sock in the washer, it's natural to panic. The first time it happens you automatically start to thrash around, trying to get to the surface. But you learn: the thrashing just uses up oxygen. In a wipe-out, survival depends on staying calm. If you relax and go with the wave's motion, eventually you pop up. *Okay,* I thought to myself, *relax.*

Then I felt the muzzle of the .45 bury into my ribs.

"You move, the gun goes off," the hulk said.

I didn't move.

In all my years tagging along with Lou, never once had a gun been pointed at me. In the last two days, I had one pointed at me twice. It would make a great story to tell Lou, a story that would entertain him in that dreary hospital room. That is, if I was still around to tell it.

The hulk drove through the city, my face buried in the seat leather. I tried to keep track of the turns for a while, but eventually gave up. I berated myself for awhile: I had been so sure that I had lost the Caddy with my sneaky driving maneuvers in Westwood, so how did he tail me to Venice? Or did the hulk already know where I lived and arrived all on his own? Either way, I was going to have to up my skills and my awareness — big time and quickly — if I wanted to make it through this.

Finally, the car stopped and the hulk cut the engine. I smelled car exhaust.

"Come on. Get up. Boss wants to see you."

He had an accent. Was it German? Russian?

Lou liked to quiz me about accents that we overheard out in public. It was a game we played, trying to pin down the accent, then asking the people where they were from. For Lou the game was about training, honing an important skill for the job. For me the game was a pastime, a curiosity, something I knew Lou liked to do. And, probably because I didn't really care, it was a game I always lost.

The hulk tugged at my shoulder. I unfolded my body and sat up. We were in an underground garage. Very few other cars. I guessed it to be about 7:00 PM. If this was an office building, most everyone would have left work by now.

"Come on" the hulk ordered. "Over to the elevator. Keep your eyes on the ground. No monkey business."

The hulk put the gun in his waistband. He adjusted his brown corduroy jacket, making sure it covered the gun. He grabbed hold of my arm, yanked me close to his side, and kept me there as we walked through the dimly lit garage. We took the elevator up. An electronic bell pinged at each floor. I heard five pings. The elevator door opened. I looked up.

"Keep your eyes down," the hulk whispered.

He thumped the top of my head with the palm of his hand for good measure.

We walked down a carpeted hallway. The carpet, dark green

with tiny gold triangles, looked new. New office building. Where? *Pay attention, Ryan. Keep sharp.* I didn't feel sharp. Maybe it was the aftereffects of Doc Flynn's drug, or the grumbling in my stomach, or being pushed around and having a gun aimed at me. I felt shaky. Walking didn't come as easy as usual.

The hulk stopped, unlocked a door, shoved me forward. I heard the door lock behind me.

"Stay here," he ordered. He let go of my arm.

As I raised my head, I saw the backside of the hulk disappear through a door. I looked around. I was standing in the center of a small, windowless waiting room. Against one wall was a low-slung modern couch. Against another wall were a couple of chairs and a magazine rack with nothing in it. There were no pictures, no ashtray, nothing else. Someone was either moving in, moving out, or not expecting much company.

I heard muffled voices coming from the inner office. I put my ear up to the door, but couldn't hear anything distinct. A few minutes later, the hulk re-emerged.

"Boss wants to see you," he said, jerking his thumb towards the open door.

***

The office was large, carpeted green and gold like the hallway, and nearly empty. Cardboard moving boxes were stacked against one wall. The only furniture was an outsized desk and the padded swivel chair behind it.

A man wearing a white tennis shirt sat in the chair. Behind him, horizontal Venetian blinds were shut tight against whatever was outside a big picture window.

The man in the white tennis shirt was tossing a tennis ball back and forth between his hands. He looked vaguely familiar. He was about 40, with jet black hair and a clean-shaven, angular face. His eyes were dark, nearly black. My wallet lay open on the otherwise empty desk. He put the tennis ball down beside it.

"Mr. Zorn, I want to apologize for any discomfort you may have experienced on the way here. My associate was only taking precautions. No harm intended."

"Who are you?" I said. "What's this all about?"

"Before I answer that — if I answer that — I need to know what you were doing at the residence of Cora Flynn, as well as at Tinseltown Treasures.

"You've gone through my wallet, so you know I'm a PI."

"You didn't answer my question."

"I was on a case."

"What case?"

"I can't say."

"Can't or won't?"

"Won't. Client confidentiality."

"Nevertheless, I need to know."

"Why?"

"It's crucial to my life."

"How's that?"

The man plucked the tennis ball off the desk and began once again tossing it back and forth from hand to hand. His ball tossing reminded me of Humphrey Bogart in *The Caine Mutiny* rolling the metal balls around in his palm. This guy, however, was much more energetic and clean-cut all-American than Bogart.

The man stopped tossing the ball.

"Is there anything I could say or do to get you to change your mind?" he asked. "Perhaps a monetary incentive?"

I shook my head. "Nope."

"Tough guy, huh."

"Just doing my job."

The man nodded. "Leon!" he shouted.

Shit. Not the hulk.

The hulk came into the room. He stood near the door, waiting for further instructions.

"Leon, please escort Mr. Zorn to the waiting room. I need to make some calls."

I had no desire to hang out with Leon in the waiting room — or anywhere for that matter — but I didn't seem to have a choice. I followed him into the waiting room. Leon lowered his enormous body onto the couch. When he sat, his knees came up as high as his chest. The couch suddenly seemed ridiculously low and puny.

I stood by the empty magazine rack.

"Where are you from?" I asked.

"Shut up," he answered.

"Germany?" I said.

He shook his head "No" and looked down at the floor.

Ten minutes later, the man in the white tennis shirt opened the connecting door. He hooked a finger at Leon who followed him into the inner office. A minute later, Leon re-emerged.

"Go in. Boss'll see you now."

"Haven't we been through this before?" I said.

"Shut up," he replied.

I went in. Leon shut the door behind me, but didn't follow. The man in the white tennis shirt came around the desk and gave me back my wallet.

"Steve Sutton," he said. "Let's take this from the top, okay? Fresh start."

Sutton smiled and shook my hand vigorously, as if we were congratulating each other after a friendly game of tennis. I must have looked at him oddly.

"You can stop staring." he said. "If I look familiar, it's no doubt due to my brief and now defunct career as a bit player in movies. The less said on that subject the better. Just thought I'd save you the trouble of wondering."

"Okay," I said. He did look familiar, but the name didn't ring a bell.

Sutton walked behind his desk, picked up the tennis ball, squeezed it, began pacing back and forth in the narrow space between his desk and the big, shuttered window. Finally he sat down and faced me, his fingers drumming on the desk.

"I'm in a jam, Mr. Zorn. I've made a couple of calls and Southland checks out. And I admire the professional discretion you displayed earlier. I'd like to hire you. I think maybe you can help me out."

"Southland doesn't do business at gunpoint."

"As I said, I apologize about Leon. He's a loyal associate, just trying to be cautious. But I suppose I do owe you an explanation."

Sutton drummed his fingers on the desk again. "Where shall I start?"

The guy was trying to be nice, but I was still feeling grouchy from being pushed around and having a gun stuck in my ribs.

"How about starting with Cora Flynn," I said, "who your loyal associate harassed, assaulted, and probably burglarized."

Sutton sighed. "An unpleasant situation with that woman. Completely uncalled for. I am truly sorry about that. Leon is not accustomed to the delicacy required in this kind of situation. Which is why I need your help."

"What kind of situation are we talking about?"

Suddenly, I felt shaky again. I needed to sit down, but there was no chair.

"As I mentioned earlier," Sutton said, "once upon a time I was in pictures. Had a six-year contract at Fox. I was young, ambitious, and, I like to flatter myself, not completely lacking in talent. I got bit parts. Thought I'd be the next Clark Gable. Ha, ha. Anyway, cut to the chase: things didn't work out. I found myself out of a job, out of the industry, still ambitious, but without hope or direction. Have you ever played Monopoly, Mr. Zorn?"

"When I was a kid."

"Well, one day I'm playing Monopoly with a couple of friends, all of us out of work actors with time on our hands, and it hits me: any child with an IQ higher than a plant figures out the way to win Monopoly is to buy buy buy. At the start of the game, buy every property you land on. Low income properties are fine. Only dopes pass on Baltic and hold out for Park Place. Just buy."

Sutton picked up the tennis ball, tossed it a few times from hand to hand. Then he put it down again. He beamed at me, as if he <u>was</u> that little kid who had just figured out the secret to Monopoly.

"So that's what I did. Took the savings I had from my Fox contract and started to invest in real estate. It wasn't much. I could only afford to buy cheap, run-down properties in out-of-the-way places like Compton, Boyle Heights, you get the idea. That's where Leon came in. Collecting rents can be tricky in those kinds of neighborhoods. Leon is ... persuasive. You understand?"

"What does any of this have to do with why I'm here?"

"I'm getting to that. Anyway, it took a while, but eventually my investments paid off. However, here's the thing: none of it was satisfying. Real estate is just buy and sell. It's dead. Just a stupid board game really. Monopoly in 3-D. Know what I mean?"

He looked at me, waiting for a nod or something like that.

"Mr. Sutton," I said, "do you have anything to eat or drink around here?"

"What?"

"Food," I said. "Water." I sounded like a caveman. That's about how I felt. Hungry, tired, shaky.

Sutton opened one of the desk drawers and tossed an Abba Zabba across the desk.

"Leon practically lives on these. Got me hooked."

"Thanks."

I unwrapped the candy bar and bit into it. I would rather have had an apple, but the Abba Zabba would have to do.

"Anyway," Sutton continued as I munched, "I missed show business. I missed being out in front. Then, a few months ago, some associates of mine got wind of the fact that a developer was scouting around for a spot to put in a new shopping mall — in an area where I have multiple properties. There's even talk of a sports arena. Great, I thought. I can make a bundle and get out from under the rent collection business at the same time. But there's a ton of zoning ordinances and political red tape involved in getting it done. So my associates proposed that I run for public office where I'd be in a position to push the whole thing through. At first I thought they were crazy. Me? What did I know about politics? But I thought it over. Why not me? Politics and acting, are they really so far apart? Suddenly, for the first time in a long, long time, I was excited to get up the morning."

Sutton's face clouded over. "Then that little shit Panozzo walked into my life."

He opened the top drawer in his desk, took out a manila envelope, and pushed it across the desk towards me.

I opened the envelope and withdrew three black and white, 8x10 glossy photographs. The first photo showed two men with towels wrapped around their waists sitting by a swimming pool. Both men held champagne glasses. One of the men was a younger Steve Sutton. The other was Chip Jordan. In the second photo, Sutton and Jordan were in the water, their arms resting on the edge of the pool. In the third photo, Chip Jordan lay on his back in the water. Steve Sutton was treading water nearby. All three photos were autographed with identical words: *To Steve, Thanks for a wonderful time. Yours, Chip.*

"That little shit Panozzo called me about a week ago," Sutton continued. "He said he had a photograph that I'd be very interested in purchasing. He mentioned Chip Jordan. I told him

I wasn't in the market to buy celebrity photos, but he insisted I would be interested once I saw it. Something in his manner alarmed me. So we met and he showed me the photo with the champagne. I was shocked, to say the least. I had never seen this photo before. Never knew it existed. That long ago afternoon with Chip had been private. Or so I had believed."

"What about these other two photos? There's three here."

"I'll get to those in a minute." Sutton sounded irritated. He picked up the tennis ball again and squeezed it a few times.

"Panozzo estimated the photo's value at $1,000," he continued. "I told him that was outrageous. He said he'd have no problem finding another buyer if I wasn't interested... and that he'd appreciate his payment in twenties. What choice did I have? I paid up."

I shuffled through the photos and examined them all again. I took an especially long look at the champagne photo. The two men were looking at each other in a certain way. I had seen that look between men and women. Allison and I had stared at each other like that. But I'd never seen it between two men. It gave me the heebies. Just didn't seem right. After being creeped out for a minute, I let it sink in: Chip Jordan was a homosexual. Chip Jordan!?!

I put the photos down on the desk. Sutton took the photos and slipped them back into the envelope.

"Okay," I said. "So Panozzo shows up with just one photo. Then what?"

"As I said: I paid up. He came to my house, showed me the photo, and I paid him. I was devastated. Here I am on the brink of a new life, and it's being snatched out from under me before it can even begin."

Sutton paused and scowled. "What I did next wasn't very smart."

"What's that?"

"I had Leon follow Panozzo when he left my house. Followed him straight to his shop in Hollywood, Tinseltown Treasures. Now I knew who I was dealing with and where to find him. The next day I drove there myself. Honestly, I don't know what I was thinking. I hadn't slept at all that night. I was beside myself. I didn't have a plan, I just went. I parked on the street and sat there. I thought about going inside to confront the little bastard. What I really wanted to do was strangle him. Snap that pretentious little bowtie right off his neck. But I didn't do a thing. I just sat in my car."

He paused. His pupils were dilated; beads of sweat were forming on his forehead.

"So that's what I was doing, just sitting and stewing, when I saw her. An average looking woman in a dress. Brunette. High heels. In one hand, she carried a pocketbook. In the other, a manila envelope. It was the envelope that got my attention. She walks into Panozzo's shop. A few minutes later, she comes out. No manila envelope."

"So no manila envelope," I said. "Panozzo runs a memorabilia shop. People must bring stuff in to him all the time."

"It's hard to describe, but it wasn't just the envelope. It was something else about the woman. When she came out, she looked this way and that. Kind of furtive, as if perhaps she was afraid someone was following her, or she was feeling guilty about something. Whatever it was, her manner struck me as odd. Maybe it's my acting background, learning to read people, or maybe it was just a hunch, but I followed her. All the way out to the Palisades. I watched her go inside her house. After a while, sitting in my car, I started to feel pretty ridiculous. What was I thinking? This was just an average housewife going into her average suburban house. So I turned around and went home. The next day, Panozzo calls. More photos. Bingo."

"Cora Flynn," I said.

Sutton nodded.

I thought about the three photographs. As weird as it was to see two men look at each other like that, it seemed like pretty weak stuff for blackmail. Which is what I told Steve Sutton.

"Panozzo intimated there were more," he said. "And of course I knew those would get worse. Much, much worse."

He picked up the tennis ball and thumped it against his desk a couple of times.

"That's why I put Leon on it. I asked him to talk with Cora Flynn. Find out if she had more photos. Not a great move, I'll admit, but I was desperate. Who else was I going to turn to? Obviously not the police. The last thing in the world I wanted was for any of this to be made public."

"Who took the photos?" I asked.

"I have no idea. I didn't know they existed until Panozzo showed up."

"How could you not know that someone was snapping photos when you were right there?"

"How the hell do I know! Don't you think I've asked myself that a thousand times over this past week?"

"No idea at all?"

"We're talking movie people here. They're all crazy. Hell, I'm an expert on that — I was one of them. Maybe Chip was into kinky stuff... taking pictures of the guys he... well, you know. Maybe he had some kind of hidden camera. Your guess is as good as mine."

I thought about that. Would Chip Jordan, a movie star, risk taking photos of himself in a homosexual act? Now that would be crazy.

"So," I ventured, "you were Chip Jordan's... uh, boyfriend?"

Sutton let loose a huge laugh. "That's a good one! Boyfriend! Hardly!" He paused and looked right at me. "Ever heard of the casting couch, Mr. Zorn?"

"Yeah, I know what it is."

"Well expand your idea beyond Harry Cohn getting his afternoon blow job from aspiring starlets."

Sutton looked at me, like he was trying to figure out if I understood what he was driving at. I nodded. I didn't want to think about this too much. If someone was homosexual — Chip Jordan, Steve Sutton, or anyone else — I figured that was their business, but I didn't want to dwell on the details.

"I'm not queer," Sutton said, as if he was reading my mind. "It was just one of those things. My agent set it up. Told me Chip Jordan wanted to get to know me better. Chip was a big star. I knew the deal. I thought — stupidly in retrospect — that this might be my big break. Little did I know. And now this."

He banged his fist down on the envelope containing the photos.

Just then, there was a knock at the door.

"Boss?" Leon called out from the waiting room.

"Come on in," Sutton said.

Leon lumbered through the door, walked over to Sutton, and handed him an envelope. It was unsealed and bulky.

"Thank you, Leon. Job well done."

The big man nodded solemnly before leaving the room. Sutton pulled a wad of cash from the envelope. He counted the bills, then put them back into the envelope.

"I need your help," he said, "If these photos, and the others you can be damn sure were taken that afternoon, get out, they'll ruin my chance in politics. They'll ruin my life. I need you to find the rest of the photos. And of course any negatives that exist. I need you to put a stop to this whole rotten situation. A few grand to shut up Panozzo I can pay, but I've been around long enough to know that this blackmail thing, once it starts, is never over. I can't keep paying out for the rest of my life."

Sutton pushed the cash-filled envelope across the desk towards me. "Five hundred dollars. Just a retainer. I'll pay whatever your fees and expenses are, of course."

I glanced at the envelope, but didn't pick it up.

"Go on. Count it. It's yours. That and a lot more if you help me."

I still didn't pick it up. I thought to myself: Do I want to work for a guy who uses a thug like Leon to do his dirty work? On the other hand, a job is a job. Bills have to be paid. And blackmail is an ugly racket. Blackmail stinks.

"Okay," I said. "With one condition."

"I'm listening."

"Mrs. Flynn stays out of this. I guarantee she has nothing to do with it."

"Seems to me she's Panozzo's partner."

"She's not."

"She brings him the photos. She's got to be in it with him."

"She's not."

"How are you so sure?"

"You said you admire professional discretion, right?"

Sutton nodded. "She's your client?"

"Was. Lay off her."

"Okay. Just find me the photos."

I picked up the cash-filled envelope and stuffed it into my back pocket.

"Anything else you want to tell me before I get started?" I said.

"I've laid all my cards on the table. And don't think it's been easy for me. I've made my share of mistakes in the past. I'm just asking you to help me make the past the past. And keep it there."

I thought to myself: Is the past ever the past?

***

I followed Leon to the underground garage. I got into the back seat of the Caddy, and Leon drove us out of the garage and onto Wilshire. We crossed La Brea, heading west. Just past the tar pits, was an enormous hole in the ground that was someday going to be an art museum. Right now it was just dirt and re-bar. I stared at the back of Leon's thick neck for a while, wondering what made a man's hair turn white before he's 40.

"Hey, Leon," I said. "Wanna stop for a bite to eat? It's on me."

He shook his head and kept driving.

We pulled into the alley behind my apartment where this all began a few hours earlier. Leon cut the engine. He turned his massive bulk around to face me.

"So you're working for the boss, huh?" he said.

"Looks like it."

Leon's gaze was steady. His eyes bore into mine. "Don't fuck it up."

CHAPTER 12

I crawled into bed and slept until the squealing brakes of the garbage truck in the alley work me at dawn. I pulled on a t-shirt and a pair of cut-offs, and headed out to the beach.

The Boardwalk was empty except for a drunk slumped against one of the columns in front of the St. Marks Hotel. The column was scratched up with graffiti. Crumpled food wrappers, cigarette butts, and broken glass had collected in the gutter. Venice smelled like Venice: one part ocean, two parts decomposing trash.

I walked across the sand towards the ocean. Seagulls swooped and squawked above the water. Down at the shoreline, a guy in black baggies stood gazing out at the surf. A red pintail Weber stuck upright in the sand beside him.

"Hey, Reno," I said.

He glanced over at me. "Shoulda been here yesterday, man."

I looked out at the waves. All gutless, ankle busters breaking up on the sand.

We both stood there for a while, staring out at the soup. Reno was one of the guys I had grown up with — Reno and Micki and Skunk and Ollie and the rest of our raggedy Venice Beach crew. With working parents and little supervision, we had spent our summers surfing, chasing girls, and living just on the edge of trouble. Sometimes going over the edge. Reno had done a couple months in Juvie for breaking and entering a beach house in Malibu. Turns out the house was owned by a movie director.

When the director came home, he found Reno passed out on the bathroom floor cradling an empty bottle of Chivas. A few years after that, Reno did six months in County for possession of weed. Now he worked for Dewey Weber, shaping the boards that were flying out of Dewey's shop ever since Gidget and the Beach Boys craze hit.

Reno and I walked back across the sand, then parted ways at the Boardwalk, me going north, Reno going south.

I went upstairs to my apartment, changed into slacks and a plain blue button down shirt. Basic PI-according-to-Lou look: Bland, unremarkable, middle of the road. Good for surveillance.

I drove to the office and called Cora Flynn. I told her about my talk with Oscar Panozzo and that I didn't think he'd be bothering her anymore. She thanked me, but sounded more skeptical than grateful. I couldn't blame her. I hadn't told her anything about Steve Sutton and Leon and how Oscar Panozzo had never even been to her house.

"Mrs. Flynn," I said causally, "were there any other photographs in that Pinnacle office like those three you sold to Panozzo?"

That brought a long silence.

"Why are you asking me this, Ryan?" she said.

"It's a long story."

"Now you're being cryptic. You're scaring me."

"Sorry. I don't mean to. It's just that a lot's happened since yesterday. There's some weird stuff going on with those photos. I got hired to look into it."

"Hired? Hired by who? What are you talking about?"

"It's got nothing to do with you. Really. Don't worry. I just need to know if there were any more photographs."

Another long silence. "No," she finally answered. "There weren't."

"You went through everything in that office?"

"Yes. Mr. Dargin had already taken away his personal items. Probably on the day he was fired. His desk drawers were empty, except paper clips, pencils, things like that."

"Thanks. I appreciate it."

"Ryan, I don't know what this 'weird stuff' is all about, but if it has nothing to do with me, with me and Joey, good. I just want this whole thing to be over. I want our life to get back to normal. I'm not saying that 'normal' was so peachy and perfect. Matter of fact, it's been pretty lousy since my husband left, but still . . . " she trailed off.

"I understand," I said. "How is Joey, anyway?"

She hesitated. She hesitated way too long. "Fine" she said. "Joey's fine."

I hung up the phone, glad that the awkward conversation with Mrs. Flynn was over. I thought about Joey. From the way Mrs. Flynn said it, I knew things were not fine. But I'd have to let that go. Nothing I could do about it. At least not right now.

So I drove to the VA hospital in Westwood.

Lou was sitting up in bed, reading the <u>Evening Outlook</u>. He seemed small and shrunken in the faded hospital gown. A pale blue cotton blanket draped over his legs. His complexion was pasty and his hair was matted. The plastic oxygen tube ran up into his nose. He grinned when he saw me.

"Hey, Ryan."

"Hey, Lou."

He flicked the back of his finger against the newspaper. "Dodgers beat the Cards. That Drysdale's got some arm, huh?"

"You bet."

"Best righty in the National League."

"I'll take Gibson over Drysdale any day."

"Okay, maybe a toss up. Hey, can you believe Mays getting a hundred grand this year? If anyone deserves it, he does. Just never thought I'd see the day they'd pay that much to a Negro player."

"Times change."

Lou nodded. "Better late than never."

"So how you doing,?" I asked.

"Can't complain. Still breathing. At least I don't have to wear that damn mask today. Cute nurse on swing. Beth's her name. I told her about you."

"Jesus, Lou."

"Maybe you'll thank me later. Say, can you get me a radio? Koufax versus Gibson coming up. Don't wanna miss that one."

"I thought you had a transistor?"

"Gone. I'm pretty sure the orderly on night shift lifted it. Screw it, though. If he's that hard up to steal from an old sick vet, let him have it. So, how's biz? Your mother said you're working your ass off. My phrase, not hers."

"We got a new case on Friday."

Lou folded the paper and set it beside him on the bed.

"Details, kid. Details."

I filled him in. I told him about Mrs. Flynn and Joey and Doc Flynn. He frowned when I told him about taking Flynn's drug. I told him about Oscar Panozzo and Leon and Steve Sutton and the photographs. I told him the whole thing, all the details, everything I could remember. Then I pulled the plastic baggie from my pocket and handed it to him.

"From Mrs. Flynn's rug," I said. "Think it's blood?"

Lou peered inside the baggie. He rubbed a bit of it between his fingers. He took the oxygen tube out of his nose and sniffed it.

"Probably blood," he said. "But does it matter?"

"What do you mean?"

"You already know the boy bashed the goon on the head with the frying pan somewhere around the couch."

"Yeah."

"So there's a high chance this is Leon's blood."

"Right."

"But if even it's Martian snot, how does that change a thing? It was right that you collected it. Good job in doing that. But what was relevant last Friday is not particularly important today."

"Yeah, I see your point."

Lou was starting to breath hard. It was a raspy breathing. He gulped for air, grabbed the oxygen tube and pushed it back up into his nose. His breath started to calm down.

He caught me watching him.

"Don't worry about me, kid. I'll be fine. Now what I'm thinking about is this Dargin big shot. I've heard of him. If he's the source of the photos, even an innocent, unsuspecting source, you're going to have to dig around there."

"Yeah. I plan to."

"Good. And another thing: Think there's any conflict of interest here?"

"Whose?"

"Yours."

"I don't get it."

"Who's your client?"

"Sutton."

"And you tell him Mrs. Flynn has nothing to do with anything."

"She doesn't."

"Are you positive?"

"Yes."

"Or, are you being protective? Protective of her and the boy."

I shrugged. It was as if Lou could read my mind. I hadn't told him about my mixed-up feelings of wanting to help Mrs. Flynn and Joey. And yet somehow he knew.

"Oh, yeah," Lou added, "and about your client wanting to make the past the past? I've got news, kid: The past is never the past. It's been more than twenty years, but every time a car backfires I'm right back at Guadalcanal."

CHAPTER 13

The sign in the window said OPEN. I parked across the street from Tinseltown Treasures, in a spot where I had a good view of the door. I put on a pair of shades and a Dodgers' cap, hoping this was enough of a disguise in case Panozzo caught sight of me.

I walked to the end of the block, crossed the street, then headed up the alley that ran behind Panozzo's shop. Both the Chinese restaurant and the dry cleaners had back doors leading out to the alley. But not Tinseltown Treasures. Panozzo, and anyone else, would have to use the front door to go in or out. Which was an excellent break. Working this job solo would be do-able. Before leaving the alley, I noted that high up on the brick wall was a utility window reinforced with wire-mesh. The window was cracked open. It was probably the john.

I got back into my car. The summer air was heating up, so I rolled down all the windows. For the entire morning I was bombarded by the clatter and clang of jackhammers, tractors, drills and forklifts at a nearby construction site. It seemed like in L.A. something somewhere was always being torn down, dug up, or built anew.

At noon, Oscar Panozzo removed the OPEN card in the window and replaced it with one that read BACK SOON. He came out of his shop, locked the door, walked to the Chinese restaurant and went inside. About twenty minutes later, he walked out of the restaurant carrying a white cardboard carry-out box. He unlocked the door to his shop, went inside, changed the sign to OPEN.

At exactly 6:00 PM, Panozzo flipped the card in the window from OPEN to CLOSED. He locked the door, walked up the block towards Hollywood Boulevard. I'd seen nobody other than Panozzo go in or out of Tinseltown Treasures the entire day. No customers. No deliverymen. Zip.

I got out of my car and followed the little bald man on foot, staying on the opposite side of the street, and keeping about half a block between us.

He went into a corner grocery store with display crates of fresh fruits and vegetables stacked at the entrance. He came out a few minutes later, carrying a grocery bag with some carrots sticking out the top. He walked north on Wilcox, turned on Yucca, walked a few more blocks, finally stopping at an apartment building trying to pass as a Swiss chalet. The building had two doors on the ground floor. Between them was a stairwell leading up into darkness. After checking his mailbox, Panozzo disappeared up the stairs. I walked part way up the block to a bus stop. I sat on the bus stop bench and watched the Swiss chalet for a while, but nobody else went in or out of the building, so I walked back to the chalet and checked the names on the mailbox. Panozzo was in #4. I tore off a small strip of paper from my notebook, went up the dark stairwell, pushed the paper into the door jamb of #4.

Then I went home.

***

Early the next morning I parked across the street from Panozzo's apartment building and walked quietly up the stairs. The strip of paper I had stuck in the door jamb last night was still there. I walked to the bus stop and waited. At 8:30 AM, Panozzo came down the steps from his apartment. He was wearing a white linen suit, white buckskin loafers, and a blue polka dot bow tie. I followed him on foot to Tinseltown, watched as he unlocked the door, went inside, and flipped the sign in the window to OPEN. I hightailed it back to my car, drove the few blocks back to Tinseltown Treasures, and settled in for another day of surveillance.

For five days, Panozzo stuck to the same schedule. Walk to work. Chinese for lunch. Return to shop with leftovers box. Walk home. Each night I put a strip of paper into his doorjamb. Each morning it would still be there. The one thing I knew about him so far: Oscar Panozzo was a man with a routine.

The other thing I knew: For five days, not a single customer came into Panozzo's shop. How the heck did this cat pay the rent, I wondered. I had a lot of time to wonder. And what did he do for fun? Was his life all work, sleep, and Chinese for lunch? What kind of life was that? Did he have any friends or family? Of course these days, if someone had been tailing me, they might be asking the same thing. When was the last time I'd hung out with my buddies, or hit the waves, or dated a girl? Which, as always, got me thinking about Allison. Was she home for the summer, or still back East? *No, Ryan,* I told myself. *Don't go there. It's over. Don't think about her.*

Day 6 began as another repeat. Without Lou to shoot the shit with — or at least to trade off shifts — the job was starting to get boring. So were the cheese and tomato sandwiches I'd been bringing along every day for lunch. *Part of the deal,* I told myself. *Suck it up. I'm on Steve Sutton's dime. He wants me to watch this cat, I'll watch.*

At noon on Day 6, when Panozzo went into the Chinese restaurant for lunch, I decided to stretch my legs. I walked past the bustling construction site at Sunset and Vine, source of the racket that had been hammering relentlessly into my head all week. A signboard at the edge of the site displayed a sketch of a round white structure covered with dimples that looked like a UFO more than a building. "Coming Soon," the sign said, "The Cinerama Dome." The words below said the Cinerama Dome was a movie theater where three projectors run the film so that it stretches across a wide curved screen. I would definitely check it out. But there was no girl right now that I wanted to take with me. Except Allison. The sign said that the Cinerama Dome right here at Sunset and Vine was the first of six hundred more to be built around the world.

I got back to my car at 12:15 PM. Ten minutes later, Panozzo walked out of the Chinese restaurant carrying his usual carry-out box. As always, he entered his shop and flipped the sign to OPEN.

Then I took a calculated risk. I pulled away from the curb and headed to Beverly Hills.

If today was like the last five days, I'd have ample time to take care of business and be back long before Panozzo closed up. If today wasn't like the last five, I was fucked.

CHAPTER 14

Victor Dargin's house was white and massive, with stately columns, and windows framed by black lacquered shutters. It looked like the kind of place Thomas Jefferson might have called home. But bigger. The house was set back from the street by a rectangle of lawn big enough for a Rams game.

To the right of the house was an open two-car garage. A silver Rolls Royce was parked in one spot. What else would you expect for a big shot movie exec like Dargin? The other spot was empty.

I drove past Dargin's mansion and over to downtown Beverly Drive. My stomach was growling, and being around all this money made the thought of my tomato and cheese sandwich seem lousy. So I went into Nate 'n Al's and ate a fat pastrami on rye while enjoying the air conditioning and the cute blonde waitress who was serving the counter. After lunch, I went back to my car and rummaged through the canvas duffle bag in the trunk, pulling out a pair of non-prescription glasses with thick black rims.

Seated inside the car again, I took off my Dodgers cap and shades, combed my hair back, and put on the black rims. I checked myself out in the rear view mirror. Even combed back, my hair was still shaggy, hanging over my ears. "Too long, too recognizable, not good for sub rosa," Lou had commented many times.

I drove back to Victor Dargin's mansion and rang the bell. Chimes echoed from within. A hit of nervousness floated up inside me. I had to play this thing right. Besides Panozzo, Victor Dargin was my only connection to the blackmail photos. Cora Flynn found them in his office. He must know something about them. But I needed to question him without throwing any heat on Mrs. Flynn.

A middle-aged Negro woman in a pink maid's uniform opened the door. Her hair was streaked with white and pulled back off her smooth, unblemished face into a tight bun.

"Good afternoon," I said. "Is Mr. Dargin home?"

"No, sir." Her voice was so soft that I had to strain to hear it.

"Do you know when he'll be back?"

"No, sir."

"Will he be back today?"

"I'm sorry, sir, I can't say."

She stood in the doorway, passive, saying nothing. She looked at me, blank and serene, like she could wait here quietly for the rest of the day.

Just then, a hunter green Jaguar Mark II pulled into the driveway. Sweet. The Jag glided into the open garage. A moment later, Victor Dargin got out. He was about 50, my height, and starting to thicken around the middle. He had a large head, bushy eyebrows, and a trim beard flecked with grey. His suit jacket fit a bit too tight.

"What's this, Althea?" Dargin barked when he got to the front door.

"This gentleman would like to speak to you, sir."

Dargin glared at me. "Do I know you?"

"No, sir," I said, taking my cue from the maid. "I'm a collector."

"What?" Dargin snapped. "A collector? I pay my bills. I'm a millionaire."

"No, no. Not bills. Can we talk inside, sir?"

Dargin sighed. "Right here will do. Thank you, Althea. That's all for now." He dismissed the maid with a wave of his hand. She went inside, shutting the door quietly behind her.

"Okay," Dargin said. "What's this all about? I'm a busy man."

"Yes, sir. I understand. I collect movie stuff. It's kind of a side business. I got a tip from a friend who heard you recently left Pinnacle Studios, and sometimes people like you, people in high positions in Hollywood, well, they accumulate things, things that mean nothing to you, things you'd just as soon get rid of, but for people like us ... well, like I said, it's a business."

"Sorry, but your friend gave you a bum tip. I don't have anything like that."

"Darn. I drove all the way up from San Diego. I hate to go back empty-handed."

"Look, like I said, I have nothing for you. Why don't you hunt around the studio trash cans. MGM and Fox are practically around the corner. The art departments toss out lobby cards, posters, mock-ups, like they were banana peels."

"Our specialty is photographs, sir," I said. "Photos of movie stars."

"Got nothing for you."

"Especially autographed ones."

Victor Dargin squinted at me. "What's your name?"

"Ryan, sir."

"Ryan, you're persistent and I admire persistence. But you caught me on a bad day. Matter of fact, you caught me on perhaps the worst day of the worst month of my entire life. So I'm going to ask you to leave now."

"I guess I could come back at another time. Maybe by then—"

"Ryan."

"Yes sir?"

"Scram."

***

I drove back to Tinseltown Treasures and resumed my watch. The sign in the window said OPEN. Steam rose from the roof vents of the dry cleaners next door. I thought about Victor Dargin. He seemed like an okay guy. I wondered what made this the worst day in the worst month of his life. Getting fired would be a drag for anyone, but for a millionaire it didn't seem like it would be worst thing in the world. And what was so bad about today?

As usual, the hammering, drilling, sawing, and other assorted construction noises continued all afternoon. As usual, no customers came in or out of Tinseltown all afternoon. As usual, the construction workers quit for the day at 5:00 PM. As usual, a few minutes before 6:00 PM, I put on my shades and Dodgers cap and rolled up the windows, ready to tail Panozzo up to his Swiss chalet. But he didn't come out of the shop.

At 6:10 the sign still said OPEN. If I was surveilling someone else, I might not think anything of it. Maybe the guy was on the phone, or busy with the books. But this was Oscar Panozzo — Mr. Routine.

At 6:20 I walked across the street and peered into Tinseltown's front window. I scanned the interior, my view partly obscured by the posters plastered to the glass. I caught glimpses of the rows of filing cabinets ... the cash register on the back counter ... a bit of the back wall ... I scanned down to the linoleum floor ... where a white buckskin shoe attached to a leg in white linen trousers jutted out from behind the counter.

CHAPTER 15

My throat tightened and my heart started pumping faster.

I crossed the street to my car, grabbed my .38 Special from the glove compartment, dashed back to Tinseltown. *Slow down, Ryan. Pay attention.*

The door was unlocked. Cautiously, I opened it. Despite my best effort, the bells jingled. I shut the door, dropped to a crouch, and listened. The only sound I heard was the muffled hum of traffic along Hollywood Boulevard. Gun pointed forward, I crept through the store.

The door to a back room was slightly ajar. I nudged it open with my foot and looked inside. Empty. I turned to the main attraction.

Oscar Panozzo lay crumpled against the wall behind the counter. His face, or what was left of it, was covered in blood. A bullet had gone straight into one eye socket. A chunk of brain and skull lay on the floor beside him. Blood had spattered onto his white linen suit and onto the wall behind him. Hanging above Panozzo's body was a Bette Davis poster, a spray of red nearly obliterating the title — *Payment On Demand.*

For a moment, I thought I was going to puke. It was the face. It was death. A wrong and sickening death. I swallowed hard. I turned away from Panozzo and took a deep breath, blew the air out slowly.

I forced myself to bend down and touch his wrist. No pulse, but I already knew that. His skin was cold and tight. I tried to remember what that meant. This wasn't the first corpse I'd seen. I'd gone to the county morgue with Lou a few times and stood around while he and the M.E. discussed this and that. I had looked at the rigid bluish bodies on the cold metal carts, torsos and chests sewn up with thick black thread, toes tagged. And there was that crazy woman who lived a few doors down from me in Venice. She was stabbed one night by the liquor store, somehow managing to drag herself through the alley, blood trailing the whole way, to the foot of my rickety stairs. That's where I found her in the morning, her head resting on the bottom step.

For some reason, though, this felt different. I didn't want to look at Oscar Panozzo, almost couldn't. Only a few days ago I had been talking to this little man about Marlon Brando and *One Eyed Jacks* and his love of silent movies. We had been standing, talking, just feet from where he now lay. Now, Oscar Panozzo's life was gone… forever and always. And the last thing between us? I had threatened him. Maybe he had it coming, if in fact he really was a blackmailer, but I had liked the guy nonetheless.

Now, kneeling here, NOT looking at the mangled and bloody corpse on the floor beside me, the worst thought of all bubbled up into my mind: Was I somehow responsible for Oscar Panozzo's death? I hadn't pulled the trigger, didn't even know who did, but I had threatened him, I had followed him, I had inserted myself into the shadows of his life. And today, at the very time I was supposed to be surveilling Panozzo but was in fact in Beverly Hills, he had been killed. If I had played it differently, if I had simply walked away after Joey was safe at home, if I had stayed in my spot across from Tinseltown Treasures today, if if if if…..

I couldn't think about this anymore right now.

Later for that, Ryan. Time to take care of business.

That's when I realized I was still holding Oscar Panozzo's wrist. Skin cold and tight. What did that mean about time of death? My mind was blank. Fuck it. That was the cops' problem, not mine.

My job was to pay attention and log it all in my mind.

I stood up and looked around. Just past the counter, the iron door to a wall safe hung open. I looked inside the safe, careful not to touch it. Empty.

I went into the bathroom. Tiny, barely room to stand. Sink, toilet, linoleum floor — all immaculately clean. On the sink was a Snow White soap dispenser. Snow White wore a blue blouse and a long yellow skirt; she had rosy porcelain cheeks and held an apple in her porcelain hand. The toilet lid was down. Above the toilet, the high transom window was wide open. Shit. Did the shooter enter and exit through that window while I was on watch? With all that construction racket, would I have heard the shots? Maybe not. No way, if a silencer was used. Or did the whole thing happen while I was interviewing Victor Dargin in Beverly Hills?

Knock it off, Ryan. You can speculate later.

I stepped around Panozzo's body, picked up the phone on the counter, dialed the LAPD Hollywood Station, and called it in. Then I went to the front of the store and set my .38 on a shelf beside a plastic snow globe enclosing a miniature Scarlett and Rhett embracing by a fence.

Five minutes later I heard sirens. Two prowl cars skidded to halt in front of Tinseltown. Four uniformed cops converged on the sidewalk. One stayed out front, the other three came inside, guns drawn. The first cop to enter was beefy with a horseshoe mustache. The cop behind him had the look of a rookie catching his first homicide — gangly, wide-eyed, jumpy — trying and failing to stay cool. The last cop zeroed in on Panozzo's white buckskin shoe and went right to it.

Horseshoe lowered his gun and approached me, the rookie tagging behind.

"You called this in?" Horseshoe was gruff, no-nonsense.

"Yes, sir. I'm Ryan Zorn. Southland Investigations. My gun's over there."

I pointed to the .38 Special.

"Get the gun." Horseshoe ordered the rookie.

The rookie picked my gun off the shelf and dropped it into a plastic bag.

"Got a stiff here," the third cop called out, still crouching by Panozzo's body.

"Okay. Call off the bus," Horseshoe said. Then, to the rookie: "Frisk him."

As the rookie patted me down, Horseshoe searched through my wallet. He examined my ID for a few seconds.

"Okay Zorn, we're gonna take you down to the station."

"What for?"

"Just want to ask you a few questions. You got a problem with that?"

Before I could answer, he shoved me forward.

"Come on. Let's go."

CHAPTER 16

Horseshoe left me in a crummy government-issue interview room. Beige walls, no windows, two metal chairs with a table between them, sickly greenish lighting. After half an hour of nothing but the hum of the fluorescents, an overweight detective entered. He had bags under his eyes, a cigarette dangling from his mouth. He wore a cheap suit which only emphasized his gone-to-seed gloom. The name tag on the lanyard around his neck read "Det. Mackie".

"Okay Zorn, what the hell were you doing over at Tinseltown?" Mackie asked grumpily.

"I was on a case."

"What case?"

"Sorry Detective, I can't say. Client confidentiality — you know how it is."

"Oh, right. My apologies. Your client's privacy certainly takes precedence over a goddamn inconsequential murder. So, let's start over. What the fuck were you doing over at Tinseltown?"

"Like I said—"

"Cut the shit, surfer boy. You're taking over for the old man now, right? Well, let me tell you: Lou's got his priorities straight. He plays ball with us, we play ball with him. You got that, Junior?"

I shrugged.

Instantly, Mackie lunged across the table. He grabbed me by the front of my shirt, and yanked me towards him. His face, fleshy and red, was just a few inches from mine. His breath reeked of coffee and cigarettes.

"Look you fucking bottom feeder," he growled, "I'm trying to solve a murder here. You got that? Now either you tell me exactly what you were doing over at Tinseltown today or else you convince me right here, right now, that you're not the motherfucker who did the deed!"

I looked Mackie in the eye and said nothing. I've never done well with certain so called authority figures — just ask my high school swim coach — and Mackie was exactly that kind. I was considering my next move when the door to the interview room opened and Detective Terekov entered, a Styrofoam cup in his hand. He took in the scene with a faint chuckle. Mackie let go of my shirt and sat down in his chair. Terekov set the cup down on the table in front of me.

"Coffee?" he said.

"Thanks," I said, not referring to the coffee.

I sipped the lukewarm coffee.

"I'll take it from here," Terekov said to Mackie.

Mackie scowled, pushed himself up from the chair, and lumbered out of the room. I knew they were playing good-cop-bad-cop, but I didn't care. I was glad to see him go.

"So Ryan," Terekov said, as smooth and affable as Mackie was tough, "what's the story here? What were you doing over at the scene?"

"I'd been surveilling the store owner for about a week. He didn't close up shop like he usually does, so I went to check out what was up. That's when I found him."

"What time was that?"

"Six-twenty. He usually closes at six."

"When did you last see him alive?"

"Around twelve-thirty. When he came back from lunch."

"Then what?"

"That's it."

"So Panozzo comes back from lunch, you see nothing else for the rest of the day."

"I was gone from about twelve-thirty to three."

"Let me get this straight: You're tailing this guy all week, and in the two plus hours you're gone he gets plugged?"

I nodded, hating to admit it. "Probably."

"Or, and I love this: he gets plugged right under your nose."

Terekov shook his head and chuckled. I knew the entire Hollywood station would get a good laugh at my expense.

"I realize you're not going to give up your client," Terekov said, "but just tell me one thing: Does this homicide have anything to do with your case?"

"I don't know."

"Bullshit, Ryan. Help me out here."

Terekov raised an eyebrow. He cocked his head to the side and waited for my response. I shrugged.

"Okay," he said, "try this one on: There's been a rash of fruit rolls around the Tinseltown neighborhood, and this guy's a fruit, right?"

I shrugged again. "I guess so."

"Here's the thing, Ryan — and I know your uncle would agree — we got a serious situation here. A murder. A perp free on the street. This isn't the time to hold anything back. Whatever you're working on, that's gotta take a back seat to this situation. You understand that, right?"

"I'm not trying to be difficult, Detective."

"I'm sure you're not. I'm sure you want to play ball with us just like Lou would. So if you have information that could help us solve this thing, I'm counting on you to do right. Like your uncle would."

I nodded. I didn't believe for a second that Lou "played ball" with the cops the way these detectives made it out to be, but I knew I had to give something.

"It must have gone down before five o'clock," I said.

"Why's that?"

"There's construction nearby that stops at five. It's loud and would have made it hard to hear the shots if they happened while I was there."

"Thanks but no thanks, Ryan. The M.E. can estimate time of death within two hours. What else you got?"

"That's it."

"How about the pick-up artist you were tracking at Kelbo's? That related?"

"I don't know."

Terekov squinted at me for a long, uncomfortable minute.

"Alright get outta here," he said.

"I'm not a suspect?"

"Of course not."

"When can I have my gun back?"

"We'll call you when … and if."

Terekov stood up to leave. The interview was over. I stood up also.

"Oh, one more thing," Terekov said, looking me square in the eyes. "This isn't a game to me, Ryan. This isn't about turf or power or earning brownie points with the captain. It's about a dead guy. A guy who shouldn't be dead. Believe it or not, I care about that. I just hope you do, too."

CHAPTER 17

I swiveled Lou's desk chair around and faced the front window. The street was dark and deserted, the nursery across the street closed up for the night. The red neon BAIL BONDS sign blinked on and off. I was still amped up from the whole bizarre day. I sat and watched the red light flicker. After a while, my mind start to relax. I dialed Steve Sutton and told him we needed to meet. Tonight. At my office.

"It's after midnight," he said. "I haven't heard from you in days, and now you wake me up in the middle of the night. What gives?"

"We need to meet right now. It's important."

"Can't this wait till morning?"

"Nope."

Sutton sighed. "Alright. But at least you come up here. I'm not even dressed yet. And last time I checked you were working for me."

"I'll be there."

Before leaving, I checked with the answering service. Mrs. Keplinger had called: Someone was hitting golf balls onto her roof again. A potential new client had called: He was sure his wife was cheating on him, but he needed proof. Cora Flynn had called: No message.

I wrote it all down. Then I got into my Falcon and drove to West Hollywood.

Steve Sutton's house was on Kings Road, just above the Strip. It was a small, Spanish style bungalow — white plaster with a red tiled roof and deep set windows. An archway in front led to a small, enclosed patio filled with potted plants and vines. The low-wattage globe by the door cast an eerie glow over broad waxy leaves and red waxy flowers and a tangle of vines climbing the walls.

Sutton opened the door before I knocked. He was barefoot and hadn't shaved, but he had spiffed himself up with a black polo shirt and starched khaki slacks. And he was frowning. I hadn't told him squat on the phone, but it didn't take a genius to figure this wouldn't be a chat about Clemente's soaring batting average.

"Come on in," he said, eyeing me warily.

I stepped into a small tiled foyer with an antique side table and a carousel coat rack.

"Well?" Sutton said, after he shut the front door.

"Oscar Panozzo is dead."

"What?!" he gasped. His eyes widened and shockwaves spread across his chiseled, unshaven face. The surprise looked genuine. But, I reminded myself, Steve Sutton was an actor ... and a wannabe politician.

"He was murdered." I added. "Yesterday."

"Are you fucking kidding me? What happened?"

I filled him in on the details, wondering if I was only telling him what he already knew.

"Unbelievable!" he exclaimed when I finished. "I hire you to follow that little shit, to watch his every move, and he's murdered. Right in front of you!"

I had it coming. And I was probably going to make it worse.

"Mr. Sutton, what were you doing between noon and five yesterday?"

"You're joking."

"No."

"Why you little ... I hired you! You aren't here to question me!"

"It's what the cops will ask if they make a connection between you and Panozzo."

"Why the hell would they be making connections? That's why I hired you — to keep this quiet."

"It's their job. They're gonna be all over Panozzo's shop, his house, everywhere. They may find photos and start asking questions."

"We can't let that happen."

"So where were you yesterday?"

"Oh, for god's sake. I was at my office all afternoon. Moving in. You can check with Bekins if you want."

"What about Leon?"

"What about him?"

"He's your muscle, right?

"I wouldn't call him that."

"Call him what you want. He does your dirty work. Goodbye Panozzo, goodbye blackmail."

Sutton shook his head. "This is ludicrous. I just want the photos, the negatives, whatever is out there. I don't want to kill anyone to get them. As a matter of fact, my position is significantly worse with Panozzo dead. How are we going to find those photos now?"

"What was Leon doing yesterday while you were moving in?" I asked.

"If you must know, Leon is no longer in my employ. I had to let him go."

"Why?"

"I realized that he's become a … a liability to me. Leon may be loyal — as a matter of fact, loyalty is probably his outstanding characteristic — but he lacks the diplomatic touch. If I'm serious about this political run, and I am, Leon is only a detriment. His handling of Mrs. Flynn proved the point. My life is changing and Leon just doesn't fit in."

"How long has he worked for you?"

"Many years."

"And you fired him? Your loyal Leon? Just like that?"

"I'm not so callous. Leon is a good man — whatever you might think of him. I've known him for a long time. As an excellent long-time employee, I rewarded him with an all-expense paid vacation to his home town. An extended vacation. He was very grateful. He hasn't been back to Yugoslavia since the war."

Suddenly I felt sorry for lumbering, hulking, loyal Leon, sent away because he had become a liability.

"Maybe you'll get lucky and he'll never come back," I said.

"One can dream," Sutton answered, not catching my sarcasm.

"What day did he leave?"

"How are these questions getting us any closer to solving my problem? You can't truly be thinking Leon has something to do with this."

I shrugged. Waited for an answer. A clock dinged once somewhere in the house.

Sutton sighed. "Okay, okay. Let's see ... He left on Wednesday. There was space on a flight to London. I gave Leon plenty of cash and traveler's checks to get home from there."

I pulled out my notebook and a pen. "What's Leon's last name? And I'll need his address. And his flight number."

Sutton scowled, but reluctantly gave me the information. I didn't necessarily believe that Leon had killed Panozzo. Maybe, just as Sutton said, he was already out of the country before the murder took place. Or maybe not.

"Leon isn't a killer," Sutton said. "I know him. He's had a hard life. He may be a little rough around the edges, but he means well."

"You might be right, but I've got to at least cross him off my list."

"List?! What list!? You're supposed to be helping me with my situation, not solving that vile little man's murder."

"I'd bet odds they're connected."

"Well, I don't see it. And I don't want you going off on some wild goose chase. Not on my dime. Just find me those photos."

"That's what I'm trying to do."

Sutton sighed again and ran his hand through his hair. "Do you want to sit down?" He motioned towards an archway that lead into the living room.

"No thanks. I gotta go. But about the photos, one thing we need to do is figure out who shot them."

"I told you, I didn't even know they existed, much less who took them."

"What about the agent? The one who set up your, uh … your meeting with Chip Jordan?"

"Dargin? No way. He wouldn't know a lens cap from a knee cap."

"Is this Victor Dargin you're talking about?"

"Yes. You know him?"

"Not really. I thought he's a studio big wig, not an agent."

"We've all got to start somewhere. Mail room, casting couch, talent agency. Same road, different pit stop."

Victor Dargin. I hadn't told Sutton that the photos originated in Victor Dargin's office. Before this moment, I didn't think it was relevant to the case. Plus, to be honest, just like Lou had warned me not to, I was being protective of Cora and Joey Flynn. Bringing up Dargin naturally led to Cora Flynn.

Now I told him. I thought Sutton would be surprised, or angry, or ream me out for not telling him sooner. Instead, he just scowled.

"Dargin," he muttered, "that son-of-a-bitch. So he and Panozzo are in this together. With that Flynn woman as the middleman."

"No, she has nothing to do with this."

"That's not how it sounds to me."

"I'm gonna have a talk with Dargin," I said. "I'll get to the bottom of it."

Sutton looked up abruptly, an expression of alarm on his face. "Is that absolutely necessary? You have to bring Dargin into this?"

"Yes."

Sutton twisted his head around, cracking his neck.

"Uh, I probably should have told you this before," he said sheepishly, "but I've already spoken with Victor Dargin."

"What? When?"

"A few days ago."

"Why?"

"I guess ... Well, I've been in a state ... my nerves are shot. The days go ticking by and you haven't come up with anything and I just ... I just couldn't sit still and do nothing. The more I thought about it, the more it made sense that Dargin had some involvement in all this. I mean, to my knowledge nobody knew about that afternoon except me and Chip ... and Dargin. So I called him. I asked him about the photos. He denied knowing anything. I kept pressing. He told me to get lost. Then he hung up."

"Did you tell him about the blackmail? That Panozzo was putting the squeeze on you?"

Sutton nodded.

"You mentioned Panozzo by name?"

"I might have."

"Might have?"

"Yes. I guess I did."

"And Tinseltown Treasures?"

He nodded.

"I wish you hadn't done that, Mr. Sutton. I wish you'd let me handle the case in my own way. I had a plan for Dargin."

"Well, you didn't tell me about any plan" he snapped. "I haven't heard from you all week. You just left me dangling in the dark."

"Yeah," I admitted. "I guess you're right about that."

"Look, Zorn, if you're not up for this, maybe you're in over your head, just tell me now. This is my life we're talking about. From what I hear, Southland is tops. Maybe there's someone else at your outfit who's… who's more seasoned."

I felt my cheeks warming; tried to will my face not to turn red. I was embarrassed. And pissed off at myself. And I didn't like Sutton condescending to me — even if I deserved it.

"I'm the only PI at Southland right now," I said. "If you want to hire someone else, that's your business."

Sutton thought it over for about two seconds. "Oh, I guess you'll do. You're into it this far. But keep me informed, okay? And be discreet."

"I will."

Before leaving, I asked him one last question. I tried to make it sound off-the-cuff, my hand on the door like I was about to leave.

"By the way," I said, "Who do <u>you</u> think killed Panozzo?"

"How the heck should I know? You're the detective, what's your theory?"

"I don't have one yet."

"Well don't worry yourself too much about it. Oscar Panozzo was a no good, son-of-a-bitch blackmailer. He's dead, we move on. Just get me those photos."

Driving home, I thought about what Sutton had said. <u>Was</u> I up for this job? Or was I in over my head? I had found Joey on my own, but that was a missing kid. This was blackmail… and now with a murder attached. And I couldn't shake the thought: If I hadn't gone to interview Dargin, if I had stayed in my spot all day at Tinseltown, could I have prevented Panozzo's death?

Ryan, don't go down that hole. Move forward, not back.

I forced myself to focus on the case as it stood right now. First there was Leon. Everything Sutton said about sending Leon off to Europe could be true — there was a certain logic to it — or it could be a bunch of b.s. I had to find out which. And there was Victor Dargin. I now saw Victor Dargin in a brand new way.

CHAPTER 18

The next morning, I bought a bottle of OJ at the corner liquor store, perched myself on a bench facing the ocean and downed the juice. The hot, dry Santa Anas had blown in during the night, charging the morning air with electricity. Firemen's nightmare. Surfer's dream.

I walked across the Boardwalk and onto the beach, stepping around the palm fronds that littered the sand. Yesterday's smog had been pushed out to sea and now hung like a dirty yellow strip on the horizon. An offshore wind was whipping up the waves. Tiny rainbows were flying off the frothy white peaks like sparks off a campfire. Perfect surfing conditions.

But not for me. Not today.

I drove to the office and returned yesterday's phone calls. I referred the potential new client with the unfaithful wife to another PI; I'd have to work full-time on the case I already had. I listened to Mrs. Keplinger complain about the latest golf ball attack, her good-for-nothing son who never visited her, and how putting fluoride in the water was a communist plot. I advised her to call back in a couple of days if the golf ball attack continued. I called Cora Flynn. The phone rang and rang. Nobody answered. I called her work number. No answer.

I called Pan Am.

"Hello," I said in my most sophisticated voice. "My brother flew to London a few days ago, but we haven't heard from him since he left. I wanted to confirm that he made his flight."

"Certainly, sir," replied a female clerk. "What's your brother's full name and flight information?"

I gave it to her.

"One moment," she said, then left me listening to a cheesy instrumental version of *Mona Lisa.*

"I have the information you requested," the clerk said when she returned to the line. "We do have a Leon Vanek booked on that flight. And it appears he did board the plane."

I felt a hit of relief that Leon had left town before Panozzo's murder. It made things simpler if my client wasn't a bald-faced liar. I thanked the woman and was about to hang up when I thought of something.

"That L.A. to London flight, was it non-stop?"

"No, sir. The plane made a stop at Idlewild."

"Idlewild. Where's that?"

"Idlewild Airport. In New York City."

"Oh. Is there any way to be certain that my brother flew all the way to London?"

"I don't understand."

"Let's say he decided, for some reason, to get off in New York. Would the airline keep track of that?"

"No, sir. The only passenger data we maintain are boarding records of international travelers, based on their passport information."

"What about arriving in London — people show their passports there, right?"

"Of course. At Customs."

"So Customs in London could tell me if he arrived."

"I'm afraid not. Customs officials don't write anything down. They just make sure the passport is valid, then let the passenger through."

I thanked the woman and hung up. I thought long and hard before dialing Max Fisher. I knew Allison might be home, but saw no good way around it.

Sure enough, Allison picked up the phone. Right away I asked to speak with Max.

"Is this just a way to get back into my life?" Allison said. "Because I've moved on."

"I know. It's cool. I only want to come over to talk to Max. It's business."

"Just don't get any big ideas if I'm home when you come over."

"I won't."

"You might."

"You mean, you might," I teased.

"Very funny. I won't."

"Neither will I."

"Don't make promises you can't keep, Ryan."

Was it my imagination, or was Allison flirting with me? Because I was definitely flirting with her. Which was the exact opposite of my plan. We had gone from "I've moved on" to flirting in about ten seconds.

I felt elated. But this was absurd. We were over. So why were we doing this? Why was I doing this?

I drove out to Malibu thinking about Allison instead of preparing what I was going to ask Max. My mind floated back from our flirting today to the first time we met. It was the summer between our junior and senior year in high school. I had a job washing dishes at a private beach club. Her parents were members. Allison and her friends would hang out behind the kitchen at the end of the day, smoking, maybe drinking a beer with "the help". All the girls were cute and rich and looking for some action after swimming and tennis and working on their suntans all day. Their parents were usually too blitzed to notice.

Allison and I hit it off from the start. It wasn't just that she was the best looking of all her girlfriends, but she was the smartest. At least that's what I thought. We were together the rest of the summer, and on into senior year. She went to Santa Monica High (where all the Malibu kids went), I went to Venice, but we hung out together every weekend and whenever else possible. That's when I started coming around her house and getting to know her family.

Entering Allison's family world was like visiting a foreign country. Dinner at my house was me and my mom, sometimes Lou, sitting around the TV watching *You Asked For It* or the *Huntley-Brinkley Report.* Lou might tell a story about work, or we might all be silent. Mostly, I'd be focused on the liquor cabinet and putting an invisible force field around it to keep my mother away. Dinner at the Fisher's was fun and boisterous and loose, filled with witty banter about movies and politics and books.

"Tell me, Ryan," Allison's father Max might say, "Whadda ya think of that Fidel Castro and his guerrillas down in Cuba? How long you think they can hold off Batista's army? I'm giving them a week. Maybe a month tops."

Then it was on to another subject. Integration, famine in China, the H-bomb, Harold Pinter's new play.

Most of the time I had no idea what they was talking about. But I soaked it up and learned a thing or two along the way.

When Allison went away to college at Smith, I stayed in Venice, working for Lou, slinging burgers on the weekends at the club. Allison and I wrote letters back and forth about how much we missed each other and how great it would be when she came back for Christmas, and for the summer. But over the months, her letters became fewer and fewer. When she told me that she had met someone else — an Amherst jock on the rowing team — the truth was I had been expecting it. Still, it hurt.

When Allison and the Amherst jock broke up, we gave it another try one summer. The sex was still great, but it was obvious to both of us that things had changed. The gap between our worlds had gotten too huge. Allison had been to Europe. She had done an internship at the Museum of Modern Art and made a big thing about meeting John Kenneth Galbraith when he came there to lecture. I was hanging out at the beach and working for Lou just enough to get by.

In September, she went back to school and that was that.

***

I turned left off PCH and negotiated the Fisher's dirt driveway which curved and dipped and curved again before ending at a sprawling peach-colored rancher. I parked alongside Max's old Studebaker Starlight. Allison's father had made a bundle writing for the movies, but you'd never know it from his car.

Max Fisher met me at the door. He was short and squat, with a mop of curly brown hair just starting to go grey. He had thick knotted arms, and ruddy weathered skin that came from living out at the beach. He was wearing his usual uniform: plaid Bermuda shorts and Mexican sandals. No shirt. He greeted me with a big smile that crinkled the skin around his watery blue eyes.

"Long time no see," he said good-naturedly.

"Yeah. Thanks for having me over."

"Come on in. Let's get a drink and go out on the deck. Still club soda?"

"Yup. On the rocks."

"You're a better man than I, Ryan."

I followed him into the living room with its beachy white rattan furniture and bank of sliding glass doors that overlooked the ocean. The living and dining areas were separated by a wet bar. Max filled two glasses with ice.

"So, whaddya think of that? A Negro intellectual on the cover of *Time*. That's something, huh!"

I looked at him blankly. Around Max, I often felt a bit behind the curve — like I was coming in on the tail end of a conversation I should have been listening to all along. Luckily Max was busy fixing our drinks and didn't notice my blank expression.

"If you ask me," he continued, "that's who Kennedy oughtta be listening to. Baldwin's a deep thinker, not to mention a hell of a writer. So what do you prefer, his novels or his nonfiction? I'll take his essays any day of the week. Now Mailer ... "

Baldwin ... Mailer ... My mind drifted while Max chatted. Was Allison at home right now? I looked around the room, hoping to see some sign of her.

"... major talent, major asshole. Misogynist as hell. Here you go."

He handed me my club soda. We went out onto the faded wood deck that extended out over the sand. A flock of sandpipers scampered along the shore, plunging their beaks into the wet sand when the water ebbed, darting away when the tide flowed back in.

"So, what's this all about?" Max asked as we settled into canvas chairs facing the water.

"It's a case I'm on. I can't say much about it, but I was hoping—"

"What kind of case? I need a little background here, Ryan."

"Blackmail. Compromising photographs of two men."

"Compromising! Hah! Last time I checked the Dictionary Of American Puritan Euphemistic Slang, 'compromising' meant sex. Homosexual sex in this instance, I assume."

I nodded.

"Okay, gotcha. So how can I help?"

"Do you know Victor Dargin?"

"Unfortunately, yes. Haven't crossed paths with that son-of-a-bitch in years. Now if you tell me that Dargin is a homosexual, I'll join the John Birch Society."

"No, nothing like that."

"Thank god, all's right with the world. Okay, so what's Dargin's connection to your case?

"I'm not exactly sure. Maybe none. But his name's come up and I want to get a handle on him. What can you tell me about him?"

"Well, let's see ... "

Max leaned back in his chair and crossed his arms behind his head, clearly relishing the invitation to walk down memory lane.

"I first met Victor Dargin at Metro. Just after the war. He was practically a kid, but ambitious as hell. Already on the way up. Kind of a junior ax man for Louis B. He was a natural at the job — kissed ass above, shit on the little guy below. I think he actually enjoyed it. When Dore Schary came to Metro ... when was that? '48, '49? ... Anyway, Schary took an immediate disliking to Dargin. Could be because Dargin was Louis B's stooge. Or maybe because Schary's one of the really decent guys in Hollywood and could smell a phony a mile away. But any way you cut it, Schary and Dargin went together like spaghetti and egg rolls."

He took a sip of his drink. "Then HUAC came to town and turned the place upside down."

I nodded vaguely, trying to remember something, anything, about HUAC. Max caught my puzzled look.

"Come on, Ryan, don't tell me you've learned nothing at Chez Fisher," Max ribbed. "Have my years of brilliant speechifying fallen on deaf ears, excuse the cliché, or should I say 'water-clogged' ears?"

I took a stab at it. "McCarthy?"

"You're in the ballpark. HUAC, the House Un-American Activities Committee, was out to get the Reds just like McCarthy was. And scare the hell out of the American public while they were at it. HUAC arrived in Hollywood in 1947, ordered the studios to purge all the Reds ... or suspected Reds ... and blacklist them out of their jobs. It got ugly. And that's an understatement.

People testifying against their friends — 'naming names' is what we called it — others refusing to name names and losing their jobs, going to jail. That was the straw that broke the camel's back between Schary and Dargin. Dargin was gung ho for the whole anti-Red thing. Schary was the only studio boss to seriously push back against the blacklist. So you can imagine how they hated each other."

Max paused and grinned at me.

"Jesus, Ryan, don't get me started. You know talking is my favorite hobby."

"Lucky for me. So then what happened?"

"Once Schary gained the upper hand at Metro, Dargin was history. That's when he went over to MCA and became an agent."

"But he didn't stay an agent."

"Man like Dargin? No way. Just a matter of time until he worked himself back into the studios. He was the number two guy at Pinnacle when they canned him last month."

"Why was he fired?"

"Beats me."

"Think you could find out?"

"Hey, I might be off in the small screen boondocks, but I've still got my connections."

"You're writing for TV?"

"Don't tell my wife." Max laughed. "She still thinks I've got class."

"How bad is it?"

"Sitcom about a Martian living in suburbia."

"Ouch."

"Could we please change the subject."

"Okay. Chip Jordan. Did you know him?"

"Well, that is an about-face. But a refreshing one. So, I'll go out on a limb here: Chip was one of the men in the photos."

I nodded.

"Of course," Max muttered. "I should have guessed. That would explain it."

"Explain what?"

"I didn't know Chip well, but that's the thing — nobody did. He was a cipher. Extremely private. I ran into him once on a picket line during the Warner's strike. That was back before his star rose — and his salary with it. Took a lot of guts for a young contract player like Chip to put his ass on the line like that. We got drunk afterwards at some dive in Burbank. Chip just got quiet. Not even a shit-load of booze got that kid to open up. Hardly a scintillating drinking buddy, but a solid character. At least I thought so at the time."

"Something changed your mind?"

"You do know he testified before HUAC, don't you?"

I shook my head.

"They held a private session for him," Max continued, "just like with Larry Parks. And although nobody to this day knows what Chip Jordan actually said, it's pretty much a given that he must have named names."

"Why did he testify, snitch out his friends?"

"Same reason as anybody, I suppose. To save his own skin. Save his career. Like I said, I didn't really know the guy. But what a coup for the Committee, snaring a young stud like Chip. He had that rebel image. Some rebel, huh? He crumbled before the Committee like a week-old cookie." Max shook his head. "I suppose you can never really predict the character of an individual until his foot's to the fire."

Just then a screen door banged shut.

"Daddy?" Allison called out from inside the house.

"Out here, Allie," Max shouted back.

Allison came out to the deck wearing a bikini with a towel wrapped around her waist. Her blonde hair, still wet from a morning swim, was shorter than before, falling just below her shoulders. My stomach took a roller coaster ride.

I told myself to be cool. But I didn't feel cool.

"Hi, Daddy. Hi, Ryan." Allison tossed the words off breezily, like seeing me again for the first time in two years was nothing.

"Where's Mom?" she asked Max.

"One of her meetings. Women Strike for Peace, SANE — I can't keep track of them all. Hey, have you told Ryan your exciting news?

"Oh Daddy, he doesn't want to hear about that."

"Sure I do," I said quickly.

"I might go to Paris. To study art history."

"It's quite an opportunity," Max beamed. "She was awarded a graduate fellowship."

"That's fantastic," I said, only half meaning it.

Allison shrugged. "I guess. It's just that there's so much happening here right now. One of my roommates from Smith is down in Birmingham working with Martin Luther King, and another friend is in Mississippi helping people register to vote. It seems kind of selfish to trot off to Paris when I could be doing something important right here."

Max smiled wryly. "I'm sure those important things will still be here to do when you return."

"I guess."

Allison let the towel fall from around her waist, tossed it onto an empty deck chair.

"Well, I gotta go change," she said. "See ya."

She turned and went back into the house.

"Now where were we?" Max said.

I had no idea.

Forget her, I told myself. *Get over it.*

CHAPTER 19

Traffic was light as I drove back along the coast highway towards town. The afternoon sun glinted silver and gold off the water. The surf lay nearly flat, the Santa Anas blown somewhere far out at sea.

As I drove, I tried to get my mind off Allison. Luckily, I didn't have to search far for a distraction. Max had given me a lot to chew on: All this HUAC stuff, whether or not it came into play in my case, had me disturbed. People snitching off their friends to save their own ass. Guys losing their jobs due to their political beliefs. Chip Jordan caught up in the middle of it all. And people like Victor Dargin thinking it was all okay. Well, it didn't seem okay to me. Not one bit.

When I reached Sunset Blvd., I made a snap decision. Instead of following PCH into Santa Monica and heading to the office, I turned left, and drove into the Palisades.

I parked under the eucalyptus in front of the Flynn house and rang the buzzer. Cora Flynn answered the door wearing a terry cloth bathrobe tied loosely around her waist. She looked haggard and pale.

"Oh. Ryan. I've been trying to reach you."

She glanced down self-consciously at the drink in her hand.

"I called back a couple of times," I said, "but didn't get an answer."

"Yes ... right ... come in."

I followed her into the house. All signs of the break-in were gone. We went down the three wide steps to the sunken living room where the glass coffee table stood on the bare cork floor. Mrs. Flynn sat down on the couch, making a big show of adding Coke to her drink. I sat opposite her in a modern bucket chair that was more comfortable than it looked.

"You cleaned the place up," I said. "It looks good."

"Thanks. Joey helped a lot."

"How's he doing?"

"Fine," she said. But she said it without conviction — and without looking me in the eye.

"Is he around? I'd like to say hi."

"No. And I'm glad he's not. I don't want him to worry."

"Why would he?"

"That's what I called you about. It's Mr. Dargin. He showed up at the studio yesterday, very upset. He made an ugly scene at the gate. Security had to physically throw him off the lot. I . . . I've been anxious and worried ever since."

"What was Dargin upset about?"

"I don't know. I wasn't there. It's just what I heard."

"What time did it happen?"

"What . . . what time? I don't know. I heard about it at lunch, so sometime before that. I didn't ask questions because I didn't want to seem too interested."

"Did you hear anything else?"

"Just that Mr. Dargin was demanding to get back into his office, but they wouldn't let him onto the lot. He punched a security guard. They had to wrestle him to the ground."

"Was he arrested?"

"No. The studio likes to handle things on their own. You know how it is."

I didn't, but I let it go. Mrs. Flynn took a sip of her drink.

"Ryan," she said, leaning forward and lowering her voice, "did I do anything illegal by taking those photos and selling them?"

"I don't know. Maybe."

"Because ... this whole thing ... with Mr. Dargin coming back ... it's got me scared and worried all over again. I can't afford to lose my job."

"You said they tossed him off the lot, so that's probably the end of it."

"But he hit a security guard! I think he might be losing it. And the worst part is I can't get the thought out of my head that this all has something to do with those photos."

"Why do you think that?"

"Just a feeling. Maybe it's my guilt talking, but I'm just ... well, spooked, I guess. I don't feel safe in my own life anymore."

She looked at me. Her eyes were unfocused. She stood up, wobbled a bit as she negotiated around the coffee table, and eventually perched herself unsteadily on the arm of my chair which wasn't really an arm at all, more just a curve in the plastic.

"But you know what?" Mrs. Flynn purred. "I feel safe when you're around, Ryan."

Her leg brushed against mine. *No, no, no, no*, my mind shouted. *I need to get up from this chair and out of the house right now.*

"Ryan," Mrs. Flynn said, her rum and Coke breath just inches from my face, "do you find me attractive?"

"We're not going there, Mrs. Flynn." I began plotting how I could get up from the chair without knocking her off the curved arm.

"Well, I find you attractive," she cooed.

Her body started to sag towards me. I reached out to steady her. In doing so, I managed to maneuver myself out of the chair, simultaneously easing her into it. She had a dazed look on her face. Hopefully, she was too blitzed to get up and make another move towards me.

"Am I too old for you?" she said. "Is that it?"

"Look, Mrs. Flynn—"

"I'm only thirty-six."

"Mrs. Flynn, I need to tell you something. Oscar Panozzo is dead."

"Who … Oscar …?"

"Tinseltown Treasures. The man you sold the photos to."

"Wha … dead?"

"He was murdered."

Her body tensed up. Her eyes tried to focus. She made an attempt to sit up straight, quickly gave up, and sank back down into the bucket chair.

"How? How did it …?"

"He was shot."

"I don't … Does this have something to do with … with the photos?"

"It might."

"Why are you scaring me like this, Ryan? What's going on?"

"Honestly, I don't know. It happened yesterday. The police are just beginning their investi —"

"Police?!" Mrs. Flynn sucked in her breath.

"I thought you'd want to know."

"But I don't. I don't want to know." She shook her head back and forth in short, quick bursts. "I don't want to know anything. I just … "

She looked towards the table where her rum and Coke glass sat in a puddle of sweat. She pushed herself out of the chair, wobbled a bit, sank back down.

"Maybe you want some coffee," I suggested.

"I don't want any coffee. I just want to keep my job. No trouble … no police … keep Joey with me.. I … I know this sounds selfish, but can you do something to keep me and Joey out of this?"

"What does Joey have to do with anything.?"

"Nothing," she said quickly. "Nothing at all."

Her face went through a couple of inscrutable arrangements. I couldn't tell if she was trying to clear her booze-soaked brain, or what.

"It's just that Joey and I … we don't need any more trouble."

CHAPTER 20

I woke up feeling pressure. It was like a pile of bricks pressing down on my chest. Each brick had a name inscribed on it. Panozzo ... Sutton ... Leon ... Cora Flynn ... Victor Dargin ...

One of Lou's favorite sayings floated up into my mind:

There are no coincidences. Coincidence is just the word people use when they don't know how things are connected.

Panozzo's murder and Sutton's blackmail. I had to figure out how they connected. Solve one and other would fall into place. I was sure of it. Not sure in the way you know if it's Monday or Tuesday, or that two plus two equals four, but sure nonetheless.

As for the bricks pressing down on my chest: it wasn't just about the blackmail. It wasn't just about proving I could solve the case — proving it to my client, proving it to Lou, or even proving it to myself. It was about Oscar Panozzo. No matter what Panozzo did or didn't do in terms of blackmailing Steve Sutton, he didn't deserve to die. What the cops did about Panozzo's murder was their business. Sometimes they solved a crime, sometimes they didn't. Sometimes even a good cop like Terekov couldn't. Besides, in this case I had more of the puzzle pieces than the cops did. Pieces that, for the sake of my client, I couldn't share with the cops. And that brick was the heaviest of all.

I drove to the office.

After half an hour of beeps and disconnects and voices too faint and crackled to hear, I finally spoke with someone who knew English. What I learned about searching for someone through JAT (Yugoslavian Airlines) or through JZ (Yugoslav Railways): Don't bother.

Lou knew a PI in London with connections to Interpol who had helped out on a couple of his cases. But Sutton hit the roof when I suggested to him that I use this guy to find Leon.

"Are you out of your mind!?" he bellowed. "Leave Leon alone. Let him enjoy his goddamn vacation. Find me those photos or I'll find myself someone else who will."

So I got into my car and hit the road.

The sky was clear and blue. The KRLA Surf Report announced three foot swells at Malibu. But I was headed in the opposite direction.

I drove south, past the monster oil drums of the Chevron refinery in El Segundo, cut east on Rosecrans and drove inland. I passed dairy farms and oil derricks, rusted farm equipment and decrepit sheds. Then miles and miles of new tract homes with neatly mowed squares of lawn. The further east I drove, the hotter it got. Finally, I reached my destination: a swath of desert some developer had paved over, put up some traffic signals and tract homes, and named Norwalk.

I pulled over at Rosecrans and Pioneer, where a goofy metal tower trying to look like an oil derrick rose up from the middle of a humongous parking lot. At the top of the tower was a red sign that said *Norwalk Square*. Along one edge of the "square" were some spindly palms and a line of stores including a Market Basket and a movie theater playing *Bye Bye Birdie*. I took off my sports coat and flung it into the back seat. I would have preferred to look professional for this visit, but the heat won.

I cruised further up Rosecrans, turned onto a treeless side street. Leon's apartment building was a two-story stucco job with a narrow walkway running along the second floor. Each unit had its own parking space marked with numbers on the pavement. The place looked like a motel without the ice maker.

Leon's apartment was on the ground level, right under the outdoor staircase. I rang the buzzer just as two small boys were coming out of the unit next door, tugging their tricycles over the threshold. They looked at me for a moment, giggled, then hopped on their bikes and began zig zagging around the driveway.

I rang the buzzer again. I knocked. The door to the next unit opened again and a chubby woman in blue stretch pants and a pink apron with ruffles, stuck her head out.

"Boys! Stay away from those cars!"

Then she caught sight of me.

"He's not home," she said.

"Who?"

"The manager. Mr. Leon. You're at his door aren't you?"

"Yes. Okay, thanks. I'll come back later."

The woman rolled her eyes. "A lot of good that'll do you."

"Why's that?"

"Mr. Leon hasn't been around all week, and I'm at my wits' end. So don't hold your breath, that's all I'm saying." She started to shut the door.

"M'am?"

"What is it?"

"Well, I came a long way, and I don't want to drive out here again unnecessarily. You say Mr. Leon hasn't been home all week?"

"That's right, and he couldn't have picked a worse time. Our bathroom sink's stopped up, probably something the twins did that they won't admit to. What's the good of a manager if he isn't around to fix things? My husband tried, but no cigar, so we've been using the kitchen sink for everything. If Mr. Leon doesn't come back soon, we're going to have to call a plumber. And cross our fingers that the landlord will reimburse."

"When's the last time you saw Mr. Leon?"

The woman squinted with one eye and looked at me closely. I must have sounded too interested in Mr. Leon. To recover, I went for my wallet, pulled out a business card, and flicked it up rapidly — too rapidly to read — covering most of it in my hand.

"Mitch Randall, Electrolux Vacuum Cleaners. I'm following up on an order placed by Mr. Leon Vanek for our top of the line Automatic Diamond Jubilee Canister model."

The woman brightened and reached for the card. I drew it back before she could grab it.

"I'll just drop this into Mr. Vanek's mail slot. He has to return eventually."

I palmed the card, pushed open the mail slot in Leon's door, and pretended to drop it through.

"So you sell vacuums," the woman said. "I wouldn't mind a new one myself. I love our Kirby, but it is getting old."

"Kirbys are excellent machines."

"But Diamond Jubilee ... that sounds special."

"Top of the line. I'm sure Mr. Vanek will be quite pleased. He must be a man who values cleanliness."

"I wouldn't know. He never lets anyone inside. You knock and he comes out. You drop the rent through the slot. He's very quiet. I never hear a peep coming from his apartment, not even the TV. I think quiet people tend to be tidy, don't you?"

"Yes, I do."

I grinned at her. She grinned back. We were having a bonding moment over tidiness.

"So, is Mr. Leon gone a lot?" I asked.

"He comes and goes. But I don't remember him ever being away this long."

"And he's been gone ... did you say a week?"

She thought for a moment. "Well ... I'm pretty sure it was last Monday that the sink overflowed. So, yes. It's been a week. One whole week of Crest and Burma Shave and god-knows-what else in my kitchen sink!"

"Sounds unpleasant."

"You don't know the half of it."

"I'm sure that's true," I said. "Well, thank you, m'am. I appreciate your help. I'll try back another time."

I turned to go, but the woman wasn't finished with me yet.

"When you come back," she said, "could I have a free demonstration of that Diamond Jubilee? The Kirby man gave us a free demonstration."

"Sure. I'll do that."

"Thanks!" she beamed. Then she glanced over my shoulder into the driveway and frowned.

"Boys!" she shouted. "I want you both in right now! I warned you. You're too close to the cars."

I waited until the woman had herded her kids back inside before peering into the mail slot in Leon's apartment door. I could see part of a low table with a portable Zenith radio and a couple of magazines lying on top. The Zenith was the kind with short wave, marine weather, the whole bit. At the extreme lower edge of my vision, I could see a pile of mail scattered on the floor just inside the door.

I walked around the building, counting windows and doors until I got to the window that matched Leon's unit. The metal mini-blinds were down, but the slats were just horizontal enough so that I could peek through. Inside was a spartan bedroom with a bed, dresser, and single chair. The bed was neatly made. The dresser drawers were shut. An extra-large, brown corduroy jacket hung neatly over the back of the chair. Tidy.

CHAPTER 21

I couldn't put it off any longer. I drove back from Norwalk and straight into Beverly Hills. I walked up to the white mansion and rang the bell. The maid with the soft voice opened the door.

"Is Mr. Dargin home?" I asked. No goofy black-rimmed glasses, no slicked back hair, this time.

"Do you have an appointment, sir?"

"No, but if you could just give him this, I think he'll want to see me."

I handed her my card. She took the card and studied it. Her eyebrows arched slightly and I thought I saw a small, tight-lipped half-smile. She looked at me and chuckled.

"One moment, sir."

After the housekeeper went inside the house, I turned to survey the front yard. Tall box hedges bordered both sides of the lawn. A driveway ran along the south hedge. In the garage, the Jaguar and the Rolls were keeping each other company.

The door jerked open behind me. I pivoted, coming face to face with Victor Dargin. He was wearing a velvet smoking jacket with a silk handkerchief poking out of the breast pocket. In his hand was my business card. He tapped his finger on the card and glared at me.

"What the fuck is this?" he barked.

"I was here the other day, and—"

"I'm not senile. I know you were here. But who the fuck <u>are</u> you?"

"I'm a private investigator,. My name is—"

"I know your name. It says it right here." He tapped his finger on the card again. "Why the fuck are you here?"

"It's about the Chip Jordan photos. I'm working for Steve Sutton."

Victor Dargin stood stone-faced for a moment.

"Alright, come in," he said, resigned and more subdued. "Fucking Sutton. Let's go out back. I don't want to disturb the wife with this unpleasantness."

I followed him down a gloomy hallway with dark, polished-wood floors. I caught brief passing glimpses into a carpeted billiards room with a green felt table, the balls racked and ready to go; a kitchen with fancy copper pots hanging above the range; a formal dining room with a china cabinet and a chandelier dripping with crystal. Two other doors were shut. The hallway ended in a sitting room with heavy upholstered furniture and thick, burgundy drapes keeping out all but a sliver of the light. Dargin pulled back the drapes and unlatched the French doors that led to the backyard.

We threaded our way through a geometric maze of low boxy hedges clipped into unnatural geometric shapes. Beyond the hedge matrix was an expanse of lawn, and beyond that a swimming pool. Chaise lounge chairs were arranged neatly around the pool on pink cement. To the right of the pool was a tennis court. We sat poolside on metal chairs at a round, glass-topped table.

"Loved the amateur hour act you pulled the other day, Zorn," Dargin smirked. "Now if only you could juggle, tap dance, or twirl a baton I'd get you an audition for Ted Mac."

"Could we just let that go, Mr. Dargin.?"

"Why not. So, what do you want? Talk."

"I'm working to clear up Mr. Sutton's … situation."

"His own fucking fault, that fucking pansy."

"What's his own fault, sir?"

"Cut the 'sir' shit, buddy boy. You're a punk PI nosing around my personal business, and no 'sir' bullshit is going to change my opinion of you."

"Gotcha. So, about Mr. Sutton—"

"Let's cut to the chase," Dargin interrupted. "I'm aware of Steve Sutton's predicament, but his pansy problems have nothing to do with me. I have enough on my plate as it is. Why he wants to dig up this crap from the past is beyond me."

"He's not digging anything up. It got dumped at his door."

"Why bring me into it?"

"Because the photographs used to blackmail him came from your office."

"Bullshit."

"We both know they did."

"Can you prove it?"

"If I have to."

I let him sit with that for a while. He didn't look happy.

"You're on thin ice, buddy boy. I'm not somebody to mess with."

"Mr. Dargin, I'm not here to cause you trouble. My job is to find everything that might hurt my client and get rid of it. Until that happens, he's a sitting duck."

"What if I told you I have no more of those photographs? No negatives, no nothing."

"I'd have to have proof."

"Oh, Christ. You know as well as I do that it's impossible to prove something *doesn't* exist."

"So what about the person who shot the photos. They might have copies. Or was that person you?"

If I had wanted to rile him up further, I accomplished it. Dargin went from zero to sixty in an instant.

"What!?" he snapped. "You think I'm some kind of perv!?"

I shrugged. Which only got him madder.

"Listen, buddy boy, my advice to you, and I'm only saying this because I suspect you're in over your head and don't know what you're doing, is leave the past alone."

"Can't do it. Not until the past leaves my client alone."

"More's the pity," Dargin hissed.

He made a big show of looking at his watch, pushing his chair back, and rising to his feet.

"I need to prepare for an important business meeting," he proclaimed. "This conversation is over."

Dargin towered over me, waiting for me to stand.

I didn't get up. "Oscar Panozzo was murdered," I said.

"What the fuck?"

I felt like a messenger on repeat, spreading the same news wherever I went. Maybe I should just write it on a card and flash it when needed. *Panozzo dead. Your reaction here.*

Dargin sat down. I guess his important meeting could wait.

"Where were you between noon and five yesterday?" I asked. "Other than when we were talking at your house."

"What? Who do you think you are? A cop? That's none of your fucking business."

"Okay," I said calmly, "so explain it to the cops. Once they connect a few dots, don't be surprised to see L.A.'s finest at your doorstep."

"Are you threatening me?"

Just then, the automatic sprinklers clicked on. Tic, tic, tic tic. I watched as the rotators began their orbit, lazily spraying the lawn with water. Tooka tooka tooka tooka. Tic, tic, tic. *Water flows uphill towards money.* One of Lou's favorite sayings. Tooka tooka tooka tooka. Tic tic tic. What was my next move? I didn't know. But at least I knew more about Victor Dargin than I did an hour ago: he was easily angered, and very, very touchy on the subject of certain photographs.

The grating sound of metal scraping across cement brought me back to the here and now. Dargin stood up.

"Get the fuck out of here," he said. "And let the chips fall."

CHAPTER 22

Dargin's maid escorted me down the gloomy hallway and out the front door. I walked to my car, which was parked up the street. Then I waited. It was just a hunch, but I went with it.

About ten minutes later, Dargin's Jag backed out of the driveway. Either Dargin had a sudden need to buy a carton of milk, or he had prepared extremely quickly for his supposed business meeting.

I tailed the Jag as it headed east on Wilshire. Through Beverly Hills ... past the gold-tiled cylinder of the May Co. building at Fairfax ... past the stinky, oozing muck of the LaBrea tar pits ... past Western and Normandie and Vermont ... and straight through McArthur Park. At the east end of the park, the Jag turned right onto Alvarado. Halfway down the block it made another right turn into the park.

Shit. With no cover of trees or other cars, I couldn't follow Dargin into the park. And there was no parking on this side of Alvarado. I slowed down to a crawl, watching the Jag pull into a small parking area just inside the park. A horn honked behind me.

"Hey, Jack, get the lead out!" a man yelled as he passed.

I hit the accelerator, made a left at 7th, pulled a U-ey in the driveway just past Langer's Deli, and headed back up Alvarado.

A Helms Bakery truck was parked across the street from the park entrance. I pulled in behind the truck. From this spot I could see the Jag and the silhouette of Dargin's head in the drivers seat.

A few minutes later, a tan Bonneville pulled into the park entrance, drove the few yards to the parking area, and parked next to the Jag. Immediately, Dargin got out of his car. He walked around his car to the Bonneville, yanked open the passenger door and got in.

I watched Dargin's head bobbing and shaking, and another man's head turned towards him, immobile and topped with a fedora. *GET THE BONNEVILLE PLATES* a voice in my head shouted. I wasn't going to blow it this time. I might not be great at memorization, but that's why they invented paper. I reached for my spiral notebook just as the Helms driver tugged down on a handle and the distinct Helms Bakery double whistle blew. The driver got out and came around to the back of the truck. He unlatched the two yellow doors which opened out like a butterfly wings. By the time he had slid open the glass-fronted drawers filled with fresh donuts and cupcakes and pastries, a crowd of customers — kids, adults, teens, oldsters, white and Negro and Mexican — had gathered at the back of the truck. I could smell the donuts. Same sugary dough smell, same double whistle, same yellow and blue truck, same cheerful crowd jingling their nickels and dimes, as when I was growing up. I figure the Helms Bakery truck will be around forever.

The customers at the truck were blocking my view of the Bonneville, so I got out and mingled with the crowd. I eyeballed the license plate while pretending to check out the warm pastries. UTG 773. UTG 773. UTG 773.

I bought a jelly donut, got back into my car, and wrote down the numbers and letters in my spiral note book. A feeling of accomplishment washed over me. Three letters and three numbers. It was a start. Maybe Dargin had pushed me over the edge with his "amateur hour" mockery, but whatever it was, I was tired of being put down. And I was tired of doing things that deserved it.

I watched the two men inside the Bonneville talk for another ten minutes. Finally Dargin got out and went back to his Jag. Both cars exited the park. Dargin turned left onto Wilshire, the Bonneville turned right. I followed the Bonneville.

Downtown, on Main Street, the man in the fedora parked and got out of his car. He wore a dark suit and tie, white dress shirt, and shiny black shoes. His posture was ramrod straight, his gait precise and measured. He walked up Main, turned onto Spring, pushed open the door to the U.S. Federal Building and disappeared inside.

CHAPTER 23

A red-tailed hawk circled above Holy Cross Cemetery. Every day since Oscar Panozzo's murder, I had scanned the obits in the *Times*, the *Herald*, and the *Hollywood Citizen News*. Eventually I had found what I was looking for in the *Citizen News*. "Oscar Panozzo, loving friend, brother, and son passed away ... services to be held ... "

I turned off Slauson Avenue and drove through the ornate metal gate. Just inside was a pond surrounded by graceful shade trees and rounded boulders. Lily pads with brilliant pink blooms floated on the perfectly rippled dark water. The trees, the water, the blooming succulents poking out from between the rocks, were all so precisely arranged and manicured that I might have entered a Disneyland cemetery made of paper maché boulders and rubber lily pads.

Just beyond the pond, three paved roads led up into rolling hills of impeccably groomed lawn. The place looked deserted. I took the newspaper clipping from my pocket to double check whether the funeral was today. Yup.

Not knowing which road to take, I chose the left. Just over the crest of the hill, a dozen or so cars were parked by the side of the road. A plainclothes cop walked the line of Fords and Chevys, taking down license plate numbers. I made a quick u-turn. I hated to be late for the service, but getting myself on the cops' list of attendees would be worse.

I drove back towards the pond and took the right fork. This road led to a humongous concrete mausoleum painted in broad, alternating verticals of blue and white. Above the entrance, a white plaster Jesus hung on the cross between two live palms. I parked in front of the mausoleum, then hurried across a wide, sloping lawn, nearly tripping on one of the flat, inlaid gravestones that dotted the entire hillside. Looking down to avoid another near-fall, one gravestone caught my eye. It was white marble with an intricate pattern of black marble roses wrapped around a cross. The inscription read:

Bela Lugosi
Beloved father
1882–1956

Just beyond Dracula's grave, stone steps led to a Disney-like grotto where a waterfall flowed over rugged volcanic rocks and through a landscape of neatly sculpted shrubs. I touched the rock to see if it was real. Answer: yes … maybe.

I followed a path alongside the waterfall, through a stone archway, past an alcove cradling a statue of the Virgin Mary, and out the other side of the grotto to another wide, slopping, grassy hill.

That's where I spotted the mourners. It was a small group, gathered close together on a vast expanse of lawn. They had formed a circle around the casket, heads bowed, under the hot noon sun. I counted sixteen men and two women. A priest stood at the head of the casket, reading from the Bible. I looked around for cops but didn't see any.

I stood at the outer edge, just behind the mourners. My mission here probably wasn't that different than the cops: get a bead on Oscar Panozzo. Find out about his pals (if he had any), his family, anything at all to figure out who the guy was and what he was up to.

As the priest droned on, my mind drifted. Religion didn't mean a thing to me. Or maybe, as Allison had once said: "Surfing is your religion, Ryan. The ocean is your church." We had both laughed about it. Her observation seemed light and funny and even a kind of compliment at the time. But later, when we broke up, and, according to Allison, my lack of ambition or interests beyond surfing were part of the reason, I didn't know if it was a compliment after all.

The click-and-whir of a camera shutter brought my mind back to the present. The cop I had seen jotting down license plate numbers was standing beside me taking photos. He methodically aimed his camera at each mourner, snapped, moved to the next. They all kept their eyes down, pretending not to notice the intrusion. All except one. She was about my age, early twenties, with long black hair, smooth olive skin, and sparkling green eyes that looked directly at the cop as he pointed the camera at her. She must have felt me checking her out. Her eyes moved off the cop. She looked at me and smiled. *I have to meet this girl*, I decided. I watched as she slipped out of her high heels, her bare feet sinking into the grass. She picked up one foot and massaged her ankle. I wondered if the massage was partly for my benefit. Then again, maybe her feet just ached from the shoes. Why did girls wear those high heels that seemed more like torture chambers than footwear? There were a hundred reasons I was glad not to be a girl, and that was one of them.

The priest finally closed his Bible, the casket was lowered into the ground, and the gathering broke up. All the men, alone or in small groups of two or three, walked slowly back towards their cars.

Only the two women and I lingered at the gravesite. After the olive-skinned girl put her shoes back on, she put a comforting arm around the shoulder of the older woman who was short and dressed completely in black. Her grey hair was tied back in an old-fashioned bun, and her face was streaked with tears. She looked enough like the gorgeous brunette that I guessed she was her mother.

I approached the grave. I could feel the girl watching me. I met her gaze.

"Are you a friend of Uncle Oscar's?" she asked.

"We only met recently."

"Were you in his club?"

"Leave the man alone, Julie," commanded the older woman.

"That's okay," I assured her. Then to Julie. "No. I only knew him from his store."

"Oh, isn't that the most darling shop! I always loved to go there. Mother never really understood Uncle Oscar, but I thought he was wonderful. So sweet and so … unique."

"This isn't the time, Julie," warned the older woman.

"Oh, Mother, I'm just so sick of that. It's never the time. Nobody in our family ever likes to talk about Uncle Oscar."

"Julie, really. We need to go. I don't want to miss the plane."

I didn't want them to leave yet — for reasons professional and personal. Doing my chivalrous best, I held out my elbow to the mother. "May I escort you back to your car?"

"Thank you," she said, looping her arm through mine and giving Julie the evil eye. I turned my attention to the mother as we began the trek through the graveyard.

"You must be Oscar's sister whom he spoke so highly of." I was laying it on thick — okay, telling a straight-up lie — but what the hell.

"He spoke highly of me?"

"Yes, quite often."

"That's so nice to hear," the mother said. "Oscar and I were close when we were young, but he left home right after high school. It seemed like he couldn't wait to leave. He just rushed away from home as soon as he could."

"Why's that?" I asked.

"Oh, Oscar was always a bit different. Not that any of us had illusions he would follow Papa onto the docks. He was much too … too refined for that kind of work."

Julie rolled her eyes. "Mother, Uncle Oscar wasn't refined. He was homosexual. And nobody could ever deal with it. That's why he left home."

"Julie. Stop. This day is hard enough already. You don't need to make it worse."

Julie rolled her eyes again and shot me a my-mother-is-so-hopeless look.

"I just hope the police catch whoever killed darling Oscar," Julie said. "Who would want to kill a sweet, gentle man like him? And to die like that… I can barely think about it, it's so horrible. And what will happen to all those wonderful movie things that he loved so much? I thought maybe the club would want them, but the police won't let anybody near anything. They say it's all part of their investigation."

Julie paused. She looked over at me suspiciously.

"So you're really not in Oscar's club, Mr. … .?"

"Ryan. Ryan Zorn. And no, I'm not in any club. I don't even know what this club is."

"It's a movie club," the mother answered much too quickly.

"Oh, Mother, it's not a movie club. Can't anyone tell the truth for a change? It's a club for homosexuals. They go to movies, sure, but they also go to concerts and plays, all kinds of things."

"How do you know so much?" snapped the mother.

"Because Uncle Oscar talked to me. I didn't judge him like the rest of you did."

"Well, you don't have to air our family's dirty laundry in front of a stranger."

"It's not dirty laundry. It's just Oscar."

The older woman sighed. We had reached their car, a rented white Impala. Julie got into the driver's seat. After opening the passenger door for the mother, I circled around to Julie who rolled down her window.

"So you're flying back home this afternoon," I said.

"Mother is. I'm staying a while longer. There's a lot to do to... to wrap things up. I'm going to Oscar's apartment tomorrow morning."

"Where's home?"

"Seattle."

"Julie," the mother chimed in, "we need to get going. I don't want to be late for my plane."

"Don't worry, Mother. We'll be there in time."

Julie put the key in the ignition and started the engine. It was now or never.

"Julie," I said, "I know this kinda comes out of nowhere, but would you like to meet before you go home to... to talk about Oscar?"

"Only to talk about Oscar, huh," she teased.

"Maybe other things too," I admitted. "And by the way: I'm really, truly not in Oscar's club."

Julie grinned. "I didn't think so. Okay, call me later at my hotel if you want. I'm staying out near the airport at the Thunderbird."

CHAPTER 24

The Thunderbird billed itself as "California's First Jet Age Hotel." It was sleek and modern — three floors built around a central courtyard with a swimming pool. The color scheme was aqua and orange. The theme was Polynesian Pop. The front of the hotel constructed of huge glass panes divided by panels of aqua and orange. Palm trees were everywhere. And the doors to each room alternated aqua and orange.

As I pulled into the hotel parking lot, the sky was getting dark. The orange neon Thunderbird sign with its outsized T flickered on. I walked towards the main building. Just as I reached out to pull open the door to the lobby, it was pushed open from the other side, and I came face to face with Detective Mackie.

"Detective," I said with a nod.

Mackie stopped short. A cigarette dangled from his lips. He had the same red face and sour look as when he questioned me at the Hollywood station a few days ago.

"The fuck you doin' here, Zorn?"

"Minding my own business."

"I doubt that."

I tried to move around him, but he blocked my way.

"I asked you a question."

"And I answered it."

"Not to my satisfaction, you didn't." Mackie poked me in the chest. "And if you think I'm some moron who buys that we meet here by coincidence, think again."

I shrugged. "Think what you want, Detective."

He put his red flushed face up close to mine. His breath smelled of coffee and cigarettes. "Keep your nose out of police business."

I wanted to tell Mackie to shove it, but the last thing I needed was trouble with the cops. Lou always made a point of getting along with law enforcement. But I knew the goodwill he had cultivated was only going to get me so far. And with Mackie, I figured that wasn't very far at all.

"I'll do my best, Detective," I said, keeping my sarcasm to a low roar.

The truth is, it wasn't just Mackie. I didn't like cops much. And they didn't tend to like me. I'm different from Lou in that way. I'm not a vet or a cop-wannabe. I don't smoke or drink or call girls 'broads'. I don't cut my hair short. I'm not one of the good old boys. Some of my buddies like Reno and Skunk even have rap sheets, and the Westside cops all know it.

Mackie and I stared at each other for a few moments. Mackie scowled, but he finally moved aside.

I went into the lobby in search of the hotel's coffee shop where Julie and I had planned to meet. When I asked the desk clerk — a skinny guy wearing the hotel's trademark orange and aqua uniform — he shook his head and said, "No coffee shop. Now Huki Lau." He pointed outside towards a covered breezeway.

He was right. The Huki Lau was no coffee shop. First clue: the gas-burning tiki torches jutting up through the high A-frame roof. Second clue: the artificial rainfall behind the bar. Just what L.A. needed: another joint serving spare ribs and exotic rum drinks.

The Huki Lau was about half full. But no Julie. I sat at a booth near the front and ordered a club soda. I was sipping the fizzy water, wondering if I should ask the desk clerk to ring Julie's room, when a dark-haired beauty in tight-fitting white Capris and a sleeveless yellow blouse came into the restaurant.

"Sorry I'm late," Julie said as she slipped into the seat opposite me. "A policeman came to my room, asking questions. I didn't even have time to put on make-up."

"You look great," I said. "What did the cop want?"

"A million questions about Uncle Oscar. Questions about his past, his finances, did he have any enemies. He even wanted a list of Oscar's friends — which I told him was none of his business."

"You actually said that?"

"I did. And I had a few questions for him myself. Like when would I be allowed into Oscar's shop? I mean, I know that's where it ... happened ... but I think I have a right to go in there. Oscar left everything to me, you see. At least that's what Niles thinks. I haven't actually seen the will."

"Who's Niles?"

"You don't know?"

I shook my head.

"I guess you really aren't in the club."

"Julie, you said that club was just for fruits."

"Not to be a big lecturer, Ryan, but 'fruits' is an insulting word. There's nothing wrong with homosexuals. I loved Uncle Oscar."

"Okay. But you didn't really think I was one, did you?"

Julie laughed. "No. Not since I noticed you staring at me at the funeral."

"Phew!" I made an exaggerated comic gesture of wiping my brow in relief.

We both laughed. I was glad to turn the whole thing into a joke, but it was a little creepy to think Julie would ever, even for a second, think I was a homo.

"Since you're not in the club," Julie said, "how do you know my uncle?"

"I'll tell you, but don't freak out."

"Why would I?"

"I'm a private investigator."

Julie tilted her head, assessing me in a new light.

"I guess this isn't a date then. You probably want to ask me a bunch of questions — just like the police did."

"Well . . . I . . . "

"That's okay, but I've got to eat first."

The waitress had arrived. She pulled a pencil from behind her ear.

"What'll it be, kids?"

We both ordered Tahiti Burgers, fries, and lemonade. I waited until the waitress was out of earshot.

"So who's this Niles?" I asked.

"Ah, question number one!" Julie teased.

"It's my job."

"Who are you working for?"

"My uncle's agency. Southland Investigations. It's just him and me."

"No, I mean right now. Why are you investigating Uncle Oscar's death?"

"I can't say. It's confidential."

"But you are investigating it?"

"Sort of."

"And you expect me to answer a bunch of questions without even knowing why."

I nodded. "Pretty much. But think about it: nobody would hire a PI if we didn't keep things private."

I should have stopped right there. But I didn't. Instead, I added something that I shouldn't have. I knew I shouldn't, but I said it anyway.

"Besides," I said, "it can actually be in your interest not to know certain things."

"What things?" she asked.

"Like if the cops questioned you again and you tried to hide what I had told you, maybe something that didn't make Oscar look too good. A cop can smell a lie a mile away."

"Are you saying Uncle Oscar did something wrong?"

"No, nothing like that." I tried to worm out of it.

I had only known Julie for half an hour and already I was looking out for her, thinking about what was good for her instead of what was best for the case.

"I'm just saying I can't tell you much about my case."

"Okay. I get it." Her eyes sparkled with challenge. "You're going to be just like that policeman. All questions, no answers. This is definitely not a date."

"Hey, I'll talk about stuff. Just not things that are confidential to the case."

"Okay. So if you could go one place in the world where would it be?"

"That's easy. Waimea Bay."

"Where's that?"

"Hawaii. North shore of Oahu. Waimea's got these humongous waves in the winter... twenty, thirty feet... and a primo pipeline that —"

"Pipeline?"

"That's a tunnel of water you can surf through. The pipeline at Waimea's supposed to be incredible. I've never been there, but I know some guys who have. The swell breaks over this hollow lava reef... "

Julie was smiling at me in a funny way.

"What?" I said.

"You're a surfer."

"Yeah."

"I don't understand half of what you're talking about, but I can tell you really love it."

"Yeah." I suddenly felt sheepish. "So what about you? Where would you go?"

"Everywhere."

"Now you're the one without answers."

Julie laughed. "I want to become a journalist and go to Africa, South America, China. Really see for myself how things are."

"Do you have to go to college to do that?"

"Not necessarily, but it helps."

"So you go?"

Julie shook her head. "I wish."

"Why not?"

"I work full time. But I'm thinking of going nights. I work for my dad's union, the ILWU. That's the longshoremen. Mostly I answer phones and file things, boring stuff like that, but once in a while I get to work on the newsletter. A few months ago, they had me interview an old dock worker who was in the General Strike of 1934. Of course I didn't get to write up the story, they gave my notes to a real writer, but still . . . I loved it!"

I nodded, thinking: Another intelligent girl. Like Allison. I had a feeling about Julie that I hadn't had in a long, long time. Since Allison and I broke up, I had dated plenty of girls. Meeting girls, dating them, wasn't my problem. My problem was comparing them all to Allison. They never measured up — looks-wise or brains-wise. Allison was smokin' hot and on top of that she was smart. She had her own ideas. She made her own decisions. She was interested in the world, not just me.

I looked at Julie. She was sipping her lemonade through an aqua straw.

"I've been wanting to tell you," I said, "that I'm really sorry about your uncle. He seemed like a nice man."

"He was."

The waitress came over with our food and put it on the table. My Tahiti burger was pierced by a toothpick with a green plastic palm frond waving at the top.

"Poor Oscar," Julie said. "It's so horrible what happened to him. I've thought and thought about it and can't come up with any reason why somebody would want to kill sweet Uncle Oscar. I just hope ... " she trailed off.

"What?"

"This might sound naïve to you, but I hope he didn't suffer at the end."

"I don't think he suffered. From what I've heard, he died really fast."

"Where'd you hear that?"

"Just around."

"What else have you heard ... around?"

"Nothing much."

"At least nothing you're going to tell me." Julie grinned. Then her face darkened. "Uncle Oscar was such a sweet man. Why in the world would anybody do this to him?"

"Julie, how well did you actually know your uncle?"

"I feel like I knew him pretty well. At least better than anybody else in the family."

"When's the last time you talked with him?"

"Well ... I haven't visited him in a few years, and we hadn't talked much recently, but still, I know his basic character. He and Niles were both such dear people."

"So who is this Niles? You still haven't told me."

"He's Uncle Oscar's lover."

She said it matter-of-factly. No judgment. I liked that.

"Is Niles a member of that club you were talking about?"

"Of course. He and Uncle Oscar started it."

"What's your opinion of Niles?"

"I don't know him that well, but I always liked him. If you mean, do I think he killed Uncle Oscar — absolutely not! They've been together for years, like a regular married couple. Except for some reason they always kept separate apartments. Niles is a set designer for the movies. He's traveled all over the world and has wonderful stories. But mostly I guess I like him for the simple reason that he made Uncle Oscar happy."

"Any chance you could introduce me to Niles?"

"I'm meeting him tomorrow at Oscar's apartment to go over some things. Right after that I'm flying home."

"So soon?" The words just slipped out. If I sounded like an over-eager hound dog, Julie either didn't catch it or let it go.

"I've got a regular job," she said. "I punch the clock, nine to five. I'm not a glamorous, independent private eye like some people I know," she teased. "Anyway, there's no reason for me to stay in L.A. any longer. Niles will let me know if he needs help going through Oscar's belongings." She closed her eyes and shuddered. "It's strange just thinking about that."

"What about us meeting up with Niles tonight?"

"Why?"

"I'd like to talk with him before the cops do. Cops have a way of spooking people, making them clam up. He might know something that could help us figure out what happened to your uncle."

"If you're trying to con me with this 'we' stuff, forget it. I'm on to you, Mr. Private Eye."

We both grinned.

"You got me," I said. "But it's true we both want to find out who killed your uncle."

"And you're going to do that better than the police?"

"I've got one murder to solve. They've got dozens."

Julie finished off her lemonade.

"Okay," she said finally. "I'll call him."

CHAPTER 25

Niles Fontenot glided toward us across the lobby. Black turtleneck, camel hair sports coat, expensive leather loafers. He moved so gracefully that he almost seemed to float.

"So good to see you again, my dear," he said to Julie, grasping her shoulders and kissing the air near both of her cheeks.

Niles was about 50, sleek and trim, with a pencil-thin mustache and salt-and-pepper hair that was meticulously cut and combed. I recognized him right off as one of the mourners at Panozzo's gravesite.

Niles nodded to me and smiled. "And you of course are the mysterious private investigator whom Julie absolutely insisted I meet tonight."

Niles extended his hand to shake. I expected his grip to be soft like a girl's, but it wasn't.

We took the elevator up to the third floor. Julie's room had two twin beds, a low dresser with a bamboo-framed mirror above it, and a folding rack with her suitcase on top.

Niles alighted on the edge of one bed. Julie sat on the other. I leaned against the wall. Niles plucked a cigarette from a sleek silver case, fit it into a silver holder, snapped open a matching silver lighter. He inhaled and blew a perfect smoke ring.

"So," Niles said, "Julie informs me that you intend to solve the deeply upsetting death of our dear departed Oscar. How may I be of assistance?"

"I'd like to find out more about his life."

"That's quite a broad topic. Perhaps you could be more specific."

"How was he doing money-wise?"

"Why on earth would you be interested in Oscar's pecuniary circumstances?"

Niles was a sharp character. I wasn't going to be able to run a bunch of nosy questions by him and expect answers without doing more explaining than I wanted to do. I wanted answers, but even more than that, I wanted access to Panozzo's apartment, his store, his personal effects. Niles was my way in. I had this one evening to convince him to let me in.

Lou had a way of getting people to talk. It seemed to come naturally to him, but he taught me that some of it was pure technique. One way to put a person at ease, to get them to trust you without them even knowing why, is to get in sync with them. You copy their movements, their gestures, even their breathing. Tap your foot if they tap their foot. Sit hunched if they do. Blink often if they blink often.

Well, I sure as shit wasn't going to copy anything Niles Fontenot did. I definitely wasn't going to cross my legs in the pansy way he was doing right now.

So much for technique.

"It's possible," I said cautiously, "that Oscar was involved in a, uh … a sketchy financial situation."

"Sketchy?" Niles exclaimed. "I hardly associate that term with Oscar."

"People do all sorts of things if they're desperate," I countered.

"Oscar? Desperate for money?" Julie blurted out. "No, not Oscar."

"You're sure?" I said.

Julie nodded. "Oscar and Niles were fine. I already told you at dinner: Niles works for the studios."

She turned to Niles for confirmation. But he looked away, refusing to meet her eyes. Instead, he leaned his head back and blew another perfect smoke ring. Finally, Niles turned to Julie.

"When we spoke recently, my dear, I failed to mention an issue of significant personal magnitude. I saw no need to burden you with my private affairs. Now I see that it may be relevant to Oscar's demise."

"What is it?!" Julie demanded.

"We broke up."

"You and Oscar? But . . . but you were so . . . so together."

"Indeed. And as with any couple, it sometimes becomes necessary to go one's separate way."

"When did this happen? Oscar never said a word to me."

"About six months ago."

"I thought you were happy together."

"We were. And then we weren't. At least I wasn't . . . . Oh, it's all quite complicated, as relationships always are. Essentially, I met someone else."

"That's not complicated." Julie's eyes flashed with anger.

"Perhaps you're right," Niles sighed.

"Who is this . . . this new person?" Julie asked. "Was he at the funeral?"

"No. This 'new person' as you call him is already ancient history."

"What do you mean?"

"The pertinent data, I'm embarrassed to admit, is that he was twenty-five and hot. I fell hard, but it didn't last long. Sometimes it's the most minuscule incident that elucidates everything. We were having drinks at the Crown Jewel one night when I asked if he would like to accompany me to an Artie Shaw performance. He said, 'Who is Artie Shaw?' I was flabbergasted! Who is Artie Shaw?! In that instant, I knew it would never work between us. Of course in hindsight it's all so dreadfully obvious and unoriginal. You know, love is blind and all that clichéd tripe."

"But Niles," Julie said, "what does any of this have to do with Oscar's murder?"

"It's the pecuniary aspect, my dear. We all know Oscar loved the cinema. He loved his collections. He loved his shop. But fiscal matters were, shall we say, not his strong suit. Essentially I subsidized Tinseltown Treasures for years. The shop had its vicissitudes. I helped out during the difficult times — which were not infrequent. After our break-up, however, Oscar completely withdrew from me. I knew through friends that in recent months he was struggling financially. Of course he could have come to me. I would have been more than happy to assist. But he never did."

"Why not?" Julie asked.

"We'll never be certain, will we. However, I presume it had to do with pride. I imagine the thought of coming to me for help after such a rejection was just too much for his dignity, his sense of manhood."

Julie looked at him skeptically.

"Yes, my dear, even we homosexuals fall victim to pernicious false pride. It's been drilled into us as little boys. An unfortunate cultural phenomena. But there it is."

"So you're saying Uncle Oscar <u>was</u> financially desperate."

"It's entirely possible," Niles replied. He turned to me "Now it's my turn to be inquisitive. What precisely is the nature of this alleged 'sketchy' situation to which you alluded?"

"Oh, he's not going to tell you anything," Julie said with a mischievous grin. "This is when Mr. Private Eye gives you the 'I must protect my client's privacy' lecture."

"She's right," I said. "But I do have a few more questions, if you don't mind."

"I certainly do mind," Niles retorted. "I must inquire again: who are you working for and why are you interested in Oscar's death?"

Somehow I suspected it would come to this with Niles. Why hadn't Lou ever told me how to keep things confidential when everybody wanted to know everything. Well, I'd just have to do my best.

"I'm working for a man who's being blackmailed because he's a homosexual," I said. "Oscar's death may be related. It's really important that I solve this case before the police get wind of things that might ruin my client. And that's connected to finding out who killed Oscar. You see?"

Niles thought about this. "Vaguely," he replied.

"I could use your help," I said. "My client could use your help."

Niles blew another smoke ring. "Fair enough," he said finally. "And in turn, you can help us."

"How?"

"By finding out who killed Oscar. I have no faith whatsoever that the police will be of much use in solving his murder. To them, Oscar is just another worthless Hollywood fairy. You know, a police detective came to my home today asking the most wretched questions. He wanted names of friends, which I absolutely refused to reveal. That made him quite testy. His less than subtle insinuation was that I myself was a suspect. Ironic, isn't it? In the eyes of the society, meaningful homosexual relationships do not exist. But a murder happens and suddenly the spouse, who moments ago did not exist, soars to the top of the suspect list just like any heterosexual better-half."

I had never thought about this before. Actually, I had never given much thought to homosexuals and their problems at all.

"So," Niles said, "do we have a deal?"

"You got a deal," I said.

Niles pulled out his checkbook. "What are your fees?"

Without really thinking about it, I shook my head. Niles and Julie both looked at me, puzzled. How could I tell them that I had talked with Panozzo about Marlon Brando and *One-Eyed Jacks* only days before his murder? How could I tell them that even without Niles' money I was determined to find out who killed Panozzo … and why.

"I … I'm already on it," I said. "It's all mixed up with this blackmail. I'm sure of it."

Niles grinned. "That might be true, but I'd feel better if you took this."

He wrote out a check and handed it to me. My eyes bugged out when I saw the amount. It was enough to pay Southland's overhead bills for months.

"Now," Niles said, "we've got a deal."

I pocketed the check. And as I did, I felt the atmosphere in the room shift. Now the three of us were in this together. I turned to Niles.

"Who was Oscar close to?" I asked. "Who did he confide in?"

"At one time it was me, of course. After our break-up, however, I fear the answer is nobody. Oscar increasingly absented himself from our circle of friends."

"This circle of friends, is that your 'club'?"

"Yes."

I took out my spiral notebook and pen.

"I'd like to talk with these friends. Can you give me their names?"

"I could. But I won't."

"It might help in —"

"No," Niles cut me off. "Privacy in our circles is paramount."

"Okay. I understand."

"Besides, as I just told you, I'm quite certain Oscar had little if any contact with any of them for months."

"Poor Oscar," Julie said wistfully. "He must have been lonely."

We all sat with that thought in silence. I pictured the pink-faced movie buff, with his tufts of white hair and rosy cheeks, his bowtie and candy-striped vest who had no customers during the day, and went nowhere at night. Oscar Panozzo had been lonely.

I turned towards the window and looked down into the hotel courtyard. The pool water was glowing aqua — illuminated by underwater lights. When I turned back to the room, Niles had lowered his head and his upper body was shaking.

Julie moved to sit next to Niles on the twin bed. She put her arms around him and they embraced.

"I'm so sorry," she said softly.

Niles shook harder as he silently cried. After a while, Julie went into the bathroom and came back with a box of Kleenex. Niles blew his nose and wiped his face dry.

"It feels good to cry," he said. He sighed deeply, then turned to me. "So, what else do you want to know?"

"Did you know Chip Jordan?"

I expected this question to surprise Niles, but he didn't miss a beat.

"Ah, Chip," he said. "Never regret thy fall, O Icarus of the fearless flight. For the greatest tragedy of them all, Is never to feel the burning light."

Julie and I both looked at him quizzically.

"Oscar Wilde," Niles said. As if that explained everything.

"The writer?" Julie ventured.

"Indeed. And to translate: Chip Jordan enjoyed fame, fortune, and a few years of fabulous partying. He paid the price with a premature exit from this earth, but what the hell, it was a good run."

"Did you know Chip Jordan personally?" I asked.

"We had our brief moment. Long before dear Oscar and I were together, of course. And all very discreet."

"Chip Jordan was a homosexual?!" Julie's mouth dropped open. "I used to have such a crush on him."

"You and half the population," Niles quipped. "Male and female."

"Did Panoz . . . uh, Oscar, know him too?" I asked.

"Oh, no. Oscar's relationship to the cinema was purely a love affair with the celluloid dimension."

"But I thought Chip Jordan killed himself over a woman," Julie said. "At least that's what the magazines said."

"Chip with a woman!" Niles snorted. "That would be hilarious were it not all so tragic."

"So you're saying he killed himself over a man?" I said.

"I'm suggesting no such thing. In fact, I believe Chip's demise had nothing at all to do with love."

Niles paused and looked directly at me. "Why is it that we are discussing Chip Jordan, may I inquire?"

"His name's come up during my investigation."

"But what is his connection to our beloved Oscar?"

"Maybe none, but I've got to follow up on everything, and you seem to know a lot about . . . about a lot of things."

"I'll take that as a compliment."

"So, about your relationship with Chip Jordan . . . ?" I could see this was one subject Niles was more than happy to discuss.

"Brief but delightful. Chip struck me as an intelligent, introspective sort. He had studied at the Group Theatre so he knew all the brightest, most talented, most progressive people. He actually read books! So you can imagine my surprise when I learned that he had testified before the House Un-American Activities Committee. Frankly, I was flabbergasted. He actually named names! His testimony may have caused people, his friends possibly, to lose their jobs, lose their livelihoods. I know I could never live with myself under such circumstances. In hindsight, I do think Chip seemed troubled. There was a darkness about him. Then, shortly after his HUAC debacle . . . "

Niles made a fist, placed it at his neck, and made a twisting motion.

". . . Chip Jordan bids the world adieu."

Julie looked perplexed. "What are you saying, Niles?"

"I'm suggesting that it wasn't a man who broke Chip Jordan's heart. It certainly wasn't a woman. I believe that Chip Jordan broke his own heart — by betraying his principles."

The three of us fell silent again. I gazed down into the courtyard again. A woman in a bikini was walking to the end of the diving board. She dove in. When she emerged, she shook the water from her long, soaking wet hair. That's when I noticed that the pool was shaped oddly. *Focus, Ryan. Chip Jordan... Steve Sutton... Oscar Panozzo... HUAC... How does it all fit together?* Ever since ingesting the LSD at Doc Flynn's ranch, my mind hadn't seemed exactly the same. Sometimes things got fuzzy, or extraordinarily clear. I watched the woman in the bikini swim to the edge of the pool. The glow of the pool water was like the glow around Doc Flynn sitting on the cabin floor. The ripples in the water were like the slow motion rippling of the air when we walked through the oak forest. *I am on a mission to save somebody...* Was that somebody Joey Flynn, neglected boy of an alcoholic mother? Was it Oscar Panozzo, a dead man who deserved better, with a killer still on the loose? Or was it all one and the same?

Suddenly, I recognized the contours of the swimming pool: It was a replica of the state of California. The diving board was anchored in cement at the Mexican border. The shallow end was at the Oregon border. A metal ladder dipped into the water around Santa Barbara. The woman in the bikini climbed out of the water on the ladder. She slipped on a pair of flip flops which lay by the edge of the pool. Now, if only I could get a handle on the shape of my case as clearly as I saw the California swimming pool.

I turned to Niles. "I'd like to take a look at Oscar's apartment."

"Ask Julie. I'm just the ex."

"But Niles," Julie said, "I don't have a key. I thought you did."

"I'll have to check. I may. That is if Oscar didn't change the locks."

"Did he have a safety deposit box?" I asked.

Niles nodded. "First National Bank. Corner of Hollywood and Highland. I believe only Oscar and Julie have access."

"Me?"

"He was very fond of you, my dear."

"What about a will?" I asked.

"Oscar and I both created wills at one time. We left everything to each other. I assume he changed his once we parted ways."

"I'd like to get a look at his safety deposit box."

"Why?"

"Who would you rather have nosing around Oscar's life, me or the police?"

"Point taken," Niles said.

After we made plans to all meet the next morning, Niles and I took the elevator down to the lobby. The desk clerk gave me a weird look. For a moment, it gave me the creeps to think the clerk might believe I was a queer because I was walking with Niles. Oh, well. Fuck it.

The night air was still warm when we hit the parking lot. Niles got into a flashy red MGB convertible. Wire wheels. Chrome bumpers. Wood-trimmed steering wheel. Leather-grained vinyl fold-down top.

"Awesome ride," I said. "That the V-8 or the 3-bearing 6?"

"Excuse me?" Niles looked puzzled. Then he broke into a smile. "Oh, the car. I haven't the faintest knowledge of the inner workings of this machine. I know only that it gets me where I need to go."

He winked at me. "In style."

That's creepy, I thought automatically. *I don't want a homo winking at me.* But I reminded myself: Niles is okay. He's a queer, but he didn't mean anything by it.

As I walked across the dark parking lot towards my car, I heard the MG's motor start up. I was thinking about Julie and how seeing her again tomorrow morning couldn't come soon enough, when I heard a voice, a low growl, at the far end of the lot behind me.

"Get outta the car, faggot."

I stopped and turned. I looked back towards Niles and his MG, but between the darkness and the parked cars filling the lot, I couldn't see either one.

"Get outta the motherfuckin' car right now, faggot." the voice growled again.

The MG's engine cut off and I started to run.

CHAPTER 26

I ran as fast as I could, weaving in and out between the parked cars.

"Hey!" I shouted. "What's going on!"

If someone was messing with Niles, I wanted them to know they'd soon have me to deal with.

As I ran, I heard a crashing sound. Then a yell. I finally reached the MG. Niles lay on the ground beside his car.

Detective Mackie stood over him, his foot on Niles' neck.

I stopped short, panting. Anyone else and I would have decked them, but even an idiot knows not to touch a cop.

Mackie turned to me. "Vamoose, Junior. This is police business."

I didn't move. Mackie glared at me. I stared back at him, not giving an inch. I was trying to send a message. Bullies don't like to be called out as bullies. They don't like to be caught in the act by someone who knows the score. I kept staring.

Finally, Mackie took his foot off Niles' neck. Then he kicked Niles in the ribs ... not real hard, but it wasn't a nudge either.

"Get up and give me a straight answer, faggot," Mackie said. "I want the names of every one of your faggot so-called friends!" He turned to me. "And you stay out of this, surfer boy."

Niles slowly got up. There was a cut over one eye and his lip was bleeding. His face was scraped up from the rough pavement. He gathered himself. He smoothed his camel hair jacket, buttoned the middle button, ran his hands through his hair to neaten it up. He adjusted his expression.

"I'd be happy to discuss any subject you suggest," Niles said, "in a civilized manner. With my lawyer present."

Mackie lunged at Niles and grabbed his shirt collar. I knew the move. He had pulled it on me at the station.

"Don't fucking lawyer me," he snarled and drew back his fist.

"Hey. Mackie." I said it calmly. "Come on, man. Leave it alone."

The detective hesitated. I guess it was just enough pause to break up the track he was on. He lowered his fist and let go of Niles' collar. He squinted at me.

"Fuck you both," he grunted. Then he turned and walked away.

CHAPTER 27

I made sure Niles was okay to drive, then we went our separate ways. I couldn't get the picture out of my head: Detective Mackie standing over Niles with his foot on his neck. It made me mad, and it also made me ashamed, because it made me remember. It had happened when I was in high school. I had never told anybody about that day. Not Lou. Not even Allison. I hadn't thought about it for years, I didn't want to think about it, not then, not now, not at all. Let the past be the past, isn't that what Steve Sutton said? You can't change the past, so why dwell on it. Besides, I had other things to think about, a case to solve. Fuck it. I was tired and mad and wasn't going to think about it now.

But I had one more thing to do before hitting the sack. I swung by the VA hospital to drop off the transistor radio I had promised Lou. Tomorrow was the big Koufax-Gibson dual which he had his heart set on listening to.

The nurse let me into his room if I promised not to wake him.

Lou was sleeping, the oxygen tube pushed up into his nose. I put the radio and a new Mickey Spillane paperback on the table beside his bed. Then I sat on the folding chair and watched him sleep. I listened to his breathing. It was even and slow and only a little bit raspy.

It would be great to talk with Lou about the case right now. There were so many strands whirling around in my mind. It would make him happy to talk, even if he couldn't be out on the street himself.

Not going to happen. At least not tonight. I stared at the monitor with its pulsing green line. *You're gonna make it, Lou*, I said silently. *It's not your time yet.* I wanted to believe it.

***

By the time I got back to Venice it was 1:00 AM. My apartment was stuffy so I opened the glass slider and let in the ocean air. I put Coltrane's *Giant Steps* on the hi-fi, lay down on the couch, and closed my eyes. Music usually does it for me. The sounds pour in until the only thing that exists is the music. That's when I can let everything else disappear and just BE.

Not tonight, though. Tonight, scenes flickered across my mind: Doc Flynn walking in his muddy work boots through the oak forest… Joey running to his mother in front of their house… Oscar Panozzo's white buckskin shoe… Detective Mackie with his foot on Niles' neck…

I needed to make sense of it all, and I needed to do it without Lou. Why would Oscar Panozzo blackmail one of his own kind? Niles said they stuck together, were protective of each other. Could desperation for money turn a switch, make a person do what they ordinarily never would?

I heard footsteps coming up the rickety back stairs. I looked at the clock. 1:45 AM. Then a knock at the door.

"Ryan, it's Tom."

I got up and opened the door, turning down the hi-fi on the way over. My downstairs neighbor stood in the doorway, a black leather jacket hanging loosely on his lean body.

"Hey, man," I said. "What's up?"

"Saw your light on. Hope it's not too late."

"No, it's cool. Come on in. You want something to drink?"

"No, thanks. We just got back from Shelley's. You missed a doozy, man. Everybody, I mean <u>everybody</u>, was there. Sinatra,

Diz, Sammy D. The place was so packed I didn't think we'd get in. Where were you, man?"

"Damn, I completely forgot."

"Well, get this: Miles comes on stage, the place goes silent, I mean si-lent. He looks at the crowd, then turns his back, just stands there with his back to us. Finally he lifts his horn, still got his back to the room, and plays one long note. Then he walks off stage."

"Then what?"

"That's it, man."

"That's some crazy shit."

"What are you gonna do. It's Miles."

"Wish I'd been there."

Tom snapped his fingers and grinned. "Hold on a sec, I'll be right back."

He jumped up and left my apartment. I heard the rickety steps creak as he went downstairs, then creak again a minute later as he came back up.

"Check this out."

Tom placed a rectangular machine about the size and shape of a hotel Bible on the dinette table. The top half was silver plastic dotted with a grid of tiny holes like you might see on a microphone. The middle section was a black plastic panel. At the bottom was a silver plastic strip with a few buttons.

"Remember that buddy of mine stationed over in Germany?" Tom said. "He got this at an electronics fair in Berlin. Runs on batteries."

Tom pressed one of the buttons at the bottom of the machine. He fidgeted with the button, pressing it over to the left. I heard a whirring sound. He pressed the button upward, then let go. A second of static, then:

...and gentlemen...Miles Davis...Huge applause...a combo starts up — piano, bass, drums. The combo vamps for a

while, until the unmistakable trumpet of Miles Davis joins in. He blows one note. The note sustains, then suddenly cuts off. The band plays on for a few minutes, then stops. After that, some rustling sounds, a few claps, glasses tinkling, nightclub murmur...

Tom pressed the button again and the nightclub sounds stopped. "What'd I tell you?" he said. "One note, then he quits."

I picked up the tape recorder and turned it over. "How do you get the tape in and out and rewind and all that?"

Tom popped open the black panel and removed a small plastic cartridge. A thin strip of magnetic tape spooled through it.

"It's called an audio cassette. You've got an hour of reel-to-reel in this tiny cartridge. My buddy in Germany, he's got one also. We record concerts and send them to each other. He just sent me this killer Cannonball Adderley set, the sound quality is shit, but you know anybody else who's got Cannonball live from Baden-Baden?"

"That's wild, man." I tapped the recorder, thinking how useful something like this would be for my PI work. "So, where can I get one of these?"

Tom shrugged. "Germany, I guess. Can't get them in the States. At least not that I know of. You can borrow mine if you want. Any time. But listen, man, that's not why I came by."

I grinned. "Yeah, I didn't figure you came up here at 2 AM to shoot the shit about Miles. So, what's up?"

"It's the cops, man. They were here looking for you today."

I nodded, not surprised.

"They got the wrong apartment, or pretended to. Tina was freaking until the cop said he was looking for you, not me."

"LAPD?"

"That's what the man said. Suit and tie. I didn't ask to see the badge."

"Flabby white guy, red face, bad attitude?"

"Naw, man. Short middle-aged cat with grey hair."

I nodded. *Terekov.*

"You in trouble?" Tom asked.

"No, nothing like that. It's just a case I'm on."

"That's what I figured, but Tina, she's jumpy. First that big white guy hanging around the Boardwalk near the liquor store, then the cop. She's always worrying. I keep telling her, 'This is Venice, baby, not Tuscaloosa. Nobody's out to get us here.' Besides, I don't do a damn thing to get the cops' attention."

"Except smoke a little weed and marry a white girl."

Tom grinned. "Well, yeah, there's that."

"So what's with this white guy?"

"I dunno. He's some kind of albino or something. Huge. Never seen him before."

"White hair but kinda young?"

Tom nodded. "You know him?"

"Sort of."

"Weird looking cat," Tom added. "Tina was positive he was checking us out, so of course she freaks and decides right off he must be the KKK or something." Tom shrugged and grinned. "Girls. They get scared so easily. At least Tina does. But what the heck."

Tom got up to leave. "Well, I gotta go."

"Thanks, man," I said as he made for the door. Thinking to myself: *What the fuck is Leon doing in Venice?*

CHAPTER 28

Julie stood at the curb in front of the Thunderbird hotel, wearing a blue blouse, white Capris, and white sandals. She smiled and waved as I drove up. My stomach did a couple of flips.

On our drive to Hollywood, Julie chatted away about growing up in Seattle. She told me about her three brothers and six cousins and how all the men in the family — with the exception of Oscar — worked on the docks or in the Merchant Marine. She told me about her girlfriends from high school who were now housewives and moms, and that there was no way she was going to be either. At least not before she had seen the world.

"Why are you so quiet," she asked when, after fifteen minutes, all I'd added to the conversation were some nods and grunts. "Is something wrong?"

"No," I lied. "I'm fine."

I wanted to tell her about what happened to Niles, and holding it back made me not talk at all. But I figured it was Niles' business to say something ... or not.

When we arrived at Oscar's Swiss chalet, Niles was just getting out of his red MG. He was dressed as stylishly as last night, an expensive-looking leather satchel hanging over his shoulder. But it wasn't his attire that stood out.

"Niles!" Julie ran towards him immediately. "What happened?!"

His face looked like he'd been in a fight. He had — but it was a one way fight. His lips were swollen and puffy. His right eye was bruised and purple. His left cheek was red with abrasions.

"Oh, this. It's the latest in fashion," Niles joked. "I call it the Tippi Hedren After-The-Bird-Attack look."

"Really, Niles," Julie insisted, "what happened?"

"Let's go inside," he replied, no longer joking. "I'll tell you in there."

We followed Niles up the staircase. He unlocked the door and we went inside.

Oscar's apartment was a homey version of Tinseltown Treasures. And even more jam-packed. In the living room, nearly every inch of wall space was covered with framed movie posters and lobby cards. Each wall had a theme. There was the Barbara Stanwyck wall, the Susan Hayward wall, the Greta Garbo wall. The mantle above the fireplace was crowded with movie-themed knickknacks. The coffee table was the holding spot for stacks of *Screenland* and *Photoplay* magazines from the 1920s and 30s.

"Voilà!" said Niles, making a dramatic sweeping gesture around the room. "Pure Oscar."

"It's so strange to be here without him," Julie said. "I really miss Uncle Oscar a lot."

"Me too," Niles murmured.

"So what happened to you, Niles?" Julie asked once more.

He told her. I looked down at the floor the whole time. Especially when Niles went on and on about how I intervened and saved him from further harm. I didn't feel deserving of the praise.

"That's so terrible," Julie said when Niles had finished. "Shouldn't we do something? Report it to the police or something like that?"

Even as she said it, we all knew how ridiculous that sounded. Report a lousy policeman to the police. Lots of luck.

"The best thing we can do is nothing," Niles said emphatically. "Just let it lie. Not only would a complaint be ineffective, it might cause retaliation. It's best if we just move forward. I know from experience."

"This has happened to you before?" Julie was aghast.

"Not me personally. But we homosexuals are handy targets. And not just for police. It happens."

Time was ticking. And the conversation was making me feel uncomfortable. I didn't want to think about the problems of homosexuals right now. I wanted to search Panozzo's apartment and his bank box before I had to drive Julie to the airport.

"Mind if I look around?" I asked.

"That's what we're here for," Niles responded.

It was a two-bedroom apartment. In the study, wedged beside a life-sized cardboard cutout of Charlie Chaplin's Little Tramp — bowler hat lopsided, feet splayed in floppy shoes, a puzzled expression on his face — and another wall full of movie posters, was an antique roll-top desk. I carefully searched through all the drawers and cubby holes. I thumbed through bills and receipts, domestic and business. I found Late Notices from utility companies, Past Due notes from the landlord. Stapled to the last rent notice for Tinseltown Treasures was a receipt for $3,000 stamped PAID IN FULL

I explored the entire apartment. I looked under the bed, under the mattress, through Oscar's clothes and pockets, inside the medicine cabinet and linen closet, behind the toilet tank. I searched the refrigerator and freezer, moved the fridge and checked behind it. I hunted beneath drawers and inside pots and pans. I searched inside the fireplace, running my hand over the sooty brick. I emptied a Laurel and Hardy piggy bank. I picked up books and magazines and shook them out.

I asked Julie and Niles if it was okay to take posters out of their frames.

"Go ahead," Niles said. He seemed tired and subdued.

I carefully pried open all the movie poster frames and checked inside. When there were no more places to search, I sat down on the couch next to Julie.

"Did you find whatever it is you're looking for?" she asked.

I shook my head. We all sat in silence, surrounded by Oscar Panozzo's life.

"I brought the will," Niles finally said.

He opened his leather satchel and took out a single sheet of onion skin paper. The heading, *Last Will & Testament*, was followed by a single typed paragraph leaving all of Oscar Panozzo's possessions to Niles Fontenot. The document was stamped by a Notary Public and dated May 3, 1961.

"Oscar's birthday," Julie observed.

Niles nodded. "Turning fifty will make you take stock."

Sitting amidst Oscar Panozzo's collections of entertainment glamour and cheer, we all seemed blue. I couldn't wait to get out of there.

***

Julie and I said goodbye to Niles, then drove the few blocks to Hollywood First National Bank.

"This building looks familiar," Julie said when we got out of the car. Her mood seemed to have lightened since we left Oscar's apartment.

"Did you come here with your uncle?" I asked.

"No. Never. That's not what I mean. It just looks familiar."

We stood on the sidewalk and both stared up at the enormous, thirteen story, white tower. At the top was a green cone-shaped roof studded with winged stone gargoyles. Like vultures surveying their prey, the gargoyles were perched on a ledge at the base of the green cone, looking down on the pedestrians walking Hollywood Blvd.

"Metropolis," I said, suddenly picturing the winged gargoyles in black & white. "It's the building from Superman."

"That's it!" Julie said. "Of course. Where he would fight those goofy crooks and bad guys. My brothers and I used to watch it all the time where we were kids."

She shot me a dazzling smile. Her smile almost put me in a good mood.

We went into the bank.

The lobby was old and grand and decaying. Dark wood paneling, high windows, lots of dust. Superman — and nearly everybody else — had left the building. It seemed as if Oscar Panozzo not only had a thing for old movies, he had a thing for old banks.

I sat on a hard wooden bench near the entrance. Julie crossed the lobby and stood with her back to me, talking to a teller. I watched the teller's mouth move, but couldn't hear his words. A short, elegantly dressed man unhooked a sagging velvet rope at the end of the counter. He motioned Julie to follow him into the belly of the bank.

Ten minutes later she was back.

"I got everything," Julie said as she handed me a cardboard file box. "But don't hold your breath for anything earth-shattering... unless..." she lowered her voice in mock seriousness, "unless *The Wizard of Oz* holds the key to Uncle Oscar's murder."

We sat together on the bench. Sitting this close to Julie was distracting me from everything else. I opened the box and removed a thick stack of 11" x 14" lobby cards. *A Star is Born, The Pirate, Babes in Arms, Wizard of Oz, Easter Parade, Listen Darling, Loves Finds Andy Hardy, Into Good Meet Me In Saint Louis, Summer Stock, Old Summertime, Presenting Lily Mars...*

Most of the cards were in English, but some were in French, Italian, even Japanese.

"I didn't know Judy Garland made so many movies," I said.

"And I'll bet Uncle Oscar has every single one."

"I wonder why he kept these cards in a safe deposit box."

"Maybe they're worth a lot of money," Julie suggested.

"Judy Garland?" I looked at her skeptically. "Besides, if your uncle had money problems and these were worth something, wouldn't he sell them?"

"You don't know Uncle Oscar. He loved movies and everything related to them. Sometimes I think he ran his store not to sell things but just so he could be around all this."

CHAPTER 29

We drove back across town to the airport. Julie talked about Oscar and her first time visiting him when she was ten years old.

"I'll never forget that trip. He took me to see *Sunset Boulevard*, *All About Eve*, and *Born Yesterday*. And then *Sunset Boulevard* for a second time. One movie each day! And they were all grown-up movies!! After that, I begged my parents each summer to let me visit Uncle Oscar again. Usually I got my way."

I listened. Nodded. Grunted.

"Ryan, are you okay?" Julie finally asked. "You're so quiet, just like this morning."

We were headed down Sepulveda, getting close to the airport. I could keep silent, drop her off at the terminal, and probably never see her again. Or I could talk.

"It's what happened to Niles," I finally said. "I'm still upset about it."

"Me too," Julie said. "I really like that you're concerned about Niles. And that you're not prejudiced against homosexuals. Most people are."

"That's the thing."

"What? What's the thing?"

"It's embarrassing. No, it's worse than embarrassing. It's something I've never told anybody."

"Now I'm really curious. You have to tell," she teased.

We crossed Manchester. I turned onto a side street and parked under a magnolia tree.

"It happened when I was in high school," I began. "My buddy Skunk had gotten a job painting houses on the weekends so he got to use the boss's truck. We were all stoked because he was the first one of us to have wheels. This one day we heard the surf was up at Zuma, so me and Skunk and our buddy Reno headed up there in Skunk's truck. But when we got to Zuma, the surf was mush. The weather was cold and cloudy and nobody else was at the beach. So we just hung out in the truck for a while, shooting the shit. Then this awesome car drives into the lot. It was an Austin Healey, a British car. I mean you hardly ever see them in the States. And this one is a silver-blue convertible, chrome wire wheels, hard top. We're stokin' out on the Healey as these two guys get out of it. They walk to the beach. We're just there, watching, shooting the shit, when all of a sudden the two guys hold hands. Ugh. I mean my philosophy is live and let live, but seeing it like that . . . well, at the time it seemed kind of disgusting to all of us. And Skunk, he got it the worst. He goes ape, talking about 'those fuckin fairies' and stuff like that.

" 'I'll show those fuckin fags,' Skunk says, and he jumps out of the truck. The two fair– uh, homosexuals, are way down the beach now where we can't see them anymore. Skunk, he goes around the back of the truck and grabs a can of paint. I'm thinking: oh, no, don't do it, man! Finally, I yell, 'Leave it alone, man,' something like that, but he waves me off. He runs over to the Healey and paints these big sloppy white letters across the side of the car. F-A-G-G-O-T. Then he runs back to the truck and we book outta there."

I look at Julie, waiting for her to tell me what an asshole I am and how she was wrong about me being an okay guy.

"That's awful, Ryan," she says.

"I know. I feel lousy about it. Really, really lousy."

"You weren't the one who did it."

"I could have stopped him."

"You tried."

"Not really. Not very hard."

"Well, it was a long time ago. I mean: high school. We're all different now."

I shrugged. Was I different? I sure wanted to be.

"And since I'm telling you the whole thing," I admitted, "here's how low my thinking can go. While Skunk was painting those letters, I was more worried about messing up the Healey than about the two guys."

Julie laughed. "Men. You are a weird bunch."

At least she was laughing.

Julie looked at her watch. "Hey, we've got to go. I don't want to miss my plane."

***

As we drove to LAX, my mood had improved 100%. Julie didn't hate me. And I didn't have to hold onto that secret anymore.

We circled passed a white flying saucer on spider legs, otherwise known as the LAX restaurant. I'd never been inside, but according to Lou the drinks were watered down, the steaks decent, and the 360° views were the best in town.

I pulled to the curb at the Western Airlines terminal and we got out of the car. I lifted Julie's suitcase out of the trunk.

"I can take it from here," she said.

We were standing close to each other. The air was soaked with the smell of jet fuel.

"I'm glad you told me about that day," she said. "I feel like I know you a little bit."

"Yeah" I said. "Thanks."

"Well … bye."

I put down the suitcase and kissed her. She kissed me back. We stood at the curb kissing for a while. Then she picked up her luggage, flashed me a smile, and walked toward the terminal. When she got to the smoky glass doors, she turned and waved. The door whooshed shut behind her.

Usually, I don't feel alone. I might be alone, but it doesn't bother me. As soon as Julie left, it did.

I drove to an abandoned onion farm at the north edge of the airport. I parked in the middle of the field, got out of the car, and hoisted myself up onto the roof of my Falcon. I lay down on my back, legs dangling over the windshield. I shut my eyes and listened to the cars whiz by on Sepulveda. Cool damp air drifted in off the ocean and settled on my skin. A jet engine started revving up, its high-pitched whine electrifying the air. I listened as the plane taxied up the runway, getting louder and louder ... until ... I opened my eyes and stared straight up into the steel underbelly of the jet as it passed over me, its engines roaring like a massive fire. The air wrinkled with fuel and heat.

I watched the plane ascend over the ocean, get smaller and smaller, until it disappeared into the milky blue sky. Then I hopped down from the car. I knew what I had to do.

CHAPTER 30

I drove out Wilshire Blvd. to Steve Sutton's office. The morning fog had burned off, and the sky was a clear, blazing blue. It was a notable improvement to be headed this way without a gun jammed into my ribs.

Sutton wasn't expecting me, which was all the better. I didn't want him to prepare some b.s. answer to what I planned to ask.

"Well, this is a surprise," my client greeted me.

He was wearing his tennis whites. The Bekins moving boxes had disappeared from his office. In their place was a leather couch, two steel frame chairs with leather hammock seats, and a bookcase holding several tennis trophies. On his desk was a crisp new blotter, a telephone with buttons for two lines, and a heavy cut-glass ashtray. Next to the ashtray, a paperback version of *How To Win Friends and Influence People* lay open.

The picture window behind Sutton's desk looked out on the Hollywood Hills. At the right edge of my view was the circular Capitol Records tower up on Yucca and Vine. Whoever thought of designing a building to look like a stack of records on a turntable was genius in my book.

"So what brings you out this way?" my client asked. "I hope it's better news than last time."

"I'm fairly certain Leon is still in L.A." I said.

"What?"

"My neighbor saw him down in Venice."

"That's ridiculous. Anyway, how in the world would your neighbor know what Leon looks like?"

"He described him and the description fit. Leon is unique. Also, I went by his place in Norwalk. His clothes—"

"Damn!" Sutton interrupted. "I almost forgot."

He pulled a notepad towards him and picked up a pen. "That woman in unit two has been pestering me about her bathroom sink. I've got to get another manager in there now that Leon is gone. And the Flower place, I need to rent out unit three. If it's not one thing, it's another. I can't tell you how much I look forward to getting out of the rental business."

Sutton scribbled something on the notepad. I could make out the upside-down words PLUMBER and FLOWER and the number 3.

When he finished writing he turned his attention back to me. "Now what were you saying?"

"Leon's clothes, at least some of them, and a bunch of other stuff is still there at his Norwalk apartment. And the mail's piling up."

"So?"

"A guy goes on a long trip — you even suggested he may never return — he would close up his place, cancel the mail, pack up his stuff. And Yugoslavia? He didn't even take his jacket."

"We're talking Leon here. Leon isn't like other people."

"What's he like?"

"Just... different. Possessions wouldn't mean anything to him."

I thought about that. Who didn't care about possessions? I couldn't think of anyone. Possessions were exactly what everybody <u>did</u> care about. To some it was the Buick in the garage. To the Gas House gang it was their berets and bongos. To me, my stereo and surfboard. I thought about Doc Flynn. What about Doc Flynn? Did possessions mean anything to him?

"Who exactly is Leon?" I asked.

"What do you mean?" Sutton said. "Leon is Leon."

"I mean what's his story? How did he come to work for you?"

"Oh, that. I picked him up hitchhiking. About ten years ago. He looked lost, this oversized oaf with white hair and ragged clothes standing by the side of the road. His arms were scratched up. I felt sorry for him, so I took him home, got him cleaned up, let him stay rent-free in one of my apartment units down in San P for a while. Leon isn't much of a talker, but eventually, little by little, he told me about his background. His mother and father had been killed during the war. He wandered around Europe by himself, stealing to survive, living in bombed-out ruins. Ate rats. He finally caught a break when some save-the-war-orphans outfit set him up with a family in the U.S. Turned out to be a sham. The outfit was bringing kids over and putting them to work in the agricultural fields, locking them up in a basement at night. Eventually Leon escaped. He roamed around L.A. He worked in bars, on the docks, in the fields. Found trouble. Anyway, my real estate business was just taking off, so I put him to work."

"I can see why he'd be loyal."

"What's that supposed to mean?"

"Nothing. You said he was loyal. I can see why, after everything you've done for him."

I wondered to myself if there wasn't more to the story, more to the bond between Sutton and Leon. But I figured that wasn't any of my business. It wasn't anybody's business but theirs.

What *was* my business, however, was to find out why was Leon hanging around my apartment. And why his boss and savior seem to know nothing about it.

CHAPTER 31

It was late afternoon by the time I reached my next, and in my mind at least, most important stop: Pacific Palisades. I walked up to the Flynn's front door and rang the bell. This being a weekday, I assumed Mrs. Flynn would be at work. At least I hoped so. I knew what Lou would have said about me checking on Joey, about letting a case get personal, about being here at all. But it didn't really matter what Lou would have said, because I was here anyway.

I rang the bell a second time. Waited. Nobody answered. So I walked up the street to the Ackerman house. Someone was playing cello scales inside. As soon as I rang the buzzer, the cello scales were drowned out by the yapping of Buster the poodle. A minute later, Mrs. Ackerman, holding Buster, inched the door open. The cold cream was gone, but the same suspicious eyes greeted me. The dog growled.

"Hello, Mrs. Ackerman ... Hi, Buster."

I showed the dog my hand. He sniffed it and began wagging his tail.

A flash of recognition crossed Mrs. Ackerman's face. She pulled the door open a few more stingy inches.

"Oh, it's you Mr. ... Mr. ... ."

"Zorn. Ryan Zorn."

"That's right. Ryan. Don't tell me Joey has run away again."

"I don't think so, but he wasn't at home so I thought he might be over here."

She shook her head. "No, I'm afraid not. We've forbidden Nicholas to play with Joey for the rest of the summer."

"Why's that? I thought they were best friends."

"Maybe we should talk inside."

I followed her into the kitchen. The cello scales had stopped.

"Keep practicing, Nicholas!" she shouted. "You still have fifteen minuets to go!"

The cello started up again. Not scales this time, but a slow, somber melody. I sat across from Mrs. Ackerman at the white Formica table.

"So what happened with Joey and Nicholas?" I asked.

"It wasn't an easy decision, but my husband and I decided Joey is a bad influence on Nicholas."

"Why?"

Mrs. Ackerman leaned towards me and lowered her voice. She obviously delighted in spilling the beans.

"We caught Joey stealing. And that's not all. We found out that Nicholas helped him run away — the time when you went looking for him. He took my husband's car in the middle of the night and drove Joey to the Greyhound bus station."

"The one in Santa Monica?"

She nodded.

"That's a ways away. Your son must be a pretty good driver. Most 11-year-olds can't even see over the steering wheel."

"Nicholas isn't 11. He's 14."

"Oh." I was surprised, but kept a neutral tone.

"It's not Nicholas's fault. I blame my husband for all this. You see, Nicholas is ... different. Not stupid. Just different. He gets teased by other boys in school. Never by Joey, though. Anyway, my husband has been letting Nicholas drive around in our church parking lot when it's empty. He says it helps Nicholas feel more grown-up. I don't like it, and I've told him as much, but you can't fight every battle, now can you?"

"No, you can't."

"Anyway, I think Nicholas will be just fine. Did you know that children develop at different rates? And he's very gifted, musically."

As if on cue, the cello music stopped and a large boy, probably five-eight but still hanging on to some baby fat, appeared in the doorway. His brown hair was cut in a bowl shape. He had large dark eyes and a blank expression on his face.

"I heard you talking about me," he said.

"Go go back to practicing, Nicholas. This is adult talk." Mrs. Ackerman spoke to her son as if he were a small child rather than a teenager.

"I heard my name," Nicholas said.

"I don't know how... if you were concentrating on your music."

"I don't want to play anymore."

"Fifteen more minutes."

"That's not what I mean. I don't want to play anymore — ever. No more lessons."

"Not now, Nicholas. We have company."

"I want to switch to drums."

"We'll see what your father has to say about that when he comes home."

"He thinks the cello's for sissies."

"I'm not going to argue with you about it. Now go."

The boy remained standing in the doorway. He didn't look defiant, or angry, or much of anything at all. He just looked blank. And now he was staring right at me.

"Hi, Nicholas," I said. "I'm Ryan."

"The one who brought Joey back," he said.

I nodded. "Do you know where Joey is right now?"

Nicholas started to say something, but bit down on his lip and remained silent.

Mrs. Ackerman turned to me. "I told you, Nicholas and Joey no longer play together, so he wouldn't know—"

"He's probably at our fort," Nicholas blurted out.

"Where's your fort?" I asked.

"By the creek."

"What creek?"

"The bottom of the hill behind Joey's house."

"Nicholas," his mother broke in, "why don't I know anything about this fort?"

The boy shrugged. I thought I detected a faint smile.

"We talked about this, Nicholas," Mrs. Ackerman lectured. "No lies, no secrets. Honesty is the key to a happy family life."

The boy stayed blank.

"Nicholas, are you listening to me?"

"Yes."

Nobody said anything for a moment.

"Nicholas," I said finally, "do you think Joey's at his fort right now?"

"Maybe."

"Really, Nicholas," his mother said, "I don't want you sending this man on a wild goose chase down that steep hill back there."

"That's okay, Mrs. Ackerman. I'll take my chances." I turned to the boy. "Thanks, Nicholas. You've been really helpful."

"You're welcome." His voice was flat.

"Okay, Nicky, now go. You have fifteen more minutes of practice. Don't think I forgot."

The boy waited at the door a moment longer. I thought he was going to say something, but he turned and left the room. A few seconds later, I heard a door slam. I didn't hear any more cello music.

"Mrs. Ackerman, you said something about Joey stealing."

"He took my husband's gun."

"What? When was this?"

"My husband noticed it missing last week. He asked me about it, but of course I didn't know anything. Why would I? I've told him a hundred times that I don't want a gun in my house. It all started after that dreadful Cuban missile crisis. My husband wanted to build a bomb shelter and stock it with canned food and water and crackers and some complicated air filtering system. Oh, and a pool table and wet bar. Why waste the space in the meantime, he said." Mrs. Ackerman shook her head and sighed. "Men. Anyway, once he found out the cost he gave up his ridiculous bomb shelter idea, but he absolutely insisted upon purchasing a gun. I mean really! What's he going to do, shoot the whole Russian army if they invade?"

"So this gun, how do you know Joey took it?"

"Nicky broke down and told us everything. We marched right over to the Flynn's to get to the bottom of it. Cora refused to believe that Joey had stolen it, but she finally let us search his room. And there it was, just like Nicholas said, under the mattress. And don't for a minute think my son isn't being punished for all this. We believe in consequences."

"Where's the gun now?"

"Locked up securely, I can assure you."

"May I take a look at it?"

"Well... I don't see why not."

Mrs. Ackerman dug a set of keys out of her purse. She fanned through them until she found the key that she was looking for. I followed her to the den where a television in a fancy wood console faced a small couch and a Naugahyde Reclina-Rocker. Next to the TV was a closet. Mrs. Ackerman opened a step stool that was stored in the closet, stood on the top rung, opened a metal safe that sat on a high shelf in the closet, and brought out a small pistol. She held the butt of the gun tentatively, between her thumb and forefinger, as if she were dangling a dead rat by its tail.

She handed me the gun. It was a black Smith and Wesson .22 pistol with a wooden grip. I sniffed the muzzle, catching the faint but distinct metallic odor of gunpowder.

"What about ammunition?" I asked her. "Was any missing?"

"I don't know. I suppose my husband would."

I gave the pistol back to Mrs. Ackerman and walked back to Joey's house. I went around to the backyard where a couple of faded canvas chairs sat on a neglected, parched lawn. I stood at the edge of the yard and looked down into the canyon below.

CHAPTER 32

I saw no creek, no fort, not even a footpath. Only a dense tangle of creosote and sumac and sage brush. I cupped my hands and shouted.

"Joey! You down there!?"

The air was still.

I walked along the lip of the canyon. In one corner of the yard was a sycamore tree with a rope swing hanging from a branch. Just past the sycamore, I spotted a break in the chaparral. I pushed aside the woody shrubs that hid a narrow path snaking down the hill.

The brush scratched against my arms and legs as I made my way down. At the bottom of the canyon was a dry creek bed. Across the creek was a cluster of oaks. Where would a couple of kids build a fort? When I was Joey's age, my buddies and I didn't build forts. We stole beer off the back of delivery trucks, built bonfires on the beach at night, and ran like hell when the cops arrived. On the other hand, not one single time did any of us get our hands on a gun.

"Joey!" I called out. "It's me, Ryan!"

I stood very still and waited. Then I saw something move in the brush beyond the oaks. It might have been a bird, or a rabbit, or a boy hiding out. I kept my eye trained on the spot where I had seen the movement, and walked toward it.

Just past the oaks were a couple of manzanitas with smooth red bark, twisty branches, and a low canopy of grey leaves. The leaves on one manzanita started to shiver. Joey crawled out from beneath the tree.

"Hi," he said.

Joey sat on the ground, cross-legged, in a way that immediately reminded me of his father sitting cross-legged in the dark mountain cabin. I sat down so we'd be eye to eye.

"How you doing, Joey?"

"Okay. Why are you here?"

"I was worried about you."

"Why?"

"I guess because it's summer and I know you're here alone a lot, and everything that's happened in the past few weeks. I wanted to see how you're doing."

"I'm okay."

I motioned to the manzanita thicket. "This your fort?"

Joey nodded.

I pictured a kid's fort to be some kind of Swiss Family Robinson tree house like you see in the movies.

"You got stuff in there?" I asked.

"No."

"So, what do you do in the fort?"

"Just sit. Watch the animals and birds."

"What do you see?"

"Squirrels. Jays. Sometimes a jack rabbit or a deer. Skunks. Owls at night."

"You come down here at night?"

Joey shrugged.

"I just came from Nicholas' house," I said. "His mother told me about the gun."

"Yeah, big deal."

"Why'd you take it?"

"To protect my mom."

I nodded. "I get that."

"I don't want to talk about this anymore. Okay?"

"Okay. One more question though."

Joey kept quiet.

"Did you fire it?"

He shook his head.

"Did Nicholas?"

"No."

"Not even to shoot at a tin can or something like that?"

Joey shook his head again.

"So what'd you do with it?"

"Put it under my mattress." Joey scratched at the hard-packed ground with his fingernails. "Just in case."

"When did you take it?"

"Last week."

"What day?"

He shrugged again. We were quiet for a while. A scrub jay landed on a nearby branch, squawked a few times, and flew off.

"Have you talked to your dad since you got back?" I asked.

"What do you mean?"

"You have his phone number."

"I'm only supposed to call if it's an emergency."

"You called him when you ran away. Of course, that qualifies as an emergency in my book. A creep hit your mom and you bashed him."

Joey looked down at the ground.

"To me," I said, "if a kid steals a gun to protect his mom, that's an emergency."

Joey kept silent for a while. "You think I should call him?" he whispered.

"If you want to."

"What would I say?"

"Whatever you want. Your father seems like an intelligent man, maybe he can help you figure things out."

"My dad is ... he doesn't like to be bothered too much. He's doing important work. Plus, he'd be mad if my mom got his phone number off the bill."

"Come on," I said. "Let's go find a pay phone."

***

The first phone booth we saw was at a Phillips 76 station on Sunset. I dug through my pockets, came out with a clump of change, and handed it to Joey. He closed the accordion door to the booth. Even with the door shut, I could hear his side of the conversation.

"Dad?" Joey said into the receiver. "Yeah, it's me ... No, everything's okay ... Yeah, she's okay ... At work.... Yeah, I know.... Uh, just that detective, Ryan .... Yeah.... I think he wants to talk to you. Okay."

Joey opened the accordion door and handed me the phone.

"Go sit in the car," I said.

Joey nodded. I kept an eye on the kid as he ambled back to my Falcon and got in.

"Doc Flynn?" I said.

Flynn chuckled. "So what's going on down there, wise-guy? Joey knows he's not supposed to call me."

"It was my idea."

"I figured."

"Look, I think Joey needs help, some guidance or something. He's getting into some bad shit."

"Details."

"He stole a gun."

Total silence.

"What are you talking about?" Flynn finally said.

"Ask Joey. Talk to him. I think he'd like that."

Flynn sighed. "You might have noticed that playing Daddy is not my strong suit."

"Yeah, I noticed."

"So, wise guy, you're at my house in the middle of the day, hanging out with my kid, maybe sleeping with my ex —"

"No, man," I interjected. "Nothing like that."

"Anyway, you're there. I'm not. What about you giving the kid some, as you say, 'guidance'? You seem to have a decent head on your shoulders."

"No, no, no. Not me, man."

"Why not?"

"I've got a life, a job."

"Oh, so it's like that. You need money. Of course you do. The way we live up here ... well, money is the least of it. But I can probably dig up some cash."

"It's not about money. I just can't take care of a kid."

"Well, neither can I."

"Someone has to."

There was silence on the line. Joey had gotten out of the car and was headed my way.

"I want to put Joey back on," I said. "That okay with you?"

Doc Flynn grunted a yes.

I opened the accordion door and handed Joey the phone.

"Dad? ... Yeah, sure ... No. ... Yeah, I will. I promise ... Okay ... Bye."

After the conversation with his father, Joey seemed dispirited.

"What'd he say?" I asked.

"Stay outta trouble, I'm the man of the house, my mom needs me to be good. You know."

I nodded. "Yeah, I do."

***

We drove back to Joey's house and I called his mother at Pinnacle Studios. She was less than thrilled to hear from me.

"Richard called ten minutes ago," she said, "out of the blue. He's nagging me about taking better care of Joey — talk about the pot calling the kettle black, as if he's around to be a parent of any kind at all — and now you. I don't need you or anyone else accusing me of being an unfit mother."

"I understand," I said. "I'm just concerned about Joey."

"What do you want me to do? I'm trying to provide for my son. I'm doing the best I can."

"I know, but your kid had a gun."

"And that's the end of the world? He gave it back, no harm done. What happened to 'boys will be boys?' "

I didn't say anything.

"Okay," she finally conceded, "so Joey made a mistake. And now that self-righteous Mrs. Busybody won't even let him play with his best friend. As if Nicholas, just because he's retarded, is so perfect. He's a nice boy, but please! No, of course everything is always Joey's fault."

I listened to Mrs. Flynn and wondered: Was it this difficult for my mother when she was raising me? I had gotten into my share of trouble. One time, Reno and I had been caught scaling the fence at the junior high, me holding a trumpet, Reno holding a guitar that we had lifted from the music room. The cops brought me home in handcuffs. Had my mother worried about me, or just figured I'd be okay? Or had alcohol blotted it all out. Unlike Mrs. Flynn, my mother hadn't seemed to care about what others thought of her, a single mother trying to raise her boy. Then again, she didn't have the stigma of being divorced. Plus, she had Uncle Lou. And I had the Venice Beach surfers who took me under their wing. Who did Joey have? He was alone all day with nobody around to notice what he did. Did he get himself to Hollywood and kill a man? There was a city bus that ran all the way up Sunset, from the Palisades to Hollywood and beyond. No. It couldn't be. Or could it?

I looked over at Joey who was lying on the couch in the sunken living room staring at the TV. Who was this kid? What was he capable of doing? I was going to have to find out.

"Hey, Joey," I said after finishing the phone call with his mother, "I gotta go now, but do you want to hang out with me sometime, go fishing or something?"

He perked up. "Tomorrow?"

"Can't do it tomorrow. How about the day after?"

"Okay."

"Alright. I'll be by day after tomorrow, in the morning."

I headed for the door, taking one last glance at Joey. He had turned back to the TV, and was staring at it blankly.

CHAPTER 33

The next morning, I called Detective Terekov at the Hollywood station. The desk sergeant said Terekov was busy but that he'd deliver my message.

I drove downtown. I parked on Hill, dropped a couple of dimes in the meter, went around the corner to the Hall of Records.

The lobby was light and clean and spacious, with acres of pristine, polished marble floors and walls. I took the elevator down to the basement, a dark and sunless maze of even more polished marble. I'd been down here many times on errands for Lou. It was amazing what they kept down here: a century of paper detailing people's liens, divorces, deeds, and court appearances. The clerk, a thin man with thinning hair and a grayish complexion, looked briefly at the form I put in front of him, picked it up and disappeared into a back room. I leaned against the wall and waited. The cold of the marble seeped through my shirt and put a chill on my skin.

When the clerk returned, he handed me a two-page list. I sat on a recessed marble bench and read through the document. Steve Sutton owned 17 separate parcels of property. I took the list to the adjoining room and searched through a file cabinet for each parcel map, writing down the corresponding street address for each piece of land. Sutton's properties were scattered all across the region, from Sunland to Norwalk to Compton to Venice.

Back at the office, I spread out a road map of L.A. on my desk. I went down the list of Sutton's properties, marking an X on the map for each one. Once all the Xs were in place, I examined the map and planned my route. I couldn't charge the trip to my client, so I did some quick math in my head. A hundred plus miles at thirty cents a gallon, twenty miles to the gallon. I'd only be out about two dollars. It was worth it.

I started in Venice. Both of Sutton's Venice properties were east of Electric Avenue. Electric got its name from the electric trains — they were call the Red Cars because they were painted, duh, red — that used to run all over L.A. My mother used to take the Red Car to work. When they shut the system down, she had to switch to the bus, complaining for years about how much better the Red Cars were.

East of Electric was the Negro section of Venice. Officially, the neighborhood was called Oakwood, but from as far back as I can remember, everyone in Venice — black and white — called it Ghost Town. Don't ask me why. A few years ago, some Mexican families moved into Ghost Town when construction of the 405 Freeway tore up their neighborhood and forced them out. That's when you started seeing V-13 graffiti scrawled on walls and garage doors, V-13 standing for Venice 13, the Mexican gang. The Mexicans and Negros didn't get along all that well, and once in a while you'd hear about knife fights, even a killing or two. But Ghost Town was Ghost Town, Venice was Venice, and we just swung with it and got on with life.

I drove by each of Sutton's Venice properties. The first was a rundown wood frame house on Vernon. The second was a stucco 4-plex with peeling paint and missing roof shingles on Flower. An elderly Negro man sat on the stoop at the 4-plex. He was holding a paper bag wrapped around a bottle. As I pulled to the curb, he set the paper bag down on the concrete behind him.

"Hi," I said as I walked up to him.

The man nodded. His skin was dark and leathery. He was wearing denim overalls and a white ribbed undershirt.

"Ryan Zorn," I said, and handed him my card. "I'm a private investigator."

The man examined the card, slowly and deliberately.

"I'm looking for Leon Vanek. They guy who collects the rent."

"What'd he do?" The man had a slow, southern, country drawl.

"Nothing. I just need to find him."

"Hmmm."

"Has he been around lately?"

"Nah."

"Have you seen him since the first?"

"Not then neither."

"I thought he collected the rent."

"We pay on time."

"Does he come by to fix things, do maintenance?"

The man snorted. "Do it look like it?"

"So when *does* he come by?"

"Evict. Or trouble."

"What kind of trouble?"

"Any."

"Been any trouble around here recently?"

"Nah. No trouble."

***

It was the same all over Steve Sutton's dilapidated empire. Nobody had seen Leon lately. He only showed up to collect late rent, evict, fix the kind of problems that took muscle or the threat of it. Plumbing or electrical? Forget about it. A Mexican woman in Tujunga who lived in a shack with chickens running around the front yard told me in broken English that Leon had shoved her husband around and broken his jaw. A Negro boy in Compton said he liked Leon because Leon gave him a candy bar.

By the end of the day, I had circled L.A. I'd driven from the beach, to the Valley, to the Eastside, to the flats south of downtown, and back west again. Out of all Sutton's seventeen properties, the only place not neglected and shabby was the apartment building in Norwalk where Leon had been the manager. It was also the only property where the tenants were white. Par for the course. Even with Leon gone, things would get fixed for the white renters in Norwalk. When I was in his office, Sutton had made a note to get that woman's sink fixed. PLUMBER FLOWER 3.

An idea hit me.

Flower. The 4-plex.

I headed back to Venice and parked in front of Sutton's 4-plex. As I walked towards the building, I heard Vin Scully's voice calling a Dodgers game from a radio or TV in one of the apartments. There were two units downstairs and two up. I went upstairs and rapped on the cheap hollow door that had a #3 hanging lopsided from a single screw. When nobody answered, I went back downstairs.

The door to Unit 1 was open. Though a screen door, I could see the elderly man who had been sitting on the stoop that morning. He was playing checkers with a woman about his age whose hair was wrapped in a colorful scarf. A radio sat on the table next to the checker board broadcasting the Dodgers game.

I rapped on the screen door's rotted wood frame. The woman started to get up, but the man put a hand on her arm and said, "I'll get it, babe." He walked slowly to the front door, using a cane. He nodded when he saw me, but kept the screen door shut.

"Hi," I said. "I was here this morning."

"I remember."

"Anyone living in number three right now?"

The man shrugged. "Not my bizness."

"I guess not." I gestured towards the radio. "What's the score?"

"Dodgers just scored eight in the sixth."

"Who's pitching?"

"Roebuck in relief."

I nodded. "Thanks. Have a good evening."

I went back up the stairs to #3. I slipped my plastic Texaco Travel Card into the door jam, pushed open the door, and went inside.

CHAPTER 34

The room was dark and reeked of cigarette smoke. All of the windows were closed and the curtains pulled shut. An old couch sagged against one wall. No table. No pictures or photos. No shelves. No books or magazines or radio or TV or phonograph. No knick-knacks, no loose change, no mail laying around. The wall-to-wall carpet, what was left of it, was stained and worn down to the matting in some places. A single metal folding chair was positioned near one end of the couch. On the seat of the chair was a beanbag ashtray filled with cigarette butts.

I went into the bedroom. There was a mattress on the floor with a rumpled blanket on top, no sheets. Next to the mattress, on the worn carpet, was another beanbag ashtray filled with ashes and butts.

The galley kitchen had just enough room for one person to stand. On the counter was a bag of unshelled peanuts and an Abba Zabba candy bar. In the fridge was a carton of milk and a few apples. The milk smelled fresh. In the trash bucket under the sink was an empty package of Marlboros and an apple core.

I walked back into the main room and sat on the couch. A lonely feeling came over me. I tried to shake it, but the feeling stuck to me like the nicotine on the ratty drapes. I imagined what Leon's life was like, living here in a dark, smoke-filled room, sustaining himself on candy bars and cigarettes... and something else.

Leon was a man on a mission.

CHAPTER 35

The phone was ringing when I got home. I'd been driving around all day; I was tired and hungry; but my first thought was: I hope it's Julie.

"Ryan, I've got the intel you wanted."

It was Max Fisher, my Hollywood connection and Allison's father. For a moment, I couldn't remember what I had asked him to find out for me. Luckily, Max kept rolling.

"I called a pal of mine over at Columbia who's up on everything," he said. "Looks like our man Dargin was canned because he refused to hire Lester Cole for a picture. The producer wanted Cole. So did the director. Even the big wigs in New York wanted Cole. But Dargin flat out refused."

"He lost his job over a writer?"

"Lester Cole wasn't just any writer. He was one of The Ten."

The Ten. My mind was blank. THE TEN. It was something I felt I should know, but no picture, no words, floated in to fill the void. *Think, Ryan. Don't be a dope.* I could hear the waves roll in on the other end of the line. Max must have been on the extension with the long cord that reached out to the deck. Allison used to take the phone out there when we wanted to talk in private. I pictured Malibu's smooth right break, the perfect waves to cross-step up the board, curl all ten toes over the nose …

"The Hollywood Ten," I said. "They went to prison for not answering HUAC's questions."

"Exactly," Max said. "And, by not answering, by invoking their First Amendment rights, they showed HUAC to be precisely what it was: a political witch hunt cloaked in Congressional clothing."

"So Dargin has a grudge against old Commies?" I ventured.

"That's putting it mildly. Guys like Dargin would just as soon everybody to the left of Nixon be shipped off to another planet. One without oxygen, if possible." Max chuckled. "He must have really blown his top over the thought of hiring a real Red like Cole."

"Sounds like Dargin is an extremist."

"Not for 1950."

"But we're not in 1950 anymore."

Max laughed. "How right you are. I guess our man Dargin hasn't gotten the news. It ain't the 50s anymore, Victor. McCarthy's dead. Trumbo got screen credit for *Exodus* and *Spartacus*. For god's sake, we have a Catholic president!"

"So Dargin is willing to lose his cushy movie job over politics."

"Which, in a perverse way, you've got to admire. He took a stand. I mean The Ten went to prison over ideological issues, of course for them it was about freedom of speech, freedom of political affiliation, whereas for Dargin it's the antithesis. It's fear of free speech, fear of new ideas, fear of things he doesn't understand. He's what I call a fear-man."

"A fear man ... " I liked the sound of it. I had only met Victor Dargin a couple of times, but I had a sense that the term fit.

"Of course," Max continued, "these are just the humble speculations of a lowly television writer. I figure a fear-man like Dargin, the more power he gets, the more he fears losing it."

"Seems to me that getting fired is more like losing power, not keeping it."

"That's the ironic beauty of it all. Dargin is a dinosaur. Tyrannosaurus Darginitis. Thrashing about in the swamp, the ground shifting beneath him. The more he thrashes, the further he sinks. It's the end of an era, Ryan, and good riddance to it. Mark my words, ever since the Supreme Court ruled on Brown versus the . . . "

I could tell that Max was revving up for an extended political monologue. "Max," I interrupted, "did your friend say anything else about Dargin?"

"Just that they're taking bets on tonight."

"Bets?"

"Yup. UA's having a private screening of the new McQueen picture tonight, some World War II epic. Dargin was invited before he got the ax. Some pals of mine are taking bets whether he'll have the balls to show up. He's not very well liked around town."

I perked up. "The screening is tonight?"

"That's what my pal said."

"What time?"

"How the hell would I know?"

I looked at my watch. "That's okay. Thanks, Max. I really appreciate your help. I gotta go."

As soon as we clicked off, I went into overdrive. This was my chance. I'd been wanting to get inside Victor Dargin's house again. I had no idea if Dargin's hostile attitude towards me when I questioned him was just his standard operating procedure, or if he was hiding something — something related to my client's blackmail, or even Panozzo's murder. Maybe I had just hit a sore spot with him, or maybe he was neck deep in the whole mess.

Anyway, it stood to reason that his house, his private kingdom, might hold some clues. To find out, I needed to get a look around. A real look. It was now or never.

I found Dewey Weber Surfboards in the phone book, dialed, and got Reno on the line.

"Hey, Reno. It's Ryan. When are you getting off work?"

"Not till late. What's up?" Reno sounded as laid back as I was amped up.

"I need you for a job. Can you take off right now?"

"No, man. No way. Dewey's pissed at me already. He said my attendance, and I quote, has not been stellar."

"What's he running down there — a sweat shop?"

"Hey, don't rag on Dewey, man. Surf was up, so I didn't get in till after two. And we've got orders like you wouldn't believe. I'm a sanding demon, man."

"Well, I'm coming down to get you anyway. I've got to. Can't you make something up, some emergency to tell Dewey?"

"Like what?"

"Like — I don't know, man. Just think up something brainy. This is important and there's twenty-five bucks in it for you. For just a couple hours."

Silence. I could practically hear Reno thinking. Twenty-five dollars for a few hours of work was way more than he made sanding boards for Dewey Weber.

"Okay, man," he said. "I'm in."

"Cool. See you in a few."

I hung up the phone, took the rickety steps down from my apartment two at a time, jumped into my car, and drove to the office.

At the office, I grabbed the key to the storage closet and unlocked it. I pulled out a crow bar, camera with flash, 10-inch steel strip, latex gloves, walkie-talkie, and two extra batteries. I switched on the walkie-talkie transceivers. Neither one had any juice. I put in new batteries, tried again. They both crackled to life.

Ten minutes later I was back in Venice, pulling to the curb in front of Dewey Weber Surfboards. Dewey's new shop on Lincoln Blvd. was a big improvement over the old one. This was a real store rather than a glorified shed. His trademark red and black logo was painted on the front of the squat brick building. On either side of the door were huge floor-to-ceiling display windows showcasing eight boards on iron racks.

I went inside. The showroom was lined with more boards on display racks. Dewey was showing a ten-footer with a thin red stripe to a teenage boy and his father.

I caught Dewey's eye.

"Getting Reno," I said.

Dewey gave me a funny sideways grin and jerked his thumb over his shoulder. I went through a connecting door into the factory which was a long narrow room with stacks of foam blanks leaning up against the walls. More boards in various stages of completion were stacked here and there. The floor was covered with a layer of fine white polyurethane dust. On one side of the room was a work bench cluttered with resin jars, draw knives, sandpaper, and boxes of fins. On the other side, a partial wall stopped just short of the ceiling. From behind it came the whirring sound of an electric planer. I went behind the half-wall where Reno was sanding a board that lay across two saw horses. He was so concentrated on his work that he didn't realize I was in the room.

"Hey, man," I shouted over the buzz of the planer.

Reno looked up and nodded. He turned off the planer and the room instantly got quiet. He brushed white dust off his clothes, face, and arms. I followed him out to the showroom where Dewey was ringing up a sale on the register. Dewey grinned at me again.

"Hasta la vista, papacito," he said with a wink.

"What was that all about?" I asked Reno as we got into my car. "Dewey's acting weird."

"Nothing, man. Don't sweat it."

"Don't sweat what?"

"Well … I told him you got a girl pregnant and she hates you now so I gotta take her to TJ for an abortion tonight."

"Jeez! You really said that?"

Reno nodded. "Best I could come up with on short notice. So, what's up for tonight?"

I told him as much as he needed to know, which wasn't much. Reno turned on the radio. Monk's *Criss-Cross* was playing on KNOB. Reno tapped his foot for a little while, then gave up. I knew he didn't go for jazz, but those were the rules: my car, my music. As *Criss-Cross* segued to a Gerald Wilson number, a '61 Corvette with whitewalls and white coves pulled alongside us at a stoplight.

"XKE or Vette?" Reno said.

"XKE," I answered immediately.

Reno whipped around to face me. "You counting the new Stingray? Split rear window, four-wheel independent suspension, retractable headlamps. The Stingray's awesome, man."

"Sorry, bro. XKE. Not even close."

"Okay, Sandra Dee or Natalie Wood?"

The light turned green and the Corvette shot ahead.

Suddenly I was bored. We had been playing this game since junior high. Liz Taylor or Ava Gardner? Platters or Coasters? Rincon or Malibu? Who gave a fuck?

"Reno," I said, "let's focus on the job, man. I don't want anything to go wrong."

CHAPTER 36

By the time we hit Beverly Hills, the summer heat had eased up. We cruised by Victor Dargin's house at 6:30 PM. The green Jag and the silver Rolls were both in the carport. At least we weren't too late. By 8:00 PM, if neither car had moved, I'd know the night was a bust. We parked part way down the block and waited.

At 6:45 PM, the Rolls backed out of the driveway. I slithered way down so that I'd be invisible from the street.

"Coming this way," reported Reno. "Male and female. Both Caucasian. Male driving."

I laughed. "You auditioning for *Dragnet*?"

"Fuck you, man." Reno poked my ribs.

A moment later, I heard the Rolls pass as it headed south towards Santa Monica Boulevard.

"All clear," Reno announced. "What now?"

I sat back up in a normal position.

"What's she wearing?"

"Jewelry, low-cut dress."

"Him?"

"Suit and tie. Squaresville."

"Great. They're probably going to that screening. Best case scenario: they're gone a couple of hours. Worst case: the maid's a live-in. Middle ground: the wife gets a headache or spills something on her dress or they're nutcases who get dressed up to go grocery shopping and they're back at any time."

Reno nodded. “Fifteen minutes,” he said. “Let’s go.”

We drove up the street and parked near Dargin’s house in a spot where my Falcon was screened from the neighbor’s view by a tall hedge. I gave Reno my extra ignition key and one of the transceivers. I put the other transceiver in my jacket pocket.

“You sure you don’t want me to get you inside?” Reno asked. “Not to rub it in, but you know I was always better at this shit than you.”

“I’m cool. Just keep out of sight.”

“Okay.”

Reno hopped out of the car and, in a flash, disappeared into the hedge. I walked to Dargin’s front door and rang the bell. Nobody answered. No voices, no footsteps. I waited extra long just to be sure.

A whitewashed brick wall extended from the left edge of the house, separating the front from the back yard. I walked along-side the wall, my back to the street. As I walked, I pulled the latex gloves out of my jacket pocket and put them on. I quickly scrambled over the wall and dropped onto the plush backyard lawn. Now I was invisible to the street. I unbuttoned my shirt and removed the metal strip from my waist band, relieved not to have ten inches of steel going up the side of my ribs.

I crouched down and turned on the transceiver.

“Reno,” I whispered. “You there?”

“Yeah, man. All good,” he whispered back. His voice came in scratchy but the words were clear enough. “Fourteen minutes.”

I put the transceiver back into my pocket, walked to the French doors, and tried the handle. No surprise that the door was locked. I looked through the glass. A second lock extended from the bottom of the door into a metal plate in the floor. Dargin was security conscious. I would be too if I had all the ritzy stuff he had. Being rich had a million benefits, but the downside was that lots of people with less wanted to get their hands on your stuff. If someone ripped me off, the only pawnable items they'd get was a primo Shure turntable and a couple of Altec speakers.

At the corner of the house was a door with a small inset window. I peered through the window into a laundry room with matching avocado-green washer and dryer. I slid the metal strip between the frame and the door jamb, then lowered it until it came to an abrupt halt against a deadbolt.

My last chance to get in through the back was the double-hung windows. I inserted the notched end of the metal strip into the spot where the top and bottom window frames met. I jiggled the strip around until the notch connected with the lock. Reno was right: he was always better at this than me. During our brief breaking-and-entering career, which had lasted part of one high school summer, this had been his job. My technique was passable but slow. With one hand, I held the frames together. With the other hand, I carefully jostled the metal strip until the lock unlatched. I opened the window and climbed through.

CHAPTER 37

I walked rapidly down the main hallway, head swiveling to ID each room: kitchen, dining room, living room, billiards. The final door off the hallway was closed but not locked. I went in.

Victor Dargin's office reeked of success: black leather chesterfield with bronze studding, mahogany bookcase filled with bound movie scripts, large mahogany desk. One wall was filled with framed photos. I swept over them quickly: Dargin with Walt Disney. Dargin with Gary Cooper. Dargin with Ronald and Nancy Reagan. Interesting, but I didn't have time for that now.

I tried opening the desk drawers. They were all locked except the shallow one at the top. Paperclips, stapler, rubber bands, matches. No keys.

I jogged up to the second floor. There were enough bedrooms up here to sleep the Kennedys. Only one room seemed lived-in. The king-sized bed was piled high with satin pillows. On one nightstand was an eye mask, a frosted-glass bottle of skin lotion, and a *Cosmopolitan* with Audrey Hepburn and Bill Holden on the cover. On the other nightstand was an alarm clock, a telephone, and a pair of reading glasses. I opened the drawer below the alarm clock. Inside was a cigar box filled with loose change and a key ring filled with keys.

I sprinted back down the stairs, unlocked the drawers in Dargin's desk, and went through each one. In the bottom drawer was a metal lock box with a standard hanging padlock. None of the keys on the key ring fit the lock, so I took a paperclip out of my pocket and broke it in half. I inserted one end of the half-clip into the lock, nudged it around until I felt the right tension. I inserted the other half and wiggled it until the padlock fell open.

Inside the lock box was a bound leather notebook sitting on top of a manila envelope. I opened the notebook and flipped through the pages. It contained a list of names — some I recognized, some I didn't. Next to each name were notations, letters and numbers. Some kind of code, I figured, which meant exactly nothing to me.

Inside the manila envelope were photographs: 8x10 black & white glossies, as well as a smaller white envelope containing strips of negatives. I shuffled through the photos. All were of Chip Jordan and Steve Sutton. Long shots. Medium shots. Close-ups. By the pool. In the pool. In the bedroom.

I locked up all the drawers, ran upstairs and tossed the key ring back into its cigar box, crawled out the back window, climbed over the whitewashed wall, and walked back to my car.

As I opened the driver's side door, Reno emerged from the hedge and slid into the passenger seat. I tossed Dargin's manila envelope and notebook onto the backseat. Then I started the engine and we cruised out of Beverly Hills.

CHAPTER 38

I sat down at my dinette table and I flipped through Dargin's notebook until I found Jordan, C. Following his name was a string of alphabet soup code. I closed the notebook and set the manila envelope and the notebook side by side on my dinette table. I stared at them for a while.

Then I went out onto the balcony and listened to the waves break on the beach. A police siren wailed in the distance. Victor Dargin had been blackmailing Chip Jordan. And I had an idea as to why.

My board leaned against the wall in the corner of the balcony, draped in a beach towel. I lifted the towel and ran my hand down the deck. The wax was uneven and starting to get gritty. The thought of scraping off the old wax and applying fresh base put me in a good mood. Out with the old, in with the new.

I went back inside, got a box of matches, and went into the bathroom. I placed the manila envelope on the shower floor. The tiles were old and cracked; most of the grout had worn away. A grayish-red mold was filling in for the grout, and nobody, not me, not the landlord, was about to fix it. I lit a match and tossed it onto the envelope. The match sizzled and went out. I touched a second match to the envelope's edge and held it there until the paper caught. I watched the paper burn. The acrid odor of burning photographic emulsion filled the room.

I watched until all that remained on the cracked shower tiles was a mound of black ash.

CHAPTER 39

"Got a book or something?"

"What for?" Joey asked.

We were standing at the Flynn's front door, Joey inside, me out. He was wearing a T-shirt, jeans, and sneakers. Ready to go.

I looked at Joey differently today. Before the whole gun situation, I figured he was just a kid at loose ends for the summer, doing his best to deal with a mother who drank too much and got herself into some scary trouble. Doing his best to protect her. Just a kid.

But now I wasn't sure: Was Joey just a kid, or had he gone over the edge?

What I did know was that Oscar Panozzo's killer was out there somewhere, maybe standing right here in front of me.

"Something to read while I work," I answered.

"I thought we were going fishing."

"We are. Later."

"Okay."

Joey went inside, returning in a few minutes with a Batman comic book and a paperback. We drove down his quiet tree-lined street, hung a right on Sunset. After a while, I glanced over at Joey who was looking out the window, his thumb idly flicking through the pages of the paperback. Just a kid? My job was to find out the truth. That's what a PI does, or is supposed to do. But me, Ryan, not the PI, was rooting for Joey to be innocent. Just a kid.

"You like to read?" I asked.

"Sometimes."

"Because this work thing might take a while."

"I don't mind. It's better than staying home alone all day."

"Don't you have other friends besides Nicholas?"

"They're all at camp or on trips. Where are we going?"

"Malibu."

"Why there?"

"I've got to talk to someone about a case."

Joey nodded. He read his Batman comic as we drove up Pacific Coast Highway.

***

Max Fisher answered the door wearing his trademark Bermuda shorts and sandals.

"Hi, Ryan." He nodded towards Joey. "So, who's your new partner?"

Joey looked at me, then at Max.

"Flynn," he said. "Joey Flynn."

"Ah, a Bond man." Max grinned. "Did you see *Dr. No*?"

Joey nodded.

"They've got another movie in the works, you know," Max said. "*From Russia with Love*."

"I read the book."

"Oh, you're a reader too. What do you have there?"

Joey handed Max his book.

"*The Phantom Tollbooth*. Never heard of it. What's it about?"

"A boy named Milo who finds a magical tollbooth and all these strange things start to happen like he finds a dog with an alarm clock built in," Joey gushed. "It's a watchdog. Get it?"

Max laughed. "I get it." He turned to me. "Where'd you find this kid, Ryan? He's sharp."

Joey beamed.

Max settled Joey out on the deck with a glass of milk and a piece of chocolate cake. Max and I went into the living room and I handed him Dargin's notebook.

"What do you make of this, Max?"

Max sat down on the couch and lit his pipe. He cocked his head to the side as he scanned the names and notations on the first page.

"Very interesting," he muttered. "Where'd you get this?"

"Victor Dargin."

"He know you have it?"

"I hope not."

"Then how . . . ?"

"Better if we skip the details." I said. "So what do you make of it? Other than some of the names, it's alphabet soup to me."

Max nodded. "Abbreviations. Look here."

He pressed the notebook open, ran his finger down the left side of a page.

"Obviously, this first column is a list of people" he said. "After each name, these are the initials for organizations, magazines, newspapers, meeting halls. I don't recognize them all, but enough to know what I'm looking at. Mostly organizations. Now, knowing that, look again. Recognize any?"

I leaned in closer and scanned the page.

"ACLU. American Civil Liberties Union?"

"There you go. The ACLU is still alive and kicking. A lot of these other groups, however, are defunct. CCLESL: Coordinating Committee to Lift the Embargo on the Spanish Loyalists. ACYR: American Committee for Yugoslav Relief. NNC: National Negro Congress. ALB: Abraham Lincoln Brigade. All progressive organizations."

"What about the people? Some I recognize, some I don't."

"A veritable roll call of Hollywood liberals and leftists. Let's see . . . Burrows, A is Abe Burrows. He wrote *Guys and Dolls*. LJC is Lee J. Cobb, terrific actor. *On The Waterfront, 12 Angry Men.* Hellman, L., is obviously the playwright Lillian Hellman. *Little Foxes, The Children's Hour.* Bernstein, L, is the great conductor and composer. Scott, H is . . . hmmm, I don't know this one. Whoever it is, she married Adam Clayton Powell and joined the NAACP."

"Could it be Hazel Scott?" I ventured. "The jazz pianist. She played on a couple of Count Basie records, even played with Bird. Then she just kinda disappeared."

"Hazel Scott! Of course. She had her own TV show for a minute — until she was accused of being a Red and they cancelled it."

Max ran his index finger beneath the notations that followed Hazel Scott's name. "Let's see . . . . NAACP, Café Society, dates, times. So: performing at an integrated nightclub. Very subversive!"

"What about all these dates and times?" I asked. "It's like someone was keeping track of everything she did. Man, I'd like to get that gig: following around celebrities to their nightclubs and meetings. Easy money."

"You wouldn't have to *literally* follow her to get most of this. Just follow her name in the papers."

"I don't think so," I countered. "Maybe some of it, but meeting times and dates? They don't print that stuff up anywhere."

"You're probably right," Max said as he flipped through the notebook pages. "Oh, this is rich!" he exclaimed suddenly. "Welles, O. FTP, HFWC, CCDMAY, HANL."

"Orson Welles. Is he a Red?"

"Nah. I don't think so. Just a fellow-traveler."

"I played pinball with him once."

"You played pinball with Orson Welles?"

"Yeah. He was shooting a movie in Venice near my house when I was in high school. They dressed up Windward Ave. to look like a Mexican town."

Max nodded. "*Touch of Evil.*"

"Right. My buddies and I used to hang out at this bar off Windward and play pinball. We were underage, but nobody gave a damn as long as we kept feeding in our dimes. Anyway, one night this big, fat man in a black overcoat walks in. He comes over to me and asks if I'd show him how to play pinball. So I did. He got really into it, until this nervous guy with a pencil behind his ear comes in and says to the fat guy, 'Mr. Welles, we're ready for your reverse.' He told the nervous guy to be patient and wait while he finished the game."

Max laughed. "Well, let's see what subversive activities Orson Welles has been up to. Besides playing pinball, that is."

He translated more alphabet soup. "Federal Theatre Project. Hollywood Free World Committee. Citizens' Committee for the Defense of Mexican American Youth. Hollywood Anti-Nazi League. Busy man."

"Those groups don't sound very subversive to me," I said.

"To some people, and Victor Dargin is one of them, cherry pie is subversive because it's red."

"Like when they changed the Cincinnati Reds to the Redlegs for a while. That was lame."

"Exactly."

"Max, a lot of what we do at Southland is surveillance, and it seems to me that it would take a whole army to follow all these people around and get this info on them."

"An army of spies," Max muttered. Suddenly, he laughed. "I'll bet old J. Edgar Hoover would have loved to sic his army of g-men on these people. It must gall Hoover that he's relegated to pursuing actual crime."

Max chuckled to himself as he re-lit his pipe. The smoky scent of apple and vanilla filled the room.

"However it is Dargin comes up with this information," Max said, "it's what he *does* with it that intrigues me most."

Just then, the glass slider opened and Joey came in. He was holding an empty plate.

"Hey, Joey," Max said. "Want some more cake?"

"No thank you."

"Want to do some sleuthing?"

"Yeah, sure!" Joey brightened.

"Max..." I warned him off with a tiny head shake.

"Okay. Okay." Max turned to Joey and winked. "We've got a tough boss."

"Stay out on the deck a while longer, okay?" I said. "I'll be done in a few minutes and then we'll go fishing."

"Okay," Joey said amiably. He went back outside.

"Good kid," Max said. "Who is he?"

"Former client's son."

"What's he doing with you?"

"It's complicated," I said in a way that closed the subject. Part of me wanted to discuss Joey and the whole complicated mess with Max — *or with Julie*, the thought floated through my mind; she seemed like someone who would be good at helping me figure things out — but, for starters, it wouldn't be fair to Joey. This was one of those things I'd have to figure out for myself.

Max picked up Dargin's notebook again and thumbed through it.

"Jordan, C." he said. "A little bird tells me that you might have a special interest in this listing."

"Yeah. I already checked it out."

"Want a translation?"

I nodded.

"Let's see... March, 1945, picketed Warner Brothers with Conference of Studio Unions. November, 1945, signed a letter supporting the American Committee for Yugoslav Review. 1948, signed a petition put out by the Committee for the First

Amendment. And, I would presume from what you've told me, this 'HS' stands for homosexual."

"Probably. Is that it?" I was hoping for more.

"Yup."

"That Warner Brothers picket line," I said, "isn't that where you told me you met Chip Jordan?"

"Yup."

"And you signed petitions, stuff like that also?"

"Yup."

"So, Max, why weren't you blacklisted?"

"What makes you think I wasn't?"

That stopped me. "Well, I . . . I just never . . . "

I looked around at the comfortable, spacious, light-filled living room we sat in. People who were kicked out of a job didn't live in Malibu, belong to a private beach club, and send their daughter to a private college back East. Besides, wasn't Max always working?

Max saw my confusion and laughed. "No, I wasn't blacklisted, thank goodness. But sometimes, especially back around '51, '52, we wondered about it. Work got a bit thin for a while. The plum jobs stopped coming my way. But it was nothing like what happened to others. I guess if they blacklisted every liberal and left-leaning writer in Hollywood, the motion picture business would come to a complete and utter halt."

I sensed movement, and looked up to see Joey standing at the sliding glass door, staring in. Max saw him also. He waved at Joey, then slapped Dargin's notebook with his palm.

"Ryan, whaddya say I hang on to this for a few days? Give me time to study it more thoroughly."

I hesitated. I didn't want the notebook out of my hands.

"What?" Max said with a chuckle. "You don't trust me? I'll put it under my pillow when I sleep."

CHAPTER 40

The iron grasshoppers were pumping away along Grand Canal. When I was a kid, there used to be hundreds of them all over Venice. The canal banks had been crammed with derricks, and storage tanks, and trolley cars taking workers to and from the oil fields. But the oil boom had passed, the sand sucked dry. The last derrick had been removed a couple of months ago. Now the last few remaining grasshoppers bobbed for the last few measly gallons of oil, stinking up the place, and keeping property values low.

Joey followed behind me on the crumbling concrete path which ran along Howland Canal. The concrete finally gave way completely and the path became a muddy track dotted with duck shit. When we got to Reno's house — it was actually an old run-down bungalow with no heat — we went around back to the shed where he kept his boards and fishing gear. I grabbed two poles and the metal tackle box, handed the box to Joey. In the main house, I took out a package of Velveeta cheese from the fridge, peeled off a few slices for bait.

We walked single file along the canals until we got to the Dell Street bridge which arched over Carroll Canal. We stationed ourselves at the top of the arch.

"This was my favorite fishing spot growing up," I said. "We used to catch mullet, goby, even perch. I hope they're still swimming around down there."

I handed Joey one of the poles and a piece of cheese. He eyed the cheese with suspicion.

"Fish eat cheese?"

"Sure. If they don't have anything better."

Joey leaned over the bridge railing and scrutinized the dark, sludgy water.

"It looks dirty," he said.

"It is. But the fish don't know the difference."

I stuck the cheese on Joey's line. He looked at me skeptically, then back down into the water. A crumpled Marlboro package tangled up in a clump of bird feathers and fishing line floated by.

"The water might be poisoned," Joey said. "So the fish would be too."

"Hey, we used to catch fish right here and eat 'em for dinner all the time. You don't see me dead do you?"

I dropped my line into the water. Joey watched me closely, then dropped in his line next to mine. He stared after it.

"I don't see any fish down there," he said.

Suddenly it struck me. "You ever fished before?"

Joey shrugged. "No."

"There's fish down there, it just takes them a while to bite. Fishing's all about waiting."

I showed Joey how to reel in his line. He practiced a few times. Then we waited. After a while, two boys on a wooden raft came paddling up the canal towards us. They had a German Shepherd with them who darted back and forth across the raft, barking at the ducks. The boys were both shirtless and barefoot. One was Negro, the other was white. They waved at us and I waved back. Joey just watched until the raft disappeared under the bridge.

"Are those boys poor?" he asked.

"I don't know. Maybe."

"Were you poor growing up?"

"We did okay. Why are you asking that?"

"Eating the fish you caught. Mr. Ackerman says fish is for poor people. Fish and casseroles."

"Lots of people eat fish. And casseroles."

"The Ackermans don't."

We both gazed into the water, looking at nothing in particular.

"If we were poor," I said after a while, "I didn't know it at the time."

"Why not?"

"Probably because everybody around us was pretty much the same. If you don't know any rich people how do you know if you're poor? What do you compare it with?"

"TV."

"We didn't have a television."

"You were definitely poor."

I laughed. "Different times, Joey. Like I said, we did okay."

"My mom worries about money."

I nodded. "Her and half the world."

"Do you?"

"Nope."

"Why not?"

"Well, I've got a job and a car and an apartment. And enough money to take a girl out. I figure anything beyond that is icing on the cake."

"I wish my mom thought that way."

"Yeah, worrying sucks."

Joey stared down into the water. A shadow passed across his face.

"I lied about something the other day," he said without looking at me.

"What about?"

"The gun." He paused for a moment. "I did shoot it."

I waited, but that was all he said.

"What'd you shoot at?" I asked.

"Nothing."

"Nothing? Nobody shoots at nothing."

"A pile of dirt. Down in the canyon. I didn't want to hit any birds or squirrels or anything, so I mounded up some dirt and shot into it."

I thought about that: A kid who takes care not to hurt animals with an stray bullet didn't seem like the same kid who would kill a man resembling an ice cream cone. Then again, Hitler liked dogs, so what did I really know.

"I wanted to practice," Joey said. "In case I ever had to use it."

"Did you have to use it?

He shook his head.

"You never fired it another time?"

He shook his head again.

"So why'd you lie about firing it when I asked you before?"

Joey shrugged. "I dunno."

I waited, but that was all the kid wanted to say. I reeled in my line to be sure I still had bait, replaced the soggy cheese with a fresh piece. Joey watched me and did the same thing. We dropped our lines back into the water.

A few hours later we called it a day. Neither of us had caught anything, and I had a feeling Joey didn't mind that at all. After returning Reno's fishing gear, ate tacos at La Cabana, a new Mexican joint on Lincoln and Rose with irritating mariachi music, but good food at the right price. I was stalling for time, hoping Joey's mother would be home before I dropped him off.

It was dark by the time we got back to the Palisades. As we pulled to the curb in front of his house, Joey's eyes got big. A Ford pick-up was parked in the driveway.

"Hey!" he said, as he yanked on the car door handle. "That's my dad's truck!"

Joey pushed open the door and was about to jump out when I grabbed him by the back of his shirt collar and held on like a mother cat gripping a kitten by the scruff of its neck.

Joey tried to shake loose. "Let go! My dad's here!"

"I know, but just hold on. I'm gonna check it out. Weird things have been happening around here lately. Stay in the car until I come out to get you."

Joey grumbled, but he stayed in the car.

I got my .38 out of the glove compartment and walked up the stone path to the house. The door was unlocked. I opened it a few inches. The house was completely dark inside, not a single light on.

"Flynn?"

No answer.

I reached around the edge of the door, felt around on the wall for the light switch, and turned it on. Down into the sunken living room, was a man stretched out on his back on the floor. I went down the three steps to the living room and bent over the unmoving body of Doc Flynn.

"Flynn?"

His eyes popped open and he grinned at me.

"Present and accounted for."

"What are you doing here, man?"

"Here? Doing? Deep question. So many levels to the answer. Well, I... goddammit, is it even possible for a person to speak without using the word 'I' or 'me'?"

"I just —"

"See what I mean. Practically impossible. At least in English. Do all languages rely so heavily on 'I'? Now that's a question worth researching. How can we ever hope to break out of the illusion of 'I', if we can't communicate without using it? Speech — no, thought itself — divides the world, doesn't it? Forces us to divide, commands us by its very nature to lose track of the whole, to live in the world of illusion. And the first division is I versus YOU."

"Mr. Flynn, why are all the lights off?"

"Another interesting, and essentially unanswerable, question. Oh sure, we make up answers all the time and believe they are the truth. Joke's on us."

I looked at him and said nothing. He grinned.

"Where's Mrs. Flynn?" I asked.

"I don't know. I could make up an answer, take a good guess, but I haven't seen her. Today. Which is what I think you are referring to. Today, Mrs. Flynn has so far been unseen. By me. The unseen."

Flynn touched a finger to the middle of his forehead. At that moment the front door swung open and Joey came bounding down the steps into the living room.

"Dad!"

"Hi, son."

"What are you doing here?"

"What am I doing here? Well, here, now, I am apparently sitting on the floor conversing with you about why I am here."

"Seriously, Dad."

Doc Flynn took a moment before answering.

"Okay. Seriously. Since your mother's been so busy, I thought you might like to hang out with your old man for a couple of days."

"That's great! I went fishing today with Ryan."

"You know what the Chinese say about fishing?" Doc Flynn said.

Joey shook his head.

"Give a man a fish, and he eats for a day. Teach a man to fish, and he eats for a lifetime."

"Well," Joey said, "we didn't catch anything so I guess we won't be eating for a day or for a lifetime."

"You're so literal."

"It was a joke, Dad."

Doc Flynn grinned. "You got me there, kid."

Watching Joey and his father interact, a feeling of relief came over me. I didn't need to be here anymore. I started for the door.

"I'm gonna split," I said.

"Just a sec." Flynn reached for something on the coffee table. "This is for you."

He stood up and held out a book. *Doors of Perception* by Aldous Huxley.

"If the doors of perception were cleansed," he recited, eyes closed, "every thing would appear to man as it is, Infinite. For man has closed himself up, till he sees all things thro' narrow chinks of his cavern."

Flynn opened his eyes and grinned. "That's Flynn quoting Huxley who was quoting Blake."

He handed me the book.

"Thanks" I said. "I'll read it."

"I appreciate you hanging out with my kid."

"Yeah," Joey added. "And thanks for the tacos and fishing."

"My pleasure," I said. And meant it.

As I walked towards the door, I heard Joey ask earnestly: "What does it mean, Dad? The doors and the caverns and all that?"

"It means ... well, let's figure it out together," Doc Flynn said. " 'If the doors of perception were cleansed ...' "

I closed the door behind me and went out into the night.

CHAPTER 41

I drove to the office feeling pretty good about myself: Blackmail photos found and destroyed. (At least the source photos, that is. If Panozzo had made more copies, they were still far from my grasp.) Joey hanging out with his father. And me more certain than ever that the kid had nothing to do with Panozzo's murder. Of course, I still needed the facts, still needed to get my hands on Panozzo's ballistics report to see what those facts had to say in the matter.

But there was nothing more I could do about that tonight, so I figured I'd go through the mail, pay bills, then call it a night.

Or so I thought.

Half an hour later, just as I was finishing with the mail, a white Savoy pulled up in front. Detective Terekov got out of the car and strolled into the office. He tossed my .38 Special onto the desk.

"You called?" he said.

I put the mail down. "I need a favor."

"Don't we all."

"The piece that killed Panozzo, what was it?"

Terekov raised an eyebrow. "Why do you care?"

"Come on, Detective. Throw me a bone."

"I just might." He squinted. "So, bone for bone, Ryan, what were you doing over at Panozzo's place yesterday, with the sister and the nancy boy?"

"Client business. Confidential. I'd tell you if I could. What about the gun?"

"Police business. Confidential."

I sighed. "Can't we somehow work together on this, Detective? We both want the same thing."

"What's that?"

"Catch the killer. Justice served."

"Do I look like an idiot, Ryan? You were nosing around Panozzo before he got got. What's your interest in all this?"

I didn't answer right away. We were at a stalemate. I'd have to give something to get something.

"It's a blackmail case," I said. "Don't ask me how Panozzo's murder fits in because I'm not exactly sure. Not yet at least."

"Was Panozzo the mark?"

I held up my hands, as in 'that's all I know.'

Terekov sighed and scratched his head. He pulled a notebook out of his coat pocket and flipped it open. He thumbed through the pages until he found what he was looking for.

"Panozzo took three .357s to the head and upper torso. One round went through the left eye socket and lodged in his brain. Another severed an artery near his heart. Got a latent from the top of the toilet seat which was a match for Panozzo's shoe. Only matches around the back window were from Panozzo as well. Perp probably entered and exited through the front door. No witnesses interviewed saw or heard a thing."

He flipped the notebook shut. "There's your bone."

"Thanks," I said. "I mean it."

And I did mean it. More than Detective Terekov would ever know. A .357. That's all I had to hear. Joey was off the hook. If an inquisitive, persistent police detective wasn't standing four feet away, waiting for me to toss him a bone, I would have felt completely happy. Happy and relieved. And a bit embarrassed for having suspected Joey at all. Eleven-year-olds don't kill grown men, except in a lousy B movie, or if they are totally psycho, or in that *Twilight Zone* about a little red-headed kid played by Bill Mumy who kills people. But in real life? It was absurd.

Suddenly, I laughed out loud. I was laughing at the absurdity, and I was laughing at myself. Mostly I was laughing from relief.

"What's so funny?" Terekov asked.

"Nothing," I said. "Life, I guess."

The detective shrugged. "If you say so."

We were silent a minute. The red neon Bail Bonds sign blinked on and off in the dark night.

"Here's another bone," Terekov said. "I'm off the case."

"Why?" I was completely surprised. "What happened?"

"Captain told us to drop it, end of story, don't ask questions, move on to the next stiff."

"They're letting Panozzo's killer just walk?"

"Sure. Why not? To the brass, he's just another pansy got his lights punched on the early side. They're calling it a robbery-homicide."

"But you don't think so," I said.

"Nope. And neither do you."

"So, what do you think it is?"

Terekov took his time before answering. "I think a corpse is a corpse. I don't give a damn if it's a Hollywood fruit or John D. Fuckin' Rockefeller, a two-bit hooker or Doris Day. They all deserve the same. Panozzo? I think he got the stinkin' end of a stinkin' stick."

"Who called off the investigation?"

"Like I said, the Captain just told us to drop it."

"Wouldn't that have to come from higher up?"

Terekov squinted at me. "What do you care?"

"I'm just asking."

"Like hell you are."

I got out my spiral notebook and searched through it until I found the license plate number of the car at Victor Dargin's

McArthur Park meet-up. I copied the plate number onto a blank page, tore out the page, and handed it to Terekov.

"My bone," I said. "It might be connected to Panozzo."

"I just told you I'm off the case."

I shrugged. Terekov shook his head, shot me a wry half-smile, and shoved the paper into his coat pocket.

I drove home thinking about the cops pulling the plug on the Panozzo investigation. I guess Niles was right: Oscar Panozzo just wasn't worth the trouble. Or was it something else? What was the real reason the cops pulled the plug? Another piece of the puzzle to log in my brain. Another piece of the puzzle which might or might not be important.

I parked in the alley and headed up the rickety steps to my apartment.

I was halfway up the stairs when I saw it.

It was on the doormat. White. Flat. Coiled in a semi-circle like a snake.

CHAPTER 42

I picked up the coiled white object and uncurled a small plastic sleeve. Inside the clear plastic was a strip of paper. Typed onto the paper was LOUIS ZORN, followed by a long number. In small print at the bottom: Vet. Admin., Los Angeles, Cal.

My muscles tightened. My breathing got shallow. Fear shot through my body. I rushed into my apartment clutching the plastic wristband and dialed the VA.

"This is Ryan Zorn," I said to the nurse on Lou's floor. I tried to slow my breathing and sound calm. "I'm calling about my uncle, Lou Zorn. How is he?"

"He's fine," the nurse said. "Sleeping, the last time I checked."

"Could you please go and check on him again?"

There was a pause and a rustling of paper.

"I'm looking at Mr. Zorn's chart" she said. "His vitals have been stable all day. He didn't eat much, but that's not unusual for his condition. There's really no need for concern."

"Please. Just go into his room and check. Right now."

"This minute?"

"Yes, m'am."

There was a long pause.

"Is something wrong?"

"I hope not. And could you check if he's wearing his patient ID wristband?"

"Of course he's wearing his wristband. We never take it off. Not even for bathing. That's why it's plastic."

"Please," I practically begged, "just check."

"Alright," the nurse said. "Hold the line, please."

It seemed to take forever until she returned. When she did, her voice had changed.

"Mr. Zorn?"

"Yes."

"Your uncle is fine, no need to worry. However, I...I don't understand how this could have happened, but his identification bracelet does appear to be missing. Do you know anything about this?"

"Maybe. I'll be right over."

When I got to Lou's floor, I noticed a cluster of white-uniformed nurses conferring in whispered voices behind the counter, back near the filing cabinets. One of the nurses caught my eye and separated from the huddle.

"May I help you?"

She was cute and petite. Her blonde hair was pixie cut and she had large green eyes. The tag pinned to her uniform said *Beth*.

"I just called about Lou Zorn. I'm his nephew. Can I go in?"

"Of course. But please let him rest."

Lou was sleeping. The oxygen tank next to his bed was breathing faithfully. A vase filled with a flowers sat on the windowsill. Lou's face seemed thinner and paler than the last time I visited. Was that only a few days ago? On his left wrist was a new ID band. The door opened behind me. It was nurse Beth. She motioned me into the hallway.

"What do you know about Mr. Zorn's wristband?" she asked. She spoke quietly and calmly, but I sensed anxiety in her voice.

"Are you the nurse I spoke with on the phone?" I asked.

"Yes. We're quite concerned about this situation. We can't understand what happened."

"Somebody cut it off."

I took the curled plastic strip out of my pocket. "I found this on my doormat."

"Doormat?"

"At my apartment. Were you on duty all day?"

"No. I'm on swing. Two to ten."

"Did anyone visit my uncle today?"

"I checked the log after you called. Your mother came this morning, but that was before my shift. Since then, only the man who delivered the flowers you ordered."

"Flowers I ordered?"

"Yes, they're lovely. I know your uncle will appreciate them when he wakes up. He's been sleeping most of the evening."

"I didn't order any flowers."

"But the delivery man … and the note … "

I rocketed back into Lou's room and bee-lined for the flowers, nurse Beth following. I hadn't paid attention to the flowers before. Now I saw the card, half hidden in the greenery. It was a small card, the kind that comes from a florist shop, with pale purple flowers imprinted in one corner. Handwritten on the card, in neat, simple script, were the words *Thinking of you, Ryan.*

I pocketed the card. Beth followed me back out to the hall.

"Beth, do you know which florist delivered the flowers?"

"No."

"What about the delivery man? Did he wear a uniform?"

"I … I don't think so."

"You saw him, right?"

"Only briefly. We were very busy this evening. I gave him your uncle's room number and he took the bouquet in himself."

"If you could think for a moment about the uniform. It would be really helpful if you could remember which florist."

"I truly didn't … Wait. May I see the card, please?"

I handed it to her. She examined it and nodded.

"Heaven Scent. I've seen these cards on other deliveries. Sometimes patients ask us to read them aloud."

"That's great, Beth. Heaven Scent. Thanks."

"I don't understand what these flowers have to do with your uncle's wristband."

"You said Heaven Scent has delivered here before."

"That's right. They're just down the street."

"Do they have a regular delivery guy? Someone you might recognize?

"Well…" she thought for a few seconds, then shook her head. "I'm sorry, but I really don't know," she apologized.

"That's alright. What about the delivery man today? Do you remember what he looked like? Maybe what he wore. Just think about it for a minute, try to picture him."

She closed her eyes and crunched up her face. "He was carrying the flowers… a large bouquet… that's funny." She opened her eyes and looked at me.

"What?"

"He was dressed in a suit."

I nodded. "Okay. What else do you remember? Was he tall, short…?"

"I'm five-two," Beth said with a smile. "Everyone's tall to me."

"Right. Bad question. What about his hair? Light, dark…?"

"Honestly, I don't remember. I think he had dark hair. Brown or black. But I'm not sure."

"Thanks. You've been really helpful, Beth."

"I hope so. We're extremely concerned about this."

"Me too."

I thought for a moment, considering what to do next.

"Listen Beth, I have to go. I'll be back, but I'm not sure when. Can someone keep an eye on my uncle's room until I get back? I mean, basically, guard it. I want to be sure no visitor, no delivery person, nobody gets into his room. Except me or my mother. Is that possible? Does the hospital have some kind of security?"

"We don't have anything like that. At least not that I know of. I suppose I could talk with my floor supervisor about it, though, given the situation."

"Never mind. Look, would you do me a big favor and stay right here and watch the room for a few minutes? I'll be back in five minutes."

She glanced at her watch. "I've still got patient rounds before my shift ends."

"Five minutes. Tops. I promise."

"Okay," she said. "I'll wait."

I jogged down the stairs to the ground floor, found a pay phone in the lobby, and dialed Reno at home. My fingers were crossed that he wasn't out on a date. He picked up on the second ring.

"Hey, Reno, it's me. Can you get over to the Westwood VA? I need you pronto, man. Paying job."

"What's going on?"

"It's Lou. Kind of an emergency.

"Lou? Is he okay?"

"Yeah, I'll tell you about it when you get here. VA hospital, second floor."

"I'll be there."

Next, I called Victor Dargin and told him I was on my way over. I hung up before he could reply. I raced back upstairs, thanked nurse Beth for helping me out, and waited outside Lou's room until Reno arrived.

CHAPTER 43

The porch light was on. As I raised my fist to knock, the door opened and Victor Dargin stepped out. He was impeccably attired in his smoking jacket and a maroon silk pocket scarf, but a five o'clock shadow roughed up his jaw.

"Hey, motherfucker," I hissed. "Stop fucking with my family."

Dargin cracked the one-sided smile of a man who enjoys a fight.

"Away from the house," he said. "Don't want to disturb the wife."

I followed Dargin across the front yard to the open garage. The light of the moon glinted off the silver Rolls.

"So buddy boy, I see you got my message."

"What do you want?"

"Ah! You *are* as dumb as you look," he smirked.

"What do you want?" I repeated.

"You stole my property. I want it back."

"Something's stolen, report it to the cops."

"Let's cut the crap. I'm not going to the cops because this is a private matter and I want to keep it that way. You're not going because you're a thief. So, moving on: I'm a reasonable man. I have no beef with you. As far as I'm concerned, you don't even exist. I simply want my property back."

"What do I get in return?"

"My word."

"Of what?"

"That we never met. I don't know you or your family. And that pansy Sutton gets a free pass. I never gave a shit about him in the first place. He was just... there."

Dargin plucked a cigar from his jacket pocket. He clicked on a butane lighter and slowly rotated the foot of the cigar around the flame.

"How did you know where my uncle is?" I said.

"Connections."

"What connections?"

"None of your fucking business. When you've been around this town like I've been, you have them. Which reminds me, you can call off your man. He's a lousy tail anyway."

"What?"

"You know what I'm talking about."

"You're nuts, man.."

"Fuck you, buddy boy. You giving me back my property or not? I made you an offer, now take it or leave it."

I decided to let Dargin wait a while before I answered. He had me pegged as a fool. That gave me an advantage — so long as I actually wasn't one. If he thought I was dumb enough to make a deal based on the word of a blackmailer, good for him.

Dargin turned the lit end of the cigar towards his mouth and gently blew on it. The fat orange ember glowed brighter. He was working really hard at effecting the pose of a guy who was relaxed, in control, not a care in the world except enjoying the aroma of his cigar in the middle of the night.

"Okay," I said, "I'll take it."

"Smart move. Now let's you and I go retrieve my property."

"I don't have it."

"The hell you don't."

"No, seriously. It's stashed somewhere. I'll get it for you tomorrow."

“No deal. My offer runs out tonight. Let’s be smart and put this behind us.”

I almost smiled. This was getting better and better. The more Dargin condescended to me, the bigger advantage I had.

I looked at my watch.

“Okay,” I said. “I’ll meet you in the parking lot by the Lick Pier at 2:00 AM. That’s the soonest I can get there.”

“Lick Pier?”

“In Venice. At the ocean end of Rose, just south of P-O-P. It’ll be empty and private. And it won’t disturb your wife.”

“I’m not going to the goddamn beach in the middle of the night.”

“You want your stuff, be there.”

CHAPTER 44

I drove to the office and dialed the LAPD Hollywood station.

"You're in luck," Detective Terekov said when he came on the line. "I'm pulling a double tonight. What's your excuse for working this late?"

"I was wondering if you had a chance to run that plate yet."

"You only gave it to me a couple of hours ago."

Something in his tone told me to pursue it anyway. "Did you run it?"

There was a long silence before he answered. "Ryan, some advice. You won't take it, but I've got to give it: Drop the Panozzo case. Whatever your angle is, I guarantee it isn't worth it."

"I thought you were glad I was on it. Considering."

"Yeah, well I changed my mind."

"Why?"

"Let's just say I saw the light. Some battles are worth fighting. This one isn't."

"I appreciate your advice, Detective, but I need to see this thing through to the end."

Terekov sighed. "Just like Lou."

"So, for Lou then. The plates."

"Let it go. I'm saying this for your own good."

"I believe it, but I'm meeting a guy tonight and it would help if I could get a better handle on him and what he's up to."

"Who's this you're meeting?"

"Movie big shot. Victor Dargin."

Terekov sighed again. "Want another piece of advice?"

"Sure."

"Don't."

"Why not? Do you know something that I should know, Detective?"

"Just what I said already."

"I need to do this."

"When you really think about it, Ryan, there's very little we *need* to do in this life."

"Yeah, I know the line: Death and taxes."

"Who said anything about taxes?"

After we hung up, I switched off the lights and sat in the dark for a while. I watched the red neon Bail Bonds sign blink on and off. I had to get moving to make my 2:00 AM meet-up with Dargin, but I wanted to think it all through first. Tonight was not a night I could afford to make any rookie mistakes.

I called Max Fisher. The phone rang and rang and rang. Finally, someone picked up.

"My dad's sleeping, Ryan," Allison said. "It's after midnight."

"Could you get him anyway? It's important. A case he's helping me with."

"Wow, you're really working hard these days."

"Yeah."

"I respect that. You know, it used to bother me that you didn't seem to care about work, about making something of yourself."

"That was a long time ago."

"Not that long. Why the change?"

"Necessity, I guess. With Lou down for the count and all. Listen, Allison, I can't really talk now. I'm jammed for time."

She ignored me. "My dad says you're working on an interesting case. With historical implications. Maybe we can get together for dinner sometime, just you and me, and you can tell me about it."

"Yeah, sure," I said vaguely. "Could you get Max now? It's a time thing."

Silence. Then, coldly: "I'll get him."

***

I drove the deserted coast highway out to Malibu. For the first time in a long time, I wasn't looking forward to seeing Allison at Chez Fisher. As a matter of fact, I hoped she had gone back to sleep.

"Hi, Ryan."

Allison stood in the doorway. Her long blond hair glowed around the edges from the light behind her. She was wearing only an oversized men's blue Pendleton shirt. The top buttons were undone. The tails hung about half-way down her smooth, tanned thighs.

She noticed me checking her out. It would be hard not to.

"Look familiar?" Allison said with a sexy smile.

"That's my shirt."

She nodded. "I kept it. I always loved this shirt."

I didn't know what to do or say. For so long I had secretly hoped to get back with Allison. I told myself a thousand times it was never going to happen. I told myself a thousand times to forget about her. Now, suddenly, I had a chance. Right this minute. All I had to do was take one step . . . kiss her . . .

"Oh," Allison said, "Max asked me to give you this."

She held out Victor Dargin notebook. I hadn't noticed that she was holding it. I guess I wasn't looking at her hands. I took the notebook.

And just like that, the spell was broken.

"Thanks," I said. I looked at my watch. "Well, I gotta go."

"What's wrong, Ryan? You seem so distant."

"It's the job. I've got to be someplace. I've got a lot on my mind."

"I understand." She smiled that sexy smile again. "There's always later."

I shook my head. "I don't think so. I think our time has passed."

Allison's smile disappeared. She looked genuinely hurt. Immediately, I wanted to soften the blow.

"I mean, like you've said yourself, our lives are different now. And you're going to Paris—"

"Or Mississippi," she interjected.

"Right. Or Mississippi. So really, there's no point in trying to start something anyway."

Allison stood there and looked at me intently. "Are you seeing someone else?"

"No," I said immediately. "It's not that at all."

I thought to myself: *Or is it? If I hadn't met Julie, would I have jumped at another chance to be with Allison?* That was something I'd never truly know. Because I had met Julie. I had met someone who was as intelligent and as beautiful as Allison, someone who, when I was honest with myself, I had more in common than with Allison. Someone I wouldn't forever be wondering if she thought she was better than me or not.

We stood there for a while longer, not saying anything. Allison tossed back her hair.

"Let's talk about it later," she said. "We could sneak into the club and swim in the pool late at night when nobody else is around. Like we used to."

CHAPTER 45

The Lick Pier parking lot sucked up the moonlight, making it even darker than the inky sea just beyond it. Someone had smashed all the streetlights up on their high concrete poles long ago, and the city had never bothered to fix them. All part of the downward slide in this no-man's land between Santa Monica and Venice.

I made a wide looping U across the buckled blacktop, and parked at the back edge of the lot. My windshield faced the Boardwalk, rear tires touching the sand. I looked at my watch. A quarter to two. I had swung by my apartment on the way here and still made it in time.

Now I surveyed the area. The Boardwalk was deserted. The liquor store and the pawn shop were both closed up for the night. The only other car in the lot was a rusted-out Chevy Impala with flat tires that looked like it hadn't moved in months. To my left, at the foot of the pier, was the Aragon Ballroom. Once home to Lawrence Welk and his Champagne Music, the Aragon now sat shuttered and decaying. Broken windows, graffitied walls, fragments of glass and plaster littering the ground around the abandoned monolith. A lonely K, last remains of *Welk*, was still affixed to the marquee.

When I was a kid, the Aragon was packed and bustling. On weekends, squares from all over L.A. came to dance to Welk's good-timey polkas and waltzes in the immense chandeliered ballroom. My buddies and I sometimes hung around outside, gawking at the fancy cars and tuxedoed musicians. Eventually some broadcasting genius turned the scene into a TV show. "*And now, direct from the Aragon Ballroom in Pacific Ocean Park, here is your host, the music maker himself....*" The TV show included a machine that spewed soap bubbles across the screen when the band played its cheesy numbers. The program was such a huge hit that they moved it over to the Hollywood Pavilion. That's when the Aragon closed its doors. And they stayed shut ever since.

I rolled down the window and listened to the waves break beneath the pier. In the distance I heard the clatter-click-clatter-click of the rollercoaster over at Pacific Ocean Park. P-O-P was Santa Monica's answer to Disneyland — a nautical-themed amusement park with rides like the Mystery Island Banana Train, Davy Jones' Locker and Mr. Octopus. The park closed at 10:00 PM, so the clatter-click must have been the maintenance crew working through the night.

After a while, the rollercoaster stopped. I listened as the surf battered away at the wood pilings under the pier. Eventually, I thought, the ocean will win. One day, none of this will be here. The pier, the Aragon, the rollercoaster, the pawn shop and the liquor store, and the Boardwalk itself will all be swallowed up by the sea.

At 2:00 AM sharp, Dargin's green Jag pulled into the parking lot. The Jag cruised slowly towards my car. It stopped about ten yards away, and Victor Dargin stepped out. I got out of my car and waited by the driver's side door.

"Nice spot you've got here," Dargin sneered when he reached my car. "I'll bet it really sparkles in the sunlight."

"I'm gonna pat you down," I said.

"What is this, some kind of surfer boy's *High Noon* meets *Asphalt Jungle* fantasy? I don't carry a gun. I'm a movie producer, not a gangster."

I patted him down. When I finished, Dargin took his time adjusting his suit jacket and getting the crease in his pant legs just right.

"So where's my property, buddy boy?"

"In the car."

"Get it."

I opened the rear door to the Falcon, reached onto the backseat, and brought out Dargin's notebook and manila envelope. I gave him the envelope. As soon as he had it in his hand, he frowned. He opened the envelope and looked inside.

"What the —!?"

He turned the envelope upside down. A stream of ash cascaded onto the ground.

"Is this your idea of a joke? Where are my photos?"

"You're looking at 'em."

Dargin stood there for a moment. He stared down at the pile of ash, then back up at me.

"Why you no good ... "

He took a step towards me. I took a step back. My shoe crunched over broken glass.

Dargin stopped. He stared at me hard, his face contorting with anger. But he didn't take another step.

"Why?" he grunted.

"Because Steve Sutton's my client and that's what he would have wanted me to do."

Dargin shook his head in disgust. "Fuck you. Just give me the notebook."

"Not until I'm totally sure there's no more of these photos ... anywhere."

"You destroyed the negatives didn't you?"

"Yup."

"So what more do you want?"

"The photographer. I don't figure it was you shimmying up a tree in the Hollywood Hills with a long-lens Nikon. Who took the photos of Jordan and Sutton?"

"That's not your concern."

"It is if that person has copies."

"Look, let me simplify things for you: Nobody gives a damn about Steve Sutton. Nobody does, nobody ever did. He was just... hmmm, how do I say it... a civilian casualty."

"You make it sound like a war."

"For Christ's sake!" Dargin snapped. "Are you truly that ignorant? Of course there's a war. Call it the Cold War, call it anything you want, but if it weren't for patriotic people like me fighting it, our country would be overrun by the Russians by now. Or the Red Chinese. But maybe you like the idea of some slanty-eyed chink dictator in grey overalls running our country. No more free enterprise. No more democracy. No more freedom."

"I don't see the free in taking pictures of a homosexual and blackmailing him to snitch out his friends to HUAC."

"So this is what it's come to," Dargin sneered. "An ignoramus PI giving *me* a lecture on freedom."

I liked Dargin calling me an ignoramus. The stupider he thought I was, the more he'd talk. Also, it gave me a chance to say some things that had been building up inside. Maybe it was getting to know Julie and Niles, maybe it was learning from Max about the blacklist and what it did to people, maybe it was everything put together, but I didn't feel like giving Dargin and his bigoted, fearful opinions a free ride. Not tonight.

"I don't see how our country is any freer with Chip Jordan in his grave," I said.

"Don't you fucking pin that on me, buddy boy. He made that decision himself."

"He was pushed."

"Jordan cozied up to the Reds when it suited him, took their acting classes, starred in their pictures, walked their Commie picket lines. When truth-time came, he couldn't take his lumps like a man."

"What truth?"

"That he's a fruit. A pinko faggot."

"Who took the photos?"

Dargin shook his head. "Ancient history. Just give me the notebook."

I held up his notebook and tapped it. "And who followed these people around? Where'd all this blackmail stuff come from?"

"Blackmail? You toss that word around like you know what it means. Blackmail's that fruit Panozzo trying to make a few bucks off something he had no business having in the first place. What I did wasn't for money, it wasn't for personal gain. Far from it. If I was selfish, just looking out for number one, I would have said no when my government called. I would have simply minded my own business, taken the easy route, cashed my fat pay check and bought the wife another mink. Someday you'll thank me, and people like me, who stood up for our country when the Communists were threatening to take over. We drew a line in Hollywood. We said, 'If you're a Commie, you're not welcome here.' It sent a message to the entire country. I'm proud of what we did."

"As far as I can see, what you're proud of is sending out your spies to get information on people you disagreed with, so you could get them fired from their jobs."

"My spies?!" Dargin laughed. "I should be so lucky! What do you think, that I dispatched an army of studio gofers to run around the country on their lunch break?"

I shrugged. "So who did follow them? Who took the photos?"

"One thing I'll give you," Dargin chucked, "you're persistent."

I waited. He said nothing. The waves kept rolling up onto the sand and ebbing back to sea.

"What about the notebook?" I said. "The blacklist's over, so why are you still compiling notes on people? Right up into this year."

"You never know when the studios may once again feel the need to weed out subversives."

"Like Orson Welles?" I said sarcastically. "Or Hazel Scott? Big subversives."

Dargin rolled his eyes. "Obviously, I'm wasting my breath, but for your information, Mr. Welles is about as dangerous as you can get. Under the guise of so-called 'film,' he's spewing propaganda against our capitalist system. And Miss Scott? A covert Communist if I ever saw one. Now, just give me my property so we can call it a night. Your client has nothing to worry about. The photos are ash, and even if they weren't, nobody gives a fuck about pansy-boy Sutton. He's a nothing. A nobody. A worthless faggot who —"

Out of the corner of my eye, I saw something move. It was by the Aragon Ballroom, at the corner of the building, where the pier meets the sand. I turned towards the movement. A dark figure was rising up, emerging like a monster from the sea, now running, flopping overcoat, one arm pointed forward. A white flash emanated from the running figure. And a popping sound.

I dropped to the ground and dove under my car. I grabbed the .38 from my waistband, then came up into a crouch behind the open rear door.

Another flash of white and another pop. Victor Dargin screamed. He skittered back a few steps, his eyes and his mouth wide open.

The shooter was almost on us. His bone white hair caught the moonlight.

"Leon! No!" I shouted.

He shot again. Victor Dargin crumpled to the ground. He started dragging himself towards my car. Leon came to a stop and held his gun steady, aiming directly at Dargin's torso.

"Put the gun down, Leon," I said. "Put it down."

He shot again. Victor Dargin stopped crawling. A split second later, I shot back. I wasn't a sharp shooter, didn't trust myself to knock the gun out of Leon's hand like they do in the movies, so I shot low.

Leon let out a yelp. He bent down and grabbed his leg. His other leg buckled and he dropped to the blacktop. He sat on the ground, holding his injured leg. He looked at me in astonishment.

"Why'd you do that?" he said. "I wouldn't hurt you."

"Leon, are you crazy? You can't go shooting people like that. Killing people."

"He was bad."

I didn't say anything. I was listening to the sirens in the distance. They were getting closer. Leon cocked his head to the side. He heard them too.

"Bad like the other one," he said.

"Panozzo?"

He nodded. "They shouldn't try to hurt the boss. It's not right. He's a good man. He helps people."

Leon was still holding his gun. He wasn't doing anything with it, but it was there. He pushed himself up from the ground and stood unsteadily.

"What are you gonna do?" I asked.

"No jail," he said. "Maybe Yugoslavia."

The sirens were getting louder. Leon turned and hobbled towards the shadows of the Aragon Ballroom. I stayed crouched between my car and the open door.

Moments later, a black and white came speeding down Rose. The squad car barreled into the parking lot and came to a skidding stop. Leon tried to run, but could only manage an awkward, lumbering limp.

"Police! LAPD! Stop where you are!" The shout came from a megaphone sticking out the side window of the squad car.

"Drop your weapon! Drop your weapon! Drop your weapon!"

Leon looked down at the gun in his hand. I couldn't see his face, but I imagined bewilderment. Then he put the gun to his temple and shot.

CHAPTER 46

Leon's massive body blew sideways. His head struck the pavement with a sickening crack. The police megaphone went silent.

Moments later, another squad car and a white Savoy screeched into the lot. I heard car doors opening and closing, voices, a crackling police radio. Now footsteps running across the pavement. Detective Terekov and a uniformed cop came around the side of my car.

"You alright?" Terekov asked.

I nodded.

"Okay, stay there."

Guns drawn, Terekov and the patrol cop inspected the scene. First Dargin, then Leon.

"Radio the station," Terekov said to the patrol cop. "Two down at the Lick Pier."

The cop jogged back to his squad car. I got up and joined the detective, who was aiming his flashlight beam at the hulking corpse lying on the blood-soaked blacktop.

"Who is he?" Terekov asked.

"Leon Vanek."

"That supposed to mean something to me?"

"It's a long story."

He nodded. "Okay, at the station."

Terekov swept his flashlight beam across the blacktop, moving it methodically, side to side, like a windshield wiper.

Eventually the beam found metal. It was a carbon-steel Smith and Wesson .357.

He left the gun on the ground, called over a uniformed cop to bag it. I followed Terekov back to my car where he pointed his flashlight beam at Dargin's notebook which lay near the rear tire.

"What's this?" he said.

"Another long story."

He picked up the notebook and flipped through the pages. They were all blank. He ran his finger down the inside center binding which was ragged from where I had torn out the pages.

"Where's the rest?" he asked.

I pointed to the diminished pile of ashes on the ground. Most of the cinders had already scattered in the ocean breeze.

"Another long story, huh," he said.

I didn't bother to answer. Suddenly, all I wanted was to lie down. I wasn't sleepy. Just plain worn out.

Detective Terekov, however, wasn't tired at all. He poked his flashlight through the open window of my Falcon, searching the car. The beam eventually landed on the rectangular object on the floor by the brake pedal. He reached in and plucked it out.

"What the hell is this?"

"A tape recorder," I said.

Terekov examined the recorder, turning it over in his hand. "This thing?"

"It's a new kind. German-made."

"Fucking clever krauts. That's why they were *this close* to getting the bomb. How does it work?"

I showed him. I rewound to the beginning and pressed PLAY. *Nice spot you got here.* Dargin's sneering voice. *I'll bet it really sparkles in the sunlight.*

We listened for a few minutes, then I pressed STOP.

"Well, fuck me," Terekov muttered. "You recorded the whole thing?"

I nodded. The detective squinted, mulling things over. He snatched up the recorder, turned abruptly, and walked briskly towards the Savoy. I took off after him.

"Detective, wait. The recorder belongs to a friend of mine. It's expensive. I've got to give it back."

"Are you fucking kidding me? This is police gold."

When we reached the police cars, the patrol cop was just clicking off the radio.

"Circus is on their way," he said to Terekov.

Terekov nodded and turned to me. "Someone will take you down to the Venice station and get your statement. I'll be staying here for a bit."

CHAPTER 47

The Venice police station was a two-story Art Deco building with squat palms at each corner and enormous succulents running across the front. I followed a shirt-sleeved detective with a military style crew-cut down a dim hallway. I followed him past division offices with windows of translucent etched glass, a small kitchen, a row of iron-barred jail cells. Each cell had a lidless toilet, a cot with a grey wool blanket, and grey cinder block walls. The cells were unoccupied except the last one where a bearded man slept curled up on the cot.

I spent what was left of the night in a small office answering questions, waiting, answering more questions. With the police getting their hands on Tom's tape recorder, I knew there wasn't much I could do to keep Steve Sutton's name out of the whole mess.

At about 5:00 AM Detective Terekov showed up. He had me go through the whole thing one more time. As we began, a man wearing a black fedora came in. I recognized him right off as the man Victor Dargin had met with at McArthur Park, the man I tailed to the downtown federal building.

"Mind if I sit in?" the man said to Terekov.

"Whatever you want."

Fedora man nodded to me. "Federal Bureau of Investigation," he said. "Go ahead, I'm just listening." He looked straight at me and didn't blink.

When we finished the interview, the FBI agent left the room. He hadn't said another word the entire time.

"So what's with the FBI?" I asked Terekov.

Terekov answered by tossing my car keys onto the table. "It's parked out back. I'll walk you out."

I followed him down another dim hallway and out the back door.

The early morning sky was streaked peach and pink. We stopped at my car which was parked by a trash dumpster. Terekov opened his briefcase and handed me Tom's tape recorder.

"Thanks," I said.

Then he held up the audio cassette itself. The plastic case was split open. The brown magnetic tape was a tangled up like a heap of leftover spaghetti.

Terekov dropped the cassette on the ground. He crushed it under his shoe like you would a cigarette, the case cracking into bits, the tape shredding.

"Some things are better left alone," he said.

He lobbed the mangled mess into the dumpster.

"Why?" I asked because I was tired and couldn't think of anything else to say.

"That tape was trouble, Ryan. This way your client's interests will remain private, and so will everybody else's."

The back door to the station opened and a Negro janitor in overalls came out. He was pushing a metal cart piled with trash bags. He wheeled the cart up to the dumpster, tossed the bags into it, one at a time, and went back inside the station.

"The official story will go something like this," Terekov said. "Leon Vanek, transient immigrant, killed Victor Dargin, movie executive. Motivation remains unclear. Money, possible extortion. Shooter committed suicide on the scene. All of Hollywood mourns the loss of Victor Dargin."

"Neatly tied-up," I said.

"Neat enough."

"Won't Dargin's family want to know more?"

"You'd be surprised what people don't want to know."

"And the newspapers, won't they dig deeper?"

"Not if certain interests don't want them too."

"Meaning the feds."

Terekov lit a cigarette and took a long drag. "Let it go, Ryan. You did your job."

"What it looks like to me," I said, "is that Dargin was some kind of middleman. Maybe the FBI fed him information that he passed on to the studios. Maybe the FBI doesn't want anybody to know where they meddle. Am I in the ballpark?"

Terekov took another drag on his cigarette.

"Get some sleep," he said.

Then he flicked me a crisp salute off his brow and went back into the station.

CHAPTER 48

When I got home, I took the phone off the hook, lay down on top of the bed, and fell asleep in my jeans and T-shirt.

Next thing I knew, my eyes snapped open. Sun was pouring into the room. *Shit.* I had forgotten to call Reno and tell him he could quit his watch over Lou. I looked at the clock: Almost noon. I could hear the faint strains of Sonny Rollins blowing "Bluesong" coming up from Tom and Tina's apartment. I called the VA and got Reno on the line.

"I can't leave now," Reno said. "We're playing poker and Lou's taking me to the cleaners. I gotta at least break even."

"Okay, but you're off the clock."

"No prob. Hey, hang on, man. Lou wants to talk to you."

"Hi, kid," Lou said in a raspy voice that bordered on a whisper. "What's going on? Your buddy here is saying zip."

"I'll tell you when I get over there. Couple of hours, tops."

"Take your time. I might be a millionaire by the time you get here." Lou's last few words disintegrated into a wheeze.

***

Before going out, I found Julie's number and dialed long distance.

"Hi, Ryan." Her voice was bright and she sounded happy to hear from me. Step number one accomplished.

"I was wondering when you were going to call," she said.

"Well, I got your uncle's case wrapped up."

"Wow. Tell me everything! Have you told Niles yet?"

"No, but I'll call him today."

"So, who killed Uncle Oscar?"

I hesitated. A dog barked somewhere up Speedway. A screen door slammed shut.

"Ryan?" Julie said. "Are you there?"

"Yeah. Listen, I was thinking of making a trip. Thinking about coming up to Seattle. Maybe I could tell you about it in person."

"Hmmm ... so you want to come all the way up here to tell me stuff we could talk about on the phone?" she teased.

"Plus a few other reasons," I said, grinning to myself.

"I hate suspense," Julie said, "but maybe it'll be worth it."

We made a plan. I didn't mention to Julie that I'd never been out of California, never even been on an airplane. But I could tell her all about all that later.

***

On the drive over to Steve Sutton's house, I had time to think. Terekov, by his silence last night, just about admitted that the FBI was in up to its neck in HUAC and the blacklist. And the LAPD's actions — destroying the audio tape I made — told me it was a serious hush job. On the tape, Dargin straight up acknowledged that he (and that meant the FBI) was still keeping tabs on people. ... just in case. What did that mean: "just in case"? It was a lot to make sense of, a lot I had never thought about before, a lot that was now lodged in my brain and wasn't going away.

Any way you cut it, though, I had solved the case. Dargin, Chip Jordan, Panozzo and the rest — the pieces of the puzzle had slotted into place. Southland Investigations was going to survive, even with Lou down for the count. And, oh yeah, it looked like I might get a new girlfriend out of the whole mess. Not too shabby.

By the time I got to West Hollywood, the sidewalk was baking and sweat dripped down my back. In the daylight, the waxy potted plants and climbing vines on his porch looked harmless. I rang the bell. Sutton opened the door. His jet black hair was slicked back, his face shaved and tanned, his eyes dark and apprehensive.

"Is this good news or bad?" he said.

"Both."

I followed him inside, through the tiled foyer, into a living room with a large arched window that looked out onto a jungle of exotic plants.

"I found the photos," I said. "And the negatives. I destroyed them all. Burned them."

Sutton looked surprised. He took a deep breath and blew out the air.

"This is great," he said. "I guess I underestimated you."

"Just doing my job."

"So, where'd Panozzo have them stashed?"

"Actually, I found them at Victor Dargin's place, but —"

"Dargin!" he exclaimed. "That son-of-a-bitch. I never liked him, should never have trusted him. So Panozzo and Dargin were in this together. And that woman ... what was she, the go-between?"

"No, no, nothing like that. She wasn't involved at all."

We sat in the living room and I told my client what I knew or surmised about Dargin, the blacklist, and Chip Jordan, and about Panozzo, Cora Flynn and their money problems. He nodded slowly as I talked, taking it in. He was subdued. No tennis-ball-tossing nerves today.

"There's one thing, though," Sutton said when I had finished. "The empty safe. I read in the paper that the police are calling Panozzo's death a robbery-homicide. That means if there were photos in the safe, some thief may have them, and they could show up again one day."

"There was no thief."

Sutton looked at me quizzically. "Something tells me this is the bad news part."

"It was Leon," I said.

"Impossible." But he said it without conviction. His body sagged.

"Leon never went to Yugoslavia," I explained. "I think he turned around in New York. Anyway, he's been following me, and Victor Dargin, and doing who knows what else. I don't think he trusted me to do the job."

"Where is he now?"

I told him the rest.

"Leon," Sutton muttered, and shook his head.

I gazed out the arched window where a hummingbird hovered around a bottle brush tree — wings beating, long needle-like beak searching inside the bristly red flower.

"Loyal Leon," Sutton said quietly. "And I repaid that loyalty by trying to get rid of him. Career first and all that."

"Anyone in your position might have done the same."

"Maybe. But I've been thinking about a lot of things. Thinking about the world and how it is. And I've decided to can the whole political, running-for-office thing. It's just not realistic. I was foolish to believe I could ever be in politics. Me. A blackmail target waiting to happen. Maybe someday a person like me ... people who are different ... won't have to hide ... or pretend to be something we're not. Maybe someday things will change. Maybe in the future things will be different."

I nodded, thinking: Sounds far-fetched. But then again, if Willie Mays can sign for a hundred grand, if a Catholic can be President, why not?

ACKNOWLEDGEMENTS

I want to express my gratitude to everyone who helped this book come to fruition.

First, thank you to those who read the manuscript at various stages, and gave invaluable feedback: Linda Evans, Nan Van Gelder, Mickey Ellinger, and Alex Street. And, thank you to Cindy Bishop who helped me get "unstuck" through her work with synchronicity.

Thank you also to those who patiently answered my questions — about police procedure, private investigations, surfboard production, and burglary methods: Lucia Wade, John Kilass, Ed Mead, Bill Harris, and Johnny Rice.

Thank you to all the members of my writing group for your encouragement and astute critiques: Jo-Anne Rosen, Nancy Bourne, Wray Cotterill, Richard Gustafson, Marko Fong, Amanda Yskamp, Judith Day, and Sarah Amador-Rusnak.

And finally, thank you to my supportive, insightful agent, David Haviland, who always believed in this book.

CPSIA information can be obtained
at www.ICGtesting.com
Printed in the USA
BVOW08s0130140917
494777BV00002B/200/P